THE ALBUM

by Sandra White

The Album is a work of fiction. Names, characters and incidents are products of the author's imagination or are used fictitiously. Any resemblance to actual events or locales or persons, living or dead, is entirely coincidental.

Published 2003 by
The Fiction Works
Lake Tahoe, Nevada
www.fictionworks.com

ISBN 1-58124-082-1
Printed in the
United States of America

To my mother, Ione Schumann,
who has entered her tenth decade
of life with grace and contentment.

Best Wishes, Steve
Sandra White

THE ALBUM

Prologue

Cath's hands were shaking badly, but with sheer determination she turned yet another page of the album. Her precious photo album—the quilted fabric worn through in spots, the once colorful yellow rosebuds faded, the embroidered names no longer recognizable.

Photos of Matt graced this page—Matt on his first day of school. His little-boy smile with two missing front teeth grinned up at her.

Next, she found Jack's photograph. Jack breaking ground for a new store—the one at the shopping mall. How she had always loved that picture of Jack.

Her tears flowed freely now, dropping on the pages, leaving dark splotches staining her memories.

The album, smooth from age and scuffed at the corners, began to slide from her lap. Struggling to hold it, she turned to another page—a montage of smiles and laughter. Matt's wedding day. Matt and Rennie. Such a happy day. The wedding of her only child—Matthew John Montgomery.

Cath's fingers scratched at the edges of the thick pages, trying to turn one more. But she couldn't summon the strength. Her vision blurred, and her hands grew numb.

The album slipped to the floor, landing with a thud, some of the old and yellowed photos breaking loose from their pages.

Half-buried in the scattered remnants of her memories lay a bottle—a pill bottle. Empty. The label bore the name, "Catherine Montgomery," and the instructions, "Take two daily for pain."

Her head, white with wisps of unkempt, curly hair, fell to her chest, and her arms, one discolored with fresh bruises, dropped to her sides. A small sob escaped her lips as she whispered, "I'm coming, Jack. I'm coming."

Chapter One

Jack Montgomery had reached the apex of his career. The department store, started as a small enterprise by his father, was now so successful he planned to open a second site across from the new shopping mall east of town.

Excited, he brought home drawings and a model of the new store to show his wife.

"Let's put the model here on the dining room table, Jack," Cath said. "Right there." She helped him slide it to one end, making room to unroll the drawings. "Now we can get a good look."

Together, they pored over the model, casting shadows in the soft light from the antique fixture overhead. Cath ran her finger down the aisles, touching the tiny replica, following Jack's guided tour through the entire store.

"Honey, it's so perfect. I'll be your first customer." She kissed him firmly on his cheek.

Immensely happy for his success, Cath delighted in sharing his pride in his new venture. As she watched him check out the miniature scale model, his now completely gray head bent over the toy-like structure, she noted how handsome he still was.

Although his tall frame no longer carried the leanness of the youth she married, he remained slim, with only a minor bulge around his middle, acquiescence to his advancing years. His straight nose, bent slightly from a break suffered at the bottom of a pile in a long-ago high-school football game, was centered in his nearly square face—a face now furrowed with concentration as he examined the store model.

"Your dad would be so proud of you, Jack. You've made his successful business into a really successful one."

"Thanks, hon." He ran his fingers through his hair—a habit he'd had as long as Cath had known him. "It is exciting, but kind of stressful, too. Let's just hope everything goes as scheduled," he added. "The ground-breaking is slated for Thursday."

"I'd like to drive out and look at the spot. I haven't been to the mall since they added the new bookstore, and I need to find a book for David's birthday before I go to the gallery next week. We can do both—check out the store site and do a little shopping."

"That's a great idea," agreed Jack, obviously pleased with Cath's enthusiasm.

"You know, sometimes I still can't believe the way Blakefield is growing," said Cath later as they drove east of town.

"Nor I. When I was growing up here as a kid, the store site was so far out in the country that if someone had suggested it would someday be a major retail spot, they'd have been told they were crazy."

Blakefield, called by some a "small city" and by others, a "large town," was the hub for a countless number of rural communities in southeastern Nebraska. Its growth in recent years had been phenomenal, spreading far beyond its original boundaries in all directions—but especially, east. Where less than a decade ago fences outlined the farms dotting the dirt roads, now a large shopping mall, boasting of three major department store anchors and several specialty shops, attracted shoppers from miles around.

Some of the old-time residents despaired over the rapid growth, fearing their community would become too cosmopolitan, too unfriendly. But so far, their fears were unfounded. Blakefield had remained a warm, affable place.

A large expanse of undeveloped land spread across from the mall, property Jack and his investors had purchased for the second Montgomery store, the first being smack in the center of town. Although he had considered space in the new mall, he elected to keep his store separate, to retain, as much as possible, the historic atmosphere prevalent in store number one. Customers had long commented how shopping at Montgomery's gave them the feeling they were entering an old-time general store—one with all the modern accouterments, one with merchandise undreamed of when Jack's father had opened the original Montgomery's.

Jack and Cath sat in the car a moment, quietly taking in their surroundings. The road, now a busy highway, led directly to the approach, soon to be the parking lot in front of the store. The land had been cleared of brush and other growth and was ready for the groundbreaking.

In Cath's mind's eye, she could see the store, Jack's model enlarged many-fold. She envisioned the shoppers, their old friends and the new residents of Blakefield, many living in homes in new near-by housing developments.

Cath stepped from the car and looked over the expanse of land, her eyes taking in the openness that would still remain behind the store when it was completed.

"It's beautiful out here, Jack. Blakefield's city fathers have done a superb job expanding and building without totally demolishing the wonder of Mother Nature."

Jack put his arm around her just at the moment she shivered slightly in the early evening dampness. "You're getting cold, Nature Girl," he commented. "We'd better be going."

As they started back to the car, he said, "You really do get inspired out in the open, don't you, hon?" He was partly teasing, partly admiring her ability to be awed in the presence of nature's elements, as he had so many times before.

"Yep, I sure do. I'm a farm girl, remember? Why do you think most of my paintings are landscapes? There's no way we lowly people can begin to create beauty equal to what's in nature, but I try. Anyhow, whenever I'm out in the open like this, I feel so free. I guess being a kid out on the country, where my boundaries were almost non-existent, I developed a real need for wide open spaces— a real need for the feelings of freedom they bring."

She laughed at herself. "I'm getting a bit too philosophical, aren't

I? And facing that mall," she said, gesturing at the bustling spot across the highway, "brings me down to earth. So let's go over there and buy a book. I don't want David to think I've forgotten his birthday."

Dreary gray clouds blanketed the sky on Thursday, the day of the groundbreaking. Shivering, Cath wrapped her coat tightly around her as the breeze whipped around the corner, bringing tears to her blue eyes—blue like some of the bounty of wildflowers native to the area, Jack always said. Her short red curls, made curlier than ever by the moisture of the day, were tossed about by the wind. A steady drizzle had ceased only moments before the scheduled ceremonies.

But nothing could detract from the high spirits of the occasion. Jack dug the shovel firmly into the damp ground and overturned the first soil at the site of the new structure amidst the shouts and whistles of his friends.

"Way to go, Dad," came a cheer that could only belong to his son, Matt.

Later that week, a photograph of Jack breaking ground for the new building hit the front page of the *Blakefield Bulletin.*

"This is a really good shot of you. I simply must have a copy for our album," said Cath.

"I think the *Bulletin* sent one to the office. Call Marcy and tell her you'd like a copy. We'll probably frame it for the office—public relations, you know," he said with a mixture of marketing sense and pride.

"I'm surprised you can still find room in the album," he added, referring to the wedding present they had received from Cath's mother, Sarah Rowan, so many years ago.

Cath picked up the album from the table, holding it almost reverently. Its thick pages bulged with photographs, each carefully mounted, all telling stories of the Montgomerys and those who touched their lives. The quilted fabric cover, although faded and worn from years of use, was still bright with yellow roses, and Cath and Jack's names embroidered across the bottom were still legible—although barely.

"It's packed, that's for sure. I really must be selective about what I put in these days, but this one's too important to bypass. I'm so delighted with the store's success, and it's all your doing."

"Not entirely, Cath. First of all, Dad had already made it quite successful by the time I took over, and then, I inherited a workforce like none other. They're really a great crew. Without them, there wouldn't have been a ground-breaking," he said with conviction, looking again at the photo.

Three days later, Jack's secretary of nearly twenty years, Marcy Landish, dropped the photo by the house. Cath placed it squarely on a fresh page in the album—so glad she had requested it. It was a wonderful photograph of her husband and depicted so well the energy he had given to his career, to the retail establishment he had inherited from his father and so successfully enhanced.

Cath's career during these mid-life years was also headed for a change. For years, she had been caught up in the hectic pace of a successful painter. Her daily life alternated between the solitude of the creative artist and the fervor of showing the results of her creativity.

The pictures couldn't be in greater contrast: A paint-smock-covered Cath with traces of ultramarine blue or cardinal red smudged across her cheek was transformed into an elegant lady in a designer suit as she drove to Omaha on a regular basis to the Fairfield Art Gallerie. There she met routinely with the gallery's artistic director, David Lakey, who handled her work, displayed her paintings, set up showings, and managed sales.

The sales were numerous. Cath had become quite successful as a local artist of acclaim.

She had begun painting when Matt started school. It was a pastime she had always loved, and she did it well, even as a child. She still had, stashed away among her childhood mementos, the award she won for her fifth-grade painting of the wildflowers along the creek behind the Rowan farm.

She treasured that award and the happy memories it brought her. Her mother had been so proud of her. Her brother, too. It had been a painting from the heart—a capturing of the feelings that playing along the creek and picking flowers from the bounty growing there always gave her. Even as a toddler, the creek had drawn her like a magnet—something that had caused her mother no small amount of anxiety.

At first, painting was just a hobby, an activity to kill time, which sometimes seemed endless with Matt in school and Jack giving his all to leading the Montgomery department store to financial success. When Jack and Cath bought their home, shortly before their son was born, she gave little thought to where she would paint, never dreaming a career as a well-known artist loomed in the future. For a while, working in a corner of the kitchen satisfied her needs. She set up her easel where ample light streamed through the curtain-bordered windows in the dining area, using the table to lay out her paints and prepare her canvasses.

It didn't take long, however, for both Cath and Jack to realize that her "kitchen studio" wouldn't suffice if she were going to take her painting seriously. Late one afternoon, when Cath was cleaning out her brushes in the sink, Jack walked in. He had come home from the store early, planning to accompany his young son to a Boy Scout troop organizational meeting.

"Cath, that's gorgeous," he said, admiration evident in his voice as he looked at the landscape his wife had just completed. A lake, water shimmering in early morning sunlight, the Rocky

Mountains rising majestically in the background, numerous tall pines dotting the landscape—a scene from a vacation they had enjoyed last summer.

Jack walked over to his wife and hugged her tightly. "You are a very good artist, Mrs. Montgomery. Do you realize that?"

Cath wiped her paint-stained hands on a cloth before she turned around and returned his hug. "Thanks, hon, I'd like to think so. I'm having fun, anyhow. Sometimes, though, I feel like I'm falling over the cookie jar out here, everything's so close. Sure wish I had a bigger space, but I really don't know where it would be. None of the other rooms has any extra space to speak of, and there's not nearly enough space or light in the garage."

"I've been giving some thought to this, Cath," said Jack, taking the cloth and wiping away a spot of paint from her cheek. "We have plenty of room out in back. Let's build a studio, a separate building where the light's just right, plenty of space. A painting studio, a place all your own."

"Are you serious, Jack? Can we afford it? It would be so wonderful!" she exclaimed, filled with animation at the prospect.

"Whoa! One question at a time. Yes, I'm serious, and yes, we can afford it. Am I not a successful retail manager?" he teased. "I've given this a lot of thought, honey, and I'd really like to do it."

So Cath's painting studio came into existence. The style was a bit more rustic than their home, a one-story, unpretentious bungalow, painted white with gray-blue trim. The studio was somewhat barn-like in appearance, complete with cupola and weather vane. Cath painted it gray-blue, a good blend with the house. Over the years, they painted the house colors other than white, but the studio barn, as it was dubbed by their son, Matt, was always repainted gray-blue.

Eventually they painted the house to match the studio. Many changes were made to the house as the years went by, but the studio barn was so ideal, it was never changed.

Large windows covered the east wall, and small openings overhead, like long and narrow skylights, allowed shafts of light from above. Floor to ceiling cupboards covered one wall for storing canvasses, unused or in all stages of completion. Bins for paints and brushes filled one shelf. For the floor, Cath selected a hard-finish tile, one that could be scraped, as well as scrubbed.

"It's perfect, Jack. Just perfect." Cath hugged her husband, glowing with excitement.

"Is it okay if I come in?" asked young Matt as supplies were being moved in.

"Of course, silly," replied his mother, welcoming him with open arms.

"But remember, son, this is your mom's domain," admonished his father. "When she's working, you need to respect her privacy. We'll have a sign made for the door: Master at Work." The threesome laughed at the suggestion.

Within days of the building's completion, Cath was ready to paint. The first day she painted in her new studio was a bright sunny one, nature heralding the beginning of the career of Catherine Rowan Montgomery as a bona fide artist.

I love this place, she thought, setting a fresh canvas on her easel, its glaring whiteness soon filled with radiant colors as she began a scene of the countryside. She painted for hours, that first day, feeling again the freedom of the open spaces she painted, the open spaces she loved so much.

She spent many hours of many years in her studio, resulting in some really exceptional work. A serious artist had been lurking inside Cath ever since she painted along the creek as a child. She captured the countryside in all directions, plus brilliantly countless landscapes of spots she visited throughout the country.

"I like David, I really do," Cath explained one night as she was preparing two of her completed paintings to take to the Fairfield Art Gallerie, "but sometimes his effervescence drives me nuts."

Over the years, Cath realized that David Lakey had known he had a major find when he met Catherine Montgomery and saw her paintings—his excitement evident every time Cath came to the gallery.

"I enjoy my trips to the gallery, though, I must admit," Cath added. "It's kind of a thrill to see my own work displayed. Anyhow, it also forces me to put on some 'real clothes.'" She looked down at her paint-covered smock and laughed.

"You're a regular Jekyll and Hyde, my dear," replied Jack, hugging her, laughing with her. "A recluse artist today, a socialite ambassador of the arts tomorrow."

"Forget the 'socialite' part, but I rather like the rest."

The next morning, Cath, donned in an aquamarine suit, perfectly tailored to fit her slim body, her red curls bouncing as she stepped out the door, bore little resemblance to the paint-covered artist of yesterday. Today she was a stylish businesswoman, exuding an air of confidence and independence as she delivered her newest creations to the art gallery in Omaha.

Later, Cath entered the "illustrating" phase of her career, signing a very lucrative contract with a commercial poster firm in Chicago. She was amazed at the monetary value placed upon posters in the offices of travel agencies and the corridors of airline-passenger terminals—posters used to entice vacationers to travel to faraway and exotic places.

Fueled by the frenzied pace of success, Jack and Cath's middle years flew by rapidly. Matt grew into a fine young man they both were proud of and married Rennie. The one child of Matt's marriage, Cath's beloved granddaughter, Julie, inherited Cath's talent and the two of them became close, partly due to their shared interest in art. When Julie met Kenneth, a promising young architect, and moved to Minneapolis after their wedding, they kept their relationship close even with distance separating them.

Finally, Cath and Jack drew their careers to a close. Jack retired from the Montgomery stores, and Cath painted only as a hobby again. Officially retired, they did all the wonderful things together they had dreamed of in their hard-working days. They lounged lazily by the pool, took long walks, nurtured their roses—and traveled, traveled, traveled.

Their travels took them from the Rockies and Cascades in the west to Time Square in New York on New Year's Eve; from Bourbon Street in New Orleans to the boundary waters in northern Minnesota. They were like children, taking in the wonders of the country.

From time to time, they would visit Julie in Minneapolis. When Cath thought of all the fabulous places they visited, she had to admit the Minneapolis trips were her favorite. Besides seeing the granddaughter they loved so much, both she and Jack enjoyed Minneapolis, where they could walk on paths around its many lakes and still be in the middle of the city. They also visited the art galleries, Walker and the Minneapolis Institute of Art, and were filled with wonder at talent that stretched through the centuries.

Julie and Kenneth had built a lovely, sprawling home overlooking the beautiful waters of Lake Minnetonka—Kenneth's own design. As Cath had predicted, Kenneth gained quite a name for himself as one of the Twin Cities' best-known commercial architects.

Many of Julie's paintings adorned the walls of their home, and while admiring the most recent, Cath said, "I told you so, Julie. Remember what I said when you were about eight—that you'd see the world differently when you grew up? You're looking at the world through the eyes of a woman now, and you express what you see very well. Your talents far surpassed mine long ago."

"I don't know, Grandma Cath. There are a couple pretty wonderful Catherine Montgomerys in the next room. I am glad I have this talent, though—undoubtedly inherited from you." She hugged her grandmother. "It gives me so much pleasure, I just get lost in it sometimes."

One warm night in late June, Jack, Cath, Kenneth, and Julie sat on the patio overlooking the lake and watched the reflection of the full moon rippling on the water.

"What a great painting," Cath and Julie said simultaneously, knowing they'd both most likely capture on canvas their version of the breathtaking sight.

Chapter Two

Jack and Cath cut back on their travels that summer. Their one and only trip was the one to Minnesota. While there, Jack caught a cold—a cold that lingered the remaining days of summer.

"I don't know why I can't shake this thing," he said one morning as they were having coffee together in early September. "I've taken everything Doc Martin tossed my way, and this damned cold's got as strong a grip on me as it did the first day."

"Why don't you go back and see him again today, Jack?" Cath looked at her husband with concern. She didn't like the way his cold had hung on. And she especially didn't like the gray pallor of his complexion or the deep purple circles under his eyes. "In fact, why don't I call his office right now?"

"Okay, honey. While you do that, I think I'll just go see if there are any more roses blooming today," he said, nodding towards the garden behind him, resplendent yet with color, but beginning to fade as the shorter days of fall encroached on summertime. "There were a couple of buds just about ready to pop yesterday. One will most likely be our 'last rose of summer.'"

Jack walked down the path leading to the rose garden they so enjoyed, and Cath went into the house. She watched him through the window as she made the call to the doctor's office. He picked up a pair of flower shears from a storage basket propped up against the studio barn at the end of the path and walked over to check the blossoms. The early morning sun brightened their colors—the flamboyant coral of the Tropicana, the sunny yellow of the Lowell Thomas, the soft yellow of the Peace, its petals tinged with pink. Most of the blooms were fully opened and would soon be gone, but there, nestled among the full blooms, atop a long stem on the Lowell Thomas, was a blossom, its petals just beginning to unfold.

Jack reached for the yellow blossom—yellow, Cath's favorite. *Perfect,* she thought as she dialed the phone.

Jack bent to cut the long stem of the rose as Cath spoke to the doctor's receptionist, setting up an appointment for two o'clock that afternoon.

She watched in horror as Jack fell to the ground. She screamed, dropped the phone, and ran to him. But he was dead before she reached his side.

Chapter Three

"Mom, are you sure you don't want to stay with Rennie and me for a few days?" asked Matt as the last visitor offering condolences left.

Hundreds had attended Jack's funeral, and many came by the house later in the day to tell Cath one more time how sorry they were for her loss. Jack's death was a personal loss for several of them, as well. He had been a beloved friend, a respected businessman and pillar of their community.

Julie and Kenneth were already on their way back to Minnesota. Only Cath, Matt, and Rennie remained in the house where Jack and Cath had spent nearly their entire adult lives—the home where Matt had grown up.

"It's going to be so empty around here for you alone," said Matt. His voice choked, the word *alone* only a whisper.

Matt and his father had always maintained a close relationship. They didn't golf together as Matt and his father-in-law, Harold Spaulding, did every Saturday morning, and Matt could rarely persuade Jack to join him for lunch at the Club. But Jack was his confidante—his advisor and best friend. He wasn't sure how the pieces of his life would fit together without his dad.

And he really was concerned about how his mother would manage without her partner, her very best friend. He didn't think they'd ever been apart for more than a few days.

"I'll be fine, Matt, really. I need some time to myself. It all happened so fast, I still can hardly believe he's gone."

Matt hugged her tightly, and together they let their tears flow anew.

As he and Rennie left a few minutes later, Matt again said, "I still think you should come to stay with us for a while." He watched his mother quietly shake her head from side to side. "Well, if you should change your mind, call me. I'll be here to pick you up in a minute."

Cath smiled, blew him a kiss, and turned back to her empty house as her son and his wife drove away.

She had intentionally spurned all offers of help cleaning up after the guests. Even Rennie had volunteered. But Cath needed to keep moving to keep the pain at bay.

Dr. Landers Martin, Jack's physician and dear friend, had offered sedatives, but she refused his offer, also. "Lan, I just can't. I'm afraid if I let you drug me to sleep, I'll really come apart when I wake up. No, let me handle this in my own way."

Landers Martin had backed away and watched her suffer from a distance, ready to run to her aid if needed. He had known Jack and Cath for a long time and had always admired her innate independent nature. But he did wish she would be willing to accept some help. She was, after all, in her seventies, and there may be problems ahead she simply couldn't solve alone.

Cath dried the last plate and placed it in the cupboard. She glanced around the kitchen, the room she and Jack had so enjoyed since remodeling it thirteen years ago. She looked up at the skylight overhead, where the bright morning sun would so often shine in to add its warmth to a clear cold winter day.

Friends had told them they were crazy to put in a skylight—that the heavy Nebraska snows would break through and land on the table where they were seated below. But the forecasters of doom had been wrong. The skylight never broke, never allowed anything in but wonderful, warm, cheerful sunlight.

The sun was setting now in the west. Pink and gold, beauty as only the Master Painter could create. She stood by the window and watched the sun disappear beneath the horizon.

I want to see it gone—see this day end. I know there'll be many painful ones ahead, but this one has to be over. It just has to be. Today was the day I said good-bye to the only man I ever loved.

Cath had always hated good-byes. She didn't like saying good-bye to Jack when he left for the department store every morning, and she especially didn't like it when she had to say good-bye to him at the airport when he left on a business trip. Every day when Matt left for school, for a few moments she'd feel this terrible sense of loss.

And when she said good-bye to Julie, a sense of grief washed over her—especially now when good-bye meant Julie was going back home to Minnesota.

All those feelings of loss were simply a series of rehearsals for this day, she thought. *Even burying Mama and my dear brother Spence were just practice for today's farewell.*

As she turned her back to the west window and slowly trudged off to her bedroom, Catherine Rowan Montgomery knew her life from this point on would have very little resemblance to what it been before.

They had been a set, Cath and Jack, and now the set was broken.

Cath picked up her photo album and sat down on her bed, clutching the album as if she feared it might disappear, that it, too, might be taken from her. Then she opened it to the first page and looked at their wedding picture—hers and Jack's—and recalled the day she mounted it, the first photograph in the album.

"What are you doing?" asked Jack as he came up behind her.

Cath turned her face and kissed him before she answered, her blue eyes bright with unshed tears. "I'm just sitting here looking at our photo album and thinking of my mother. I love this album, Jack. I think it's my favorite of all our gifts."

She turned to him to explain. "Don't get me wrong. We received wonderful presents. The china and silver from your folks are more beautiful than anything I've ever had in my whole life. I'll treasure them always. But my mother put so much effort into making this for us. It's just like she's given us a bit of herself."

"She has, honey. Sarah is a very giving woman. She's had to be both mom and dad to you for a long time, Cath, and her love for you is very obvious. It's amazing you didn't turn out to be a spoiled brat," he added, smiling.

Jack pulled up a chair beside her, and together they examined their wonderful gift from Sarah, marveling at the impressive handiwork.

"No wonder it's so heavy," said Jack. "It looks like she's glued three or four pieces of paper together for each page."

"Umm-hmmm. That's what I think, too. It feels like wallpaper. That's it! Remember all those odds and ends left after she and Spence papered the bedrooms last year? She's used pieces of wallpaper glued together to make these thick pages—they'll last forever. And look, she's cut them exactly. There isn't a raggedy page in the whole book. She must have spent hours on this, Jack."

"And loved every minute of it, I bet."

Cath rubbed her hand tenderly over the cover, the quilted yellow-rose fabric. Across the bottom Sarah had embroidered, *Catherine and Jack Montgomery—1934*.

"Now for the first entry," said Cath as she picked up the wedding photograph.

She dipped her finger into the paste she had made from flour and water a few minutes ago, stirring it until it was smooth and just right. With the same finger, she carefully rubbed the sticky concoction across the back—side-to-side, corner-to-corner. She placed the photo squarely in the middle of the page, taking great care to keep it straight. Then she ran the heel of her hand across it, pressing gently to make it secure.

"There," she said, patting the photograph. She reached over and squeezed Jack's hand as she scrutinized her entry.

Page one of the album.

A smiling Cath and Jack looked up at them, lovely and handsome in their wedding finery.

With weariness and an aching heart, Cath closed the album, placed it back on the table, and crawled into bed, keeping well away from the side that had been Jack's—as if touching it would remind her too much of its emptiness. Eventually, exhaustion took over, and Cath drifted into a restless sleep.

The day was finally over.

Chapter Four

Cath buried herself in the pages of her album the first few weeks after Jack's death. Night after night, she relived her wedding day—and the days when Jack first entered her life. She remembered meeting Jack as if it were yesterday.

She attended a country school when she was a young child—a school that she loved from day one. When she turned fourteen, it was time for her to go into Blakefield for high school, just as her brother, Spence, had done. And there she met John Richard Montgomery, better known as Jack.

Jack was a senior when Cath started Blakefield High, three years older than Cath, popular, and well known. After all, his father owned Blakefield's only department store.

Jack's quiet, easy-going ways made him a favorite with boys and girls alike. He wasn't courting the affection of any one girl in particular, but any number of them would have loved to declare Jack Montgomery as her "beau." Even though he would occasionally take one or the other of them to a picnic, or dance with one at some community celebration, he more or less treated all the girls the same. He enjoyed their company—all of them. Not any one more than another.

That is, until he saw Catherine Rowan at the start of his senior year.

She was new, a freshman, although you might not have realized it just by watching her. Not even on that first day.

It wasn't her long red hair, although it was beautiful, trailing curls halfway down her back, loosely tied with a ribbon the color of new leaves on the willow trees in the spring. It wasn't even her blue eyes, clear and snappy. They sort of reminded Jack of a blue sapphire ring his rich Aunt Sophie always wore on her pinky finger.

It wasn't any of Cath's physical traits that got his attention that first day and drew him to her like a magnet. It was the air of confidence in her step.

The other new freshmen—there were only nineteen—milled around the hall as if totally lost. A few of them were from Blakefield, but most, like Cath, were from further out in the country. Six were from the country school Cath had attended up to this point, including her cousin, Elmie, one of her Aunt Irene's sons.

Jack observed that they seemed to follow Cath's leadership. No wonder, with the confident aura around her. He could see himself following her, too—anywhere.

Jack watched her from a distance for three days. The school was small, and it wasn't difficult to spot Cath going to her classes, usually surrounded with a small crowd of her classmates. On day four, he followed her into the library. She was seated at one of the library tables, old and nicked, with many an initial from years gone by carved on its surface. With a window at her back, the bright fall sun streamed through the high pane and bounced off her hair, reflecting it like newly polished copper.

Jack sat down across from her, but closer to the end of the table so as not to appear too obvious. He attempted to look as if he were engrossed in a book he had picked up randomly from the shelf on his way in. Glancing at the title of the book, *Basic Sewing Instruction,* he realized he had made a poor choice. It was a home economics book, a book on the rudiments of a skill he had no desire to develop. He really hoped she wouldn't notice, and held his hand over the title as he propped it up on the table, supposedly reading.

After a few moments, when he had not dared to even look up, he thought he could feel her eyes on him. He raised his head cautiously and met their sparkling blue.

"Why have you been spying on me?" she asked without hesitation.

"Wh . . . wh . . ." he stammered, not knowing what to say and feeling the warmth of an unwelcome blush starting at his neck and creeping up his face.

"C'mon. You can do better than that," she teased. Then she laughed. It was a pleasant laugh—a beautiful laugh, soft and rippling.

"Hi. I'm Cath Rowan," she said, smiling as she put out her hand.

Jack clasped her hand. He hadn't met a girl who shook hands before. Although his was much larger than hers, she was the one with the really firm grip.

"I'm Jack Montgomery. Boy, do I feel like a fool. So you knew I was watching you, huh?"

"Mm-hmm. You were pretty obvious. For the past three days, every time I rounded a corner, there you'd be. I decided it just couldn't be coincidence."

Even her voice captivated Jack. Clear, but soft. Much lower than you'd anticipate from a girl her size.

There was no question, Jack was totally captivated by this girl from the country. Her smile was absolutely infectious. And those eyes—all but mesmerizing him.

He also liked the way she dressed. Her clothes looked new and fit to perfection, but they were plain. Plain in a pleasant sort of way, not overdone or fancy. She didn't wear any of the silly frills that Jack saw on so many of the other girls.

Sarah had made Cath three outfits for starting high school, and Cath was very proud of her new wardrobe. The dresses weren't from expensive fabric, and they were without any unnecessary ornament. But they fit her beautifully, complementing her small young figure. The spring green one she had chosen for today set off her copper-colored hair perfectly.

Although very much a redhead, Cath's skin was tanned to a golden brown. A small smattering of freckles dotted her nose. She wore no make-up, as some of Jack's classmates had begun to experimentally do. Cath's face was clear and natural—and still smiling.

Jack looked at her hands as they lay on the table. They were deep brown, her nails cut very short. This girl wasn't a stranger to work.

"I need to get to class," she said, rising.

"Mind if I walk with you?" Jack asked, still wondering if she thought him a fool for his badly executed "spying."

"I'd like that," she said, emphasizing her statement with another of her brilliant smiles.

They saw a lot of each other after that. She and Jack just seemed to belong together. She had never had a beau before, and she never had another. Only Jack.

And Jack never had another girlfriend after he met Cath. No one else even began to measure up.

They were busy young people, each having outside responsibilities in addition to their schoolwork. Cath still had much to do on the farm, helping Sarah and even Spence. She often worked beside her brother in the fields.

Jack had regular duties at his father's store. He was rarely free on Saturdays, and often worked after school, as well.

But when they were free, they were together, oftentimes, at each other's home. Emma Montgomery, Jack's mother, was captivated by this spirited young beauty, as was John Montgomery, Sr.

And Sarah Rowan liked Jack. Even Spence approved of him— and he certainly scrutinized him. Any friend of Cath's was bound to get the "once-over" from her big brother.

Jack went to business school in Lincoln for two years after graduating from high school. His father wanted him to bring a "good head on his shoulders" to the store that would someday be his. When he completed his formal education and was awarded his business-school diploma, Jack was ready for full-time employment at Montgomery's department store.

The following year, Cath graduated from high school—at the top of her class. She had never lost the love of learning that captivated her the first day she walked into the classroom.

Sarah had always hoped this bright child of hers would be able to go on to school—maybe teachers' college. But the money just wasn't there. No matter how hard she tried, Sarah was never able to save any large sums. Every time she got close, something on the farm needed repairing or replacing.

"Mama, I don't care if I don't go to college," said Cath, kissing her mother lovingly on the cheek. She put her arm around her mother's waist and laid her head on Sarah's small shoulder. "I'll continue to learn by reading, just like always. You know I will. Anyhow, I think Jack is going to ask me to marry him."

Sarah didn't say a word, just put her arms around Cath and held her close, tears blinding her vision. She had watched the love grow between these two young people and knew it would probably be only a matter of time before they decided to spend their lives together.

She blinked back her tears and held Cath at arm's length. Smiling at her lovely child, she said, "Whatever will make you happy is what I want for you Cath. You seem terribly young for marriage, and so does he. But he's a very nice young man, and I think he truly does love you."

Jack certainly wouldn't argue with that. Cath was on his mind every minute of every day. One week after Cath told her mother that she thought Jack was going to ask her to marry him, he presented her with a ring.

"The diamond's small, I know, Cath. But I thought it was kinda pretty, and—"

"Pretty? It's beautiful! And Jack, it isn't either small." She waved her arm around in circles, totally delighted with her ring. And of course, her response to his proposal was an excited, "Yes!"

Chapter Five

Jack never replaced the engagement ring with a larger diamond, which he could easily have afforded later—Cath wouldn't hear of it. Every time she looked at her ring, she recaptured that wonderful feeling she experienced when Jack first placed it on her finger and asked her to be his wife.

Cath smiled as she looked down at her wedding picture. She had been so excited about it all, the ring, the dress—her young husband's declaration of love for her. Even in the photo, old now and faded, her face glowed with excitement.

Cath awoke on her wedding day thinking, surely there could not possibly be a more perfect day than this. Soft, fluffy clouds adorned the sky, and a gentle breeze carried the sweet fragrance of the flowers blooming along the creek and roadside. Too eager for her wedding day to arrive, she had slept very little the night before. This was her day—hers and Jack's.

A flurry of activity filled the house, hastening the fleeting time, and soon Cath saw her Uncle Elmer drive up, ready to take her to the church to get ready for the ceremony. Spence would be following shortly with her mother and Aunt Irene.

"Is it done, Sarah?" asked Irene with a hint of impatience. "We should be getting to the church."

"It's done," announced Sarah proudly, placing the large photo album on the worn table in front of her.

The old table was in perfect harmony with the rest of the room. It sat on floorboards smooth with years of wear, their wood-color scrubbed pale gray. Only two of the chairs arranged tidily around the table matched, not the others. Those two were of lovely highly polished maple, a gift from Sarah's great-aunt. Of the others, one was painted a sickly shade of green and another upholstered in a faded mauve fabric. The fifth was of unfinished pine.

An embroidered sampler, sewed to perfection, hung on the wall, each letter of the alphabet and the traditional "Home Sweet Home" bearing homage to the Rowan abode. A border of lilies-of-the-valley and assorted colorful wildflowers surrounded the letters. The sampler, along with the faded rose-hued hand-sewn curtains and three of Cath's paintings of wildflowers growing along the creek added bright spots of color to the kitchen of the Rowan family farmhouse.

The room was old and shabby, but cheerful and absolutely spotless. Many had marveled at Sarah's ability to give so little the atmosphere of so much.

The lives of Sarah and her children had been meager for a long time, but they didn't seem to be aware of their own struggling. All three were energetic and ambitious, and as far as anyone could tell, they were happy.

Spencer Rowan, known to nearly everyone as Spence, managed the farm—had since he was a boy. Some years it was very successful; other years, it was a tremendous challenge. Even though the Rowan land sat in the midst of prosperous Midwest farmland, the region had unpredictable weather—too much or too little sun, too much or too little rain—and millions of insects.

No one was ever turned away from the Rowans if they needed a meal, however, and even though Sarah relied on her sewing for income, it was not unheard of for her to quietly give a quilt to a neighbor in need rather than sell it. She taught her children compassion, and she taught them independence and pride.

"It's all right to be poor," she said, "but that doesn't mean you have to sacrifice your dignity. Never give up your dignity. And never turn your back on someone who's having a really hard time."

Sarah picked up the album, the gift she had secretly been working on when Cath was absent from the house.

"She'll like it, won't she, Irene?" Some doubt crept into Sarah's voice as she thought of the more elegant gifts her only daughter would be receiving today, her wedding day.

"Oh, honey, of course she'll like it," said Irene, hugging her sister, feeling her sister's thinness in the hug.

Irene vacillated between envy and worry over Sarah's slender frame—envy because she didn't share this trait with her sibling, worry because she questioned how well Sarah cared for herself. When they were children, after their parents died, they managed to see each other regularly, even though they never stayed with the same relatives. Many a time, they would sneak out in the wee hours of the morning, making their way across moonlit fields to compare notes on their lives—to share stories of their day-to-day living. Irene always managed, even then, to remind Sarah to take better care of herself.

"You'll kill yourself working so hard, honey."

Sarah and Irene were as close as adults as they had been when they were children, almost of one mind, people said. Often, they came up with ideas at the same time, as if they communicated by thought.

Yet, physically, they were dissimilar—almost direct opposites. Sarah was a small thin woman, very serious. When she was widowed so young, she became more independent and determined than she had ever been—and she had always been known for her independence and determination.

At the time her daughter was married, her reddish-brown hair was streaked with only a few strands of gray. Her skin was taut and smooth, defying the sometimes-brutal Nebraska winds, and her bright blue eyes sparkled with her indomitable spirit. Outwardly, the only apparent concession to her advancing years was her glasses—her very thick glasses. Years of toiling over her work as a women's tailor and quilt-maker, often after Cath and Spence were in bed for the night, had taken a toll on Sarah's eyesight.

Irene was a physical antithesis to Sarah. She was as round as she was tall, and although only three years older than her sister, her once raven-black hair was as white as snow before her thirtieth birthday. Her mouth seemed permanently curved in a smile, and her gray eyes always gave one the impression she was laughing at you—or with you.

Irene and her husband, Elmer, had six children in five years—Abby, Betsy, Carl, Diane, Elmer, Jr., and Frank. When the children were very young, Irene said she either smiled all the time or cried. But those who knew and loved her realized she was only joking. She truly adored all six of her children—and the chaotic lifestyle that came with her boisterous offspring.

Uncle Elmer did say he was worried when Irene insisted on naming their babies according to the alphabet, beginning with little Abby. He claimed that he had a suitcase secretly packed. In case Irene became terribly fond of the name Zachary, he was making a quick exit.

Everyone knew he was joking, too.

Aunt Irene's ample size provided her with a wonderful lap for her many offspring. And she always had room on her lap for Cath right along with her own six. When he was very small, Spence would also join the group of youngsters gathered around his aunt for her very special cookies and even more special hugs.

"Cath will cherish the album for years to come, Sarah," Irene said to her sister.

As she spoke those reassuring words, Irene thought for a moment about all her widowed sister had given to Cath. Most of all, love. Spence was ten years old when his dad died; Cath, a baby, barely two.

Young Spence had found his father, dead at age thirty-eight from a heart attack, lying in the field beside the wagon. Those who knew of the profoundly close relationship between Larry and his boy worried about Spence, about the depth of his loss. Not to mention the trauma of his finding his father lifeless, lying face down in the lush green field under the clear Nebraska skies.

The boy was frighteningly composed as he ran home to his mother, breathlessly bringing the news of his tragic discovery. He didn't even cry—at least not when and where any one could see him. And he stayed stoically by his mother's side every moment as she went through the motions of preparing her husband for burial. It was as if Spence had swallowed his sadness. Sadness for the loss of the father he adored, the father in whose footsteps he planned to walk.

When Spence was about eight, his dad had taught him the ways of the farm. Spence became Larry's right-hand man, the two blond heads of father and son seen daily bobbing across the fields, working together. Hair, golden and plentiful on father-arms, glistened in the sun, arms muscular from the heavy labor of the farm, arms suntanned below rolled-up sleeves of faded shirts, working side-by-side with little-boy arms, sunburned from hours spent outdoors.

After his father was buried, Spence's grief seemed to disappear, replaced by an intense drive to work, to make the farm a success. A man's fervor for work. A man, age ten.

The family barely squeezed by some years. Probably wouldn't have if it hadn't been for Sarah's gift for sewing. Sarah Rowan was known as "the best women's tailor in southeast Nebraska." She had learned her skills as a seamstress from her Aunt Amanda.

Sarah was orphaned at an early age, losing both her parents within a single winter when a flu epidemic ran rampant through her family's Midwest prairie town. She spent her teen years moving from relative to relative, always paying for her care with hard work, often with very little thanks. Her work was expected.

The one caretaker who was different was her Aunt Amanda. Dear Aunt Amanda. Her great-aunt, actually. While Sarah did her household tasks, Amanda worked right beside her, and when they finished the housework, they would sew.

By the time Sarah was sixteen years old, her sewing talents equaled those of her aunt, and when she married Larry Rowan two years later, she was excited about bringing those talents to her new home.

Sarah had spent countless hours sewing in preparation for her only daughter's wedding. She designed and stitched Cath's wedding gown of fine batiste covered with yards and yards of ivory lace—lace from Irish ancestors, saved for just such a day as this. The bodice was covered with tiny pleats and tinier-still buttons.

An elegant gown for a lovely young woman.

And then Sarah's own dress—deep blue like her eyes, tailored perfectly. Perfect like everything Sarah did. She rarely made anything new for herself, but for Cath's wedding nothing other than new would do.

Labors of love for Cath.

"Ma, Cath and Jack will be married before we get to the church if we don't hurry," said Spence, straightening his tie for the umpteenth time.

Although it was uncharacteristic for Spence Rowan to wear such finery as a starched white shirt and tie, it emphasized his suntanned face. He was an exceptionally handsome young man, and the eyes of many a young woman would follow him today, imagining themselves going down the aisle of the church on his arm—as Mrs. Spencer Lawrence Rowan.

But it never happened. Spence lost his heart once and only once—lost it to Margaret Murphy, the vivacious and beautiful daughter of Pat Murphy, publisher of the daily newspaper in nearby Harris Valley. She even accepted his engagement ring. For a while. But Meg, as everyone called her, couldn't imagine living the rest of her life on a farm.

And Spence couldn't fathom living anywhere else.

"Cath wouldn't even think of starting without us, Spence," said his mother indignantly as she straightened the bow on the gift. She'd saved a piece of soft floral fabric left from one of the many quilts she had sewn and wrapped it lovingly around the album. A colorful pattern of small, yellow rosebuds was scattered across the white background of the cloth, matching the cover of the album. A bright yellow hair-ribbon added the finishing touch.

"You're right, Ma, she wouldn't. That means we're probably holding up the whole shindig, so let's go."

Spence offered his mother his arm as they left their sixty-year-old farmhouse and headed for the wedding of Catherine Ann Rowan and John Richard Montgomery—better known as Jack—on a beautiful summer day in the Year of Our Lord, 1934.

He looked back at the family home and its surroundings as he dutifully assisted his mother and Aunt Irene into his less-than-new automobile.

Studying the old farm house with its peeling yellow paint and sagging front porch, Spence felt a tug of sadness as he realized this would no longer be Cath's home. Now, Cath would become a member of another family. She would be a Montgomery and live in town.

That is, if he'd get to church so the wedding could get take place.

Only moments before the ceremony was to begin, Spence drove to a hurried stop in front of the small white church that had served the families of the area for so many years. A tall steeple housing the only church-bell for miles around was the one accouterment belying its simplicity. Spence grabbed one of the few remaining parking spots on the grassy field directly surrounding the church. Guests— as many as could possibly squeeze into the small building—had come to celebrate the marriage of Jack and Cath, two of the area's "own kids."

Cath was pacing the entryway to the church, anxious for her mother, brother, and aunt's arrival. She, Uncle Elmer, and Cousin Abby had driven to the church early, before any guests were scheduled to arrive. Abby was to help her dress, the lovely gown draped over Cath's lap in the back seat of her uncle's car.

"I can hardly believe this is mine. Abby, it's just so gorgeous."

"Mmm-hm," agreed her cousin. "I can hardly wait to see it on you. You're going to look so beautiful." Her voice revealed pleasure, with just a mild hint of envy.

Cath donned her gown, with Abby's able assistance, in the church basement, which smelled a bit musty but was very clean. After Cath had smoothed the dress around her small waist, and Abby had completed fastening what seemed to her an endless number of tiny buttons, Cath turned and viewed herself in the white-framed mirror hanging on the wall, its tiny capillary-like cracks distorting her reflection only slightly.

"Oh, Abby," she exclaimed, placing her hands over her mouth in surprise. "Is this really me?"

"It sure is. And just like I said, you look so beautiful." Both young women's eyes glistened with excitement.

Guests began to arrive, friends and relatives alike. Cath and Abby stayed hidden downstairs, peeking around the corner of the doorway occasionally, seeing only the feet and ankles of those arriving. Cath knew her mother would come downstairs to see her as soon as she arrived.

"What can be keeping our mothers?" asked Cath anxiously as it got close to the time for the ceremony to begin. "I won't go ahead without Mama and Spence."

"They'll be here, Cath, don't worry. Nothing could keep them away. Maybe they got a flat tire—Spence's old car, y'know."

"Well, I'm going up to watch for them," said Cath with determination, holding up the folds of her long gown as she climbed the stairs to the entryway.

She had been glancing out one of the small windows that flanked the doorway of the church, worried about what could be keeping her brother, mother, and aunt when she saw the shiny black of Spence's car round the corner and come to an abrupt halt. Both ladies grabbed their hats with white-glove-covered hands and shouted simultaneously, "Spence!"

Cath smiled as she remembered how hard Spence had worked polishing his car. He was proud of the results, and so was Cath. Jack, too. Spence's car, although not too new, was as handsome as any parked in the fields around the wedding site.

And he was handsome, too, Cath had noted as she watched him through the door of the church, her small slender mother on one arm and her dear plump Aunt Irene on the other.

The picture was so vivid in her mind that even now, so many years later, Cath drew a quick breath, recalling that wonderful day as clearly as if it had been yesterday. Her recollections always ended with her thinking of Jack—Jack looking so strikingly grand in his fine suit, a sampling of the best flowers of the field in his lapel, his gray eyes laughing to match his smile.

Jack's eyes always laughed along with his lips.

Jack and Cath had taken many memorable photos on their trip to Minnesota in June. As Cath entered them in the album, she picked up one of Jack posing on a bridge and ran her fingers over his face, lightly touching, remembering their walk across the bridge spanning the Mississippi, the sun shining brightly, shimmering on the water below. She remembered the light, joyous feeling they had shared.

A lone tear dropped on to the photograph. Cath quickly blotted it away.

She mounted an entire page of photos of that trip—the last photos she'd ever have of Jack.

Chapter Six

The first few weeks after Jack's death were excruciatingly lonely for Cath. Family and friends consoled and comforted her, frequently inviting her along on their outings and activities. But she remained adamant that she work through her grief and loneliness her own way.

Cath picked up the threads of her art again and soon spent most of her days in her studio. She fully restocked her supplies, selecting tubes of paint, colors the range of the rainbow, and canvasses from the smallest to those so large she could barely get her arms around their width. Vigorously stirring colors until she reached just the right hue, she filled canvas after canvas with a combination of the bright and soft colors of nature.

Often, Cath was so wrapped up in what she was creating, she forgot to stop for lunch, or for a break of any kind. One day, as she stepped away from her work, she was amazed to find it was growing dark outside—and she had begun painting in mid-morning!

She devoted herself wholeheartedly to her talent. She immersed herself in her art, producing some really excellent paintings during the grief-stricken weeks and months following Jack's death. Perhaps some of her very best paintings. Cath's emotions dug very deeply into her creativity.

In many ways, the new paintings were reminiscent of her earlier work—long before her commercial contract for travel posters. Now she reverted back to scenes of the countryside surrounding Blakefield, scenes showing the big Nebraska skies.

Painting was good for her now; it kept her occupied through the many phases of her grief. As she entered her studio each day, some of the aching heaviness of her sadness lifted. Often she wouldn't start painting right away, but would sit and soak up her surroundings, remembering when Jack had planned this building for her, the joy she had felt when she first started spending her creative time here, and the comfort it still gave her. That old, comfortable, this-is-where-I-belong feeling.

But there came a time when she had to admit painting had become an obsession. For months that threatened to stretch into years, Cath had been taking time for almost nothing else. She had been driving herself relentlessly, turning out painting after painting, hoping her determination to work at doing her very best would help her rise above the pervading emptiness she felt inside.

In time, she began to heal. When Jack had been gone for nearly three years, Cath decided it was time to return some degree of balance to her life—time to include more of the world outside the confines of her studio. It was time to again tap into her own strength—to rise above the grief and her creative obsession.

She began to go out more often, to accept the invitations that had never ceased coming, to visit friends, to spend less time alone. She still painted, but not every single waking hour. She opened her life to others again and even planned to do some traveling.

A trip to Minnesota was foremost in her plans. She hadn't visited Julie and Kenneth but once since Jack's death, and then only briefly, when their twins were born.

The year following the death of her grandfather, Julie gave birth to twin boys, Jack and Hal, named after their great-grandfathers. The twins were not identical, not in appearance and not in personality. One had dark hair, the other light; one was quiet, the other overflowing with energy and mischief. As they grew older, it was apparent that the boys were as unlike as their namesakes. Unlike, but inseparable.

Although Cath had visited Julie when she brought the babies home from the hospital, she had kept that visit very short. She didn't want to encroach on the privacy of this, her favorite young family. And besides, it had been winter then, and the days threatened of blizzards that would hold her there for God only knows how long.

"There could be worse things than being trapped here with us in a snowstorm," teased Julie. "And it isn't as if you're going back to balmy Florida. Why, there's as much winter in Blakefield as there is here on the shores of Lake Minnetonka."

"Don't I know it. That's one of the reasons I need to get back. And honey, you and Kenneth need to be alone with these wonderful babies of yours. They're going to be around for many years, and you'd better get to know each other very well."

Julie smiled and looked down at her sleeping sons. "Aren't they beautiful, Grandma Cath?"

Cath felt a lump in her throat as she watched this young woman so dear to her step across the threshold to motherhood. She recalled how rich and fulfilling that phase of her own life had been, the years when Matt was with her and Jack, and she was very happy for Julie and Kenneth.

"Besides, I really hate to think of your going back to your empty house," Julie went on. "I worry about you, Grandma Cath. Why do you have to get back so soon?"

"Because it's home, honey. I'm fine, really. I need to go home, and you need your privacy."

Cath had avoided trips to Minnesota ever since that trip two years earlier. She just couldn't help remembering the last time she and Jack were there together, and the memories seared her with pain. But now, although Julie and her family had visited Blakefield a couple of times since the twin's birth, Cath realized she missed going to Julie's home and was eager for this trip. There was an easy coming and going for Cath at Julie's. Caring feelings were mutual, and Cath and Julie had the common bond of their love for painting.

Kenneth and Julie often discussed Cath's long absence from their home; they enjoyed having her there and had hoped she would be a vital part of their twins' lives.

"It surprises me somewhat that Cath has withdrawn so much in her grief, Julie," Kenneth said. "I know she and your grandfather were still very much in love, but each was also mighty independent—he with those great stores of his and she with her studio, her trips to Omaha, and then, to Chicago for the poster thing."

"She was—is—independent, that's for sure. I think that's part of her self-imposed isolation, Kenneth. She knows that only she can work out how her life can be worthwhile without Grandpa. I do miss her visits, though."

"I know you do; so do I."

"I had hoped she'd come to stay for some prolonged periods of time—even talked to her about it, as you know. But Kenneth, it really upset her. I think she thought I was implying I didn't think she could take care of herself, something I hadn't even considered. I know she can take care of herself. I just hate to think of her being so doggoned lonely."

She sighed. "You know, Kenneth, sometimes I think my great-grandmother did too good a job teaching her kids to always stand on their own. You know how Grandma Cath is, and my great-Uncle Spence was even worse."

"In what way?"

"Independent. Bull-headed. I can remember Grandma Cath, and even Dad, trying so hard to convince him he needed help on the farm as he grew older. It took years to persuade him. After the Bakers came to help out, he lived only three years, but at least his last three years were a bit easier. I adored my great-Uncle Spence, but he was a stubborn one."

"Like Cath?"

"Exactly."

When Cath called to say it was about time she paid them a visit, only three days after they had last discussed her, they were delighted. Trips to Minnesota became frequent again, and Cath enjoyed every one of them.

Chapter Seven

During the twins' early years, Julie painted very little. She dabbled in the colors more for diversion than professionally. It was just too difficult to concentrate on a painting with two small heads chasing one another through the legs of the easel.

But when the boys were old enough for school, she felt it was time to get back into her field. Excited when the time came for her first showing since she had resumed her career, she wanted to share the thrill. She called her grandmother.

"Grandma Cath, can you believe it! This is the first showing I've had in more than seven years, and I'm as nervous as I was the very first time. I feel like a novice all over again."

"You'll be wonderful, honey. You're good. You know you're good. The critics have liked your work for a long time now. Your talent hasn't left you, Julie, just because you've taken a brief hiatus. It'll always be there."

"Thanks, Grandma Cath. You're the best one-woman booster club anyone could hope for. I have an idea. You know what would be great?"

"No. What would be great, Julie?" asked Cath with a smile in her voice. She was delighted with Julie's news. She had wondered when Julie would again be ready to resume her career, to show her outstanding work.

Kenneth had been encouraging Julie for some time now, but Cath had been silent. She had long ago vowed not to meddle in her granddaughter's career decisions, and stick to that vow she would. However, nothing could keep her from expressing her pleasure once decisions had been made. Now Julie had come up with some "great idea."

"Fly up for the show Friday night," Julie insisted. "I know it's short notice, but I asked Mom and Dad, and they can't come." She paused. "Well, that's not totally true. Dad will be in Chicago, and Mom won't come. You know how she resents the fact that I became an artist when she wanted me to be a pianist, or an attorney—or Wall Street broker, or whatever."

Cath didn't comment on Rennie's refusal to share the joy of her daughter's artistic success. Rennie had fought Julie on this since the beginning, and Renata Spaulding Montgomery was unaccustomed to not having her own way.

Plus the last thing Rennie had wanted was for Julie to follow in her grandmother's footsteps.

"Of course I'll come. I'd be honored. I'll call Janice Masters at the travel agency and tell her to get me set up, and then I'll call you with my flight information. It's about time I visit again, anyhow. I haven't seen those growing boys of yours in too long. How are they?"

"Active, but wonderful. They never cease to amaze me. They are as different from one another as brothers could possibly be, but they're great pals. I really do wish their great-grandfathers had lived to get to know their namesakes. Grandpa Jack was gone, of course, before they were even born, and Grandpa Harold saw them just that once when I brought them to the hospital right before he died. They were only three weeks old then.

"I can hardly wait to see them, to see all of you. Let me phone Janice, and I'll call you right back."

"Just a minute, Grandma Cath, I have one more request to make of you. And please don't say no."

"Hmmm, this sounds mysterious. What is it, Julie?"

"Bring a couple of your paintings and show with me. You could send them express, and they'll be here before you are. Please. It would mean so much to me."

"Oh, Julie, I don't show any more. Just paint a bit to keep myself busy. But I'm honored, honey, really I am."

"Grandma Cath, please," she begged. "You know I never would have become an artist without you. Mom's fought me every step of the way. She refuses to share my success even now. Dad's always supported me, but only weakly because he's forever playing the peacemaker role between Mom and me. But you helped me realize I had talent, and I owed it to myself to see what I could do with it."

"You would have done it without me, Julie. You would have found your way as an artist without anyone's help."

"Don't be so sure," said Julie with a catch in her voice that Cath recognized as tears.

Cath wondered just what had gone on between Julie and Rennie this time. There had been so many battles over Julie's career choice that Cath was weary of them. She was also angry. Very angry. Darn that Rennie. Couldn't she share her daughter's joy just once?

"Honey, as long as you want your old gram to show with you, she'd regard it as the honor of her life."

"Thanks, Grandma Cath," Julie said, relief, along with excitement, showing in her voice. "It'll be so wonderful. I've sort of wanted to do this ever since I was a little girl—show my paintings along with my grandmother."

"I'd better get busy then. I'll get my plane reservations first, before I select a couple 'best of the best' and see about shipping arrangements. Goodness child, you've given me a busy day!"

"I know—isn't it fun? I can hardly wait to see you. This will be a really memorable time for both of us."

And a memorable time it was.

As expected, Julie's paintings received raving praise. She sold several—at quite a handsome prices, in fact.

Cath had a good offer on one of hers, too—a picture of the countryside around the farm where she grew up. The scene depicted the small creek and the old bridge that crossed it, a grove of fruit trees, and the old barn, barely standing, in the background. But even though the offer was tempting, she decided she couldn't bear to sell this painting, one of her early ones. Jack had always liked it, and it had been Spence's very favorite. As Spence grew older, he would often stand in front of his sister's painting for long periods of time—probably re-living his many happy years in its surroundings.

Of like minds, as always, Julie understood Cath's refusal to part with this particular painting. She, too, remembered carefree days as a small child, running along the banks of the creek and sitting on the edge of the bridge, swinging her feet, without a care in the world. She was glad her grandmother chose not to sell it, to keep it because of its strong, sentimental attachments and memories.

"That's why I love being around you, Grandma Cath. You're just so genuine, so unspoiled."

"I'm not so sure your great-Uncle Spence would have agreed with you, Julie. And I know your great-great Aunt Irene wouldn't have. She was always admonishing Mother about all the attention she gave me—warned her about spoiling me. Although," she added, "that's rather funny considering the way she spoiled her own and me."

"Well they were wrong. You're perfect just the way you are."

"Julie," said Cath, laughing, "grandparents are always perfect in the eyes of their grandchildren."

The two hugged, and Cath said, "I guess it's about time for me to get my things together and head for the airport. But before I go, one more photo of these two," she said, nodding in the direction of the twins, currently rolling on the floor with their dog.

Buster, the one-year-old chocolate-colored Labrador, seemed to be enjoying the activity equally as much as the boys. Jack and Hal, although not accustomed to being still for very long, posed once again for Cath, each with an arm wrapped around Buster's neck.

The photo turned out perfectly, and Cath placed it with pride along with the countless others in her album. "There," she said, even though no one was around to hear. "I'm getting to be just as good a photographer as you were, Jack."

Chapter Eight

Cath didn't make any more visits to Minnesota that year. She began to feel rundown and frequently ran unexplainable fevers. Her energy sporadic, some days she felt like doing everything; on others, nothing.

After a complete examination, hoping to get to the root of her general malaise and her fevers, Cath was told that she most likely had a virus of some kind, and it would undoubtedly "play itself out in due time." Extensive rest was advised.

Cath followed the advice, and within a couple of weeks, she did feel better.

Better, but not well.

Then, she began to experience sharp pains in her lower abdomen. When blood appeared in her urine, she again went through a thorough examination and several laboratory tests.

This time there was no doubt. Cancerous cells were found in her bladder.

Although not an anxious woman, she nonetheless felt the fear so often paralyzing to those who first hear the word "cancer" applied to them. She wanted it dealt with immediately and made the decision to have surgery as soon as possible.

"There's no reason for surgery not to be totally successful," the oncologist, Dr. Bruce Hazelton, told Cath and a worried Matt. "I think we've caught this in the very early stages, and you're generally in good health, Catherine."

Cath entered the hospital, and after a series of preparatory steps, made the long trip down the hospital corridors to the operating room.

Matt sat alone in the waiting room, agonizing and praying for his mother's recovery. Even though Matt had begged her, Rennie hadn't come with her husband, using the excuse that Julie was flying in from Minneapolis and she needed to wait for her arrival. He felt almost like a child, afraid to be alone.

Matt was attempting to read a newspaper when Rennie and Julie walked in.

"Daddy!" Julie rushed into his arms for a long embrace. She noted the deep concern evident on his face and matched it with a worried countenance of her own. "Have you heard anything yet?"

"Am I ever glad to see you," said Matt, hugging her tightly. "I was afraid you weren't coming. And no, I haven't heard a thing."

"You couldn't have kept me away. You know how much I love Grandma Cath," she said with a catch in her voice.

"Julie, don't you think it sounds a little childish for you to still call your grandmother, 'Grandma Cath.' After all, you're no longer a little girl."

"I'm quite aware of that, Mother," responded Julie icily, her voice revealing a mixture of anger and sadness. "But Grandma Cath is what I've always called her and always will."

"C'mon you two," said Matt, not wanting to cope with another one of the endless mother-daughter disagreements right now. "We're all a bit stressed. Why don't you just sit down, and I'll see if I can find someone who knows how it's going."

Just as Matt started down the corridor from the waiting room, Dr. Hazelton approached. Matt stopped in his tracks, glad to see someone who might be able to answer his questions about his mother, but at the same time, fearful of what the answers might be.

"Your mother came through the surgery very well, Mr. Montgomery," assured the doctor. "She's resting comfortably in recovery right now."

"Thank God," said Matt, exhaling a sigh that sounded as if he had been holding his breath. "And thank you, Doctor. Can we see her?"

"Of course, but she's sleeping and probably won't be aware you're there for quite a while. She's still pretty dopey and will undoubtedly sleep for some time. Why don't you just relax over a cup of coffee? They brew a pretty good cup in the cafeteria down on first."

"Good idea. I know I could use it. Thanks again." Matt warmly clasped the physician's hand. "We'll look in on my mother in a little while. I'm really anxious about her. My dad died a few years ago, and . . ."

"I understand. Just check with the nurse when you get back from the cafeteria. She'll show you to your mother's room. I'll be talking to you more later on. We'll need to discuss follow-up treatment," he said as he turned to walk away. "But right now relax a bit. She's going to be okay."

Matt just nodded, a lump in his throat.

"What did you find out, Dad?" asked Julie as Matt came back into the waiting room. She tried to read his expression even before giving him a chance to respond, and was immediately relieved not to see the despair she had so dreaded.

"The doctor said the surgery went well, and Mom is resting now. He asked that we wait a bit before going in to see her, since all she's going to do for a while is sleep. He suggested that we go down to the cafeteria on the first floor for what he says is a 'pretty good cup of coffee.'"

"But she's okay, Dad? Grandma Cath's okay?"

"Yes, honey, she's okay. I'll be talking to the doctor later about what follow-up treatment he advises—chemotherapy or whatever. God, I hate to think of Mom going through that," he added, speaking so softly it appeared he was talking just to himself.

But Julie heard his comment and placed her arm around him—a gesture attempting to give reassurance. "I know, Dad. But for now, let's just be grateful she's come through the surgery. And maybe the doctor won't even be suggesting anything too intensive."

Matt looked doubtful, but Rennie said, "He claimed they discovered the cancer in the early stages. Don't borrow trouble by worrying about something before you even know whether or not you have it to worry about."

Matt turned to Rennie and was about to comment on her uncaring remark, but then thought better of it.

"Let's go for that coffee, Dad," said Julie, knowing he needed some stress release, or he'd be lying in one of the hospital beds soon himself. "Besides, I'm starved."

As the three sat around a table in the cafeteria, sipping their coffee and eating what was really very acceptable apple pie, some of Matt's strain from the last few days lessened. His world revolved around three women. Two were sitting there with him, and the other was upstairs sleeping, hopefully beginning to win a battle against cancer.

He looked at his wife and covered her perfectly manicured hand with his own. From the day he had met her, Rennie had always looked picture-perfect, and today was no exception. Matt figured he looked as if he had slept in his clothes. The usual corporate-attorney correctness had been unimportant to him this morning. He barely recalled dressing.

But Rennie was as tastefully attired as usual in a coral-colored linen suit, accented by antique gold jewelry and a coral and green floral scarf perfectly arranged around her neck. Although aging was being very kind to Mrs. Matt Montgomery, she despised the wrinkles that had become quite pronounced on her neck. Rarely was Rennie seen without a scarf. Two entire dresser drawers were filled with scarves of every color and design conceivable—most of them pure silk.

Her nails were painted coral, an exact match to her ensemble. Holding her hand, Matt took a deep breath and said, "I want Mother to come live with us, Rennie. She's no longer strong enough to live alone, and heaven only knows, we have at least five times as much room as we need."

The Montgomerys' current house was large by any standards. Matt and Rennie's home well reflected Matt's successful career and Rennie's own inherited wealth. Their first home had been deemed "too small" when Julie arrived on the scene.

"Son, there is nothing 'too small' about your home," his dad had said when Matt told him of their plans to move, to buy a larger home.

"Rennie really wants the house over on Baker Boulevard, Dad. You know the one. Circle drive, corner lot."

"I know the one. It looks like a great house, but it also looks huge.

Are you sure you want to take on that much right now? You have a brand new baby daughter."

But move they did, in spite of Jack's arguments. Their home was featured in *House Beautiful* two years later, when Julie was but a toddler.

It was one of Rennie's happiest experiences.

And now Matt wanted to move his mother into her home—her perfect home. Rennie flinched, nearly yanking her hand from her husband's. She had feared he might suggest this—had, in fact, feared it since his father's death.

And she really dreaded the thought of Cath coming to live in her home.

She probably loved Cath, at least at the moment she thought she might. She really had felt bad when they learned Cath had cancer. But the idea of having her around every day was not a pleasant one, especially if she wasn't well.

Old and sick. Oh, God!

"Of course she can't live alone, darling. She's ill. But she's not going to be ill forever. You said the doctor assured you she'll most likely fully recover. Wouldn't it be better to bring her to a nursing home for a while, and—"

"Mother!" exclaimed Julie. "You can't be serious."

"No, Rennie, that wouldn't be better," Matt agreed with Julie. "I'm not going to stick my mother out of sight and out of mind. She's going to live with us."

Rennie could tell by the determination in Matt's voice that she'd never win this battle. At least not at the moment. Matt Montgomery was very much a Rowan, and she repeatedly saw the old Irish stubbornness, which was so much a part of Cath, also apparent in her husband. If Cath was going to live with them, she guessed she'd just have to make the best of it.

With a sigh of resignation, she said, "Of course, Matt. We'll fix up the back bedroom downstairs. She'll have her own bath right there, and she can be back out of—" Rennie caught herself before she added, "back out of my way," thus revealing how she really felt about this infringement on her privacy in her own home. She continued, "Where any noise won't bother her."

Matt caught the near slip and guessed what it was Rennie was about to say. *Well, no matter,* he thought. *Mother's going to be with us where she can be cared for—that's that.*

Chapter Nine

Cath argued with him when Matt first brought up the idea of selling her house. She was due to leave the hospital at the end of the week, and her recovery was going well. She wasn't certain she could ever bear to sell her house. It had been home for such a long time.

"Really, Matt, I'm not sure I'm ready to part with my home. I'm getting better, and I'm sure I'll soon be on my feet. I ought to be able to go right back to the way I've been living the past few years. I'm perfectly capable of taking care of myself, you know—or at least, I will be before too long."

She asked Matt for some time to think things over, and he agreed.

Lying in her hospital bed after he left, she reviewed all the changes they had made to the house they proudly purchased as a young couple. It had seemed like a castle to Cath then. In later years, when they easily could have afforded a larger, more lavish home, Cath and Jack decided to stay just where they were. They liked their house—and the exceptionally large yard that ran behind it, the spacious yard that became home to the studio barn and rose garden. Cath had insisted on a big yard, accustomed to the acreage of her family's farm.

Through the years the décor in their home had changed many times. Cath was somewhat ahead of her time in the decorating arena; for years she preferred muted warm colors for flooring and pale ivory for the walls. But the bathroom and kitchen had been torn apart with many a metamorphosis, as white appliances were replaced by a hideous green, followed by gold, and then again, white.

Cath chuckled to herself as she remembered Jack's words when they tore up their pink and black bathroom, replacing it with tasteful tan and white. "Please tell me, Cath, that we really didn't ever think that this pink and black stuff looked great."

But realistically, she knew that, although her mind remained alert, her body was failing her. She didn't bounce back from illnesses like she used to, and finally the thought of having to maintain the house grew worrisome to her. Even if she hired help, it might not be enough to keep her beautiful home cared for as she and Jack had done together for so many years.

Maybe it was time for a young family to enjoy it. Fill it with the love of a couple and child, as she and Jack had done. Fill it with their own special memories to look back on in their later years.

When Matt returned, she said, "I've decided you're right about selling the house. But I won't be a bother to you and Rennie. I'll stay out of your hair. Soon maybe I can find a small apartment or something of my own again."

Matt smiled at his mother's declaration of independence. And she could be right—she might be able to take care of herself again some day. But he had promised his dad ever since he was a teenager that if anything happened to Jack, he would take care of his mother, and nothing was going to deter him from that promise.

"Mom, I know you can take care of yourself. You always have. But it isn't necessary. You always took care of me, and now it's my turn. Your full recovery may take a while, and I want you where I can keep an eye on you on a daily basis. Seeing me again every day won't be so bad, will it?" he asked in an attempt to add some levity to the conversation.

Cath smiled at the thought of seeing her son daily. She'd like that very much. And she really had been terrified of the cancer. She didn't relish the thought of being alone if all that blood turned up in her urine again. Maybe she shouldn't be so stubborn—get on with growing old.

So the home or Catherine Rowan Montgomery was placed on the market by a realtor Cath knew and trusted. The home where she had come as a bride, where she and Jack had raised their son. Where they had barely begun to grow old together and where she had lived independently as a widow.

Plans were made for Cath to make her home with Matt and

Rennie.

Julie flew home to Minnesota as soon as she knew her grandmother was out of immediate danger, but promised to come back soon.

"Dad," she said, "though I hate leaving you with all of this, I do need to get back to Kenneth and the boys." She knew her mother not only wouldn't be of any help getting Cath settled, she would most likely do all she could to make it more difficult for Matt. Julie knew her mother very, very well.

"Of course you need to get back to your family, Julie. I'll manage just fine. Kenneth probably needs to be rescued by now."

They laughed, both guessing it was probably true. Matt had two very active grandsons.

"I'll come back in a couple weeks to help pack up Grandma Cath's things, Dad. Her personal things, plus her paintings and paints and everything from her studio."

"Thanks, honey. That'll be a big help. I'll have someone move her bedroom furniture and any other furnishings she can use in that room. We'll trade what's in there now for her furniture as soon as she's well enough to be up for longer periods of time. I want her to be happy living with us."

"Of course you do, Dad. And she will be. Well, I guess I'd better get on the plane before it goes without me. Tell Grandma Cath I'll see her again soon. Tell Mom, too."

Julie gave her father a quick kiss and ran to board her plane.

Matt hired a company to pack and move his mother's possessions—and sell those she'd no longer be using. He told her of this the day after she signed the sales contract.

"Can't we wait until I'm up to doing my own packing?" Cath insisted. "I don't want some strangers going through my things, deciding what I should keep. And the studio. What about my studio?"

"Mom, please relax. It's going to be okay. Louise Collins works for this company. You remember Julie's friend, Louise, don't you? And Julie plans to come back to help, too."

He relayed his parting conversation with Julie to his mother now, taking her hand and consoling her that "everything would be all right."

"If you say so, Matt. I do remember Louise. A very hard-working, levelheaded girl, if I recall. And you know I don't trust anyone more than our Julie. I'm sure she understands which things I'd like to keep."

She reflected on the plans and mused, "I guess I should really thank you for not making me go back to the house to take things out—to close it up. Even the thought hurts. It also makes me miss your dad so much, Matt." Her weary eyes glistened with tears.

"I'm rather anxious about it myself," Matt agreed. "All my memories until college are there—not to mention dad's presence. And yours. I'm glad Julie's coming back for my good, as well as yours, Mom. It'll make it easier for both of us."

Matt gently squeezed her hand, reassuring her again that it truly would be all right. She closed her eyes and gave way to a deep and restful sleep. Matt watched her for a moment, then gently lifted his hand from hers and tiptoed quietly from the room.

Matt settled his mother into the large, first-floor bedroom of his and Rennie's home. It sat far back, at the end of a long hall, distant from the living room. It was a lovely, spacious room, with wide windows from which Cath could view the attractive landscaping of the Montgomery home.

And yet, Cath was filled with an astounding emptiness.

Lying in bed, she checked her surroundings. It seemed so foreign, almost like she was living in someone else's body. She had a dislocated feeling—a feeling of not belonging.

She thought Matt and Rennie's home was one of the most beautiful in Blakefield. The decor bordered on perfection, and she had always enjoyed visiting and had some fond memories of happy occasions in this house, particularly during Julie's childhood.

But now, all she felt was an intense sadness, a separation from the familiar and endeared.

You're being foolish old lady, she argued to herself.

She recognized that part of her gloom stemmed from her illness—an illness that only time and several weeks of chemotherapy could hope to draw to a close. She also realized it was only natural she would feel despair over leaving her own home, hers and Jack's.

Their home had been the site of boundless happiness, a place to share with friends—a warm and welcoming spot. It exuded warmth and comfort. Sofas and chairs covered with floral fabric, large footstools—used both for propping up feet and sitting—colorful paintings on the ivory-colored walls, and plants everywhere, as well as floral bouquets whenever the seasons would allow. And when they didn't, it wasn't unusual to see a delivery truck from Delbert Florists pull up in front of the Montgomery house with a colorful and fragrant out-of-season bouquet. Cath loved flowers.

On the far end of Jack and Cath's living room was a massive piano with heavy turned legs and carved panels. The piano had been in Cath's Aunt Irene's home. Although all six of Irene's children had "tinkered" with playing, none had taken it seriously, and when Irene died, Abby, the eldest, offered the family heirloom to Cath.

"If you don't want it, Cuz, we'll sell it. But I did want to offer it to you first. Maybe Matt could become a Rowan virtuoso. None of our kids are interested. God knows, it didn't take with any of the six of us," she added, "in spite of Mom's efforts."

"I'd love to have it, Abby. I don't play a note, as you're aware, but who knows, maybe Matt has some latent talent."

He didn't have, but the piano remained. Cath kept it tuned, and in spite of its age and antiquated appearance, it had beautiful tone. Rarely did anyone play it—no one but Rennie—Rennie when Matt first brought her home to meet his mom and dad, and many times after that.

Other heirlooms had been tastefully displayed throughout the house—Jack's mother's boudoir chair, his father's clock—the one that had sat on his desk in the back room that served as his office at the original Montgomery store. The chandelier in the dining room came from Jack's parents' home—and from his grandparents' home before that.

Cath treasured Sarah's quilt rack, prominently displayed in the guest bedroom, holding one of Sarah's lovely hand-made quilts. Sarah's rocking chair, although too fragile to use, sat in the corner of Cath and Jack's own bedroom.

Thinking about her home—now sold—tore at Cath. As she drifted off to sleep, she wondered, *Did I make a mistake?*

Chapter Ten

Cath lay tucked between cool, ultra-fine cotton sheets in the stunning Queen Anne poster bed central in Rennie and Matt's guest room—the room she now called home. She was awake but daydreaming, thinking of days long gone by.

Her reverie was broken by loud voices coming from the kitchen. Matt and Rennie's voices. Arguing.

She couldn't hear what they were saying, but she had the uncomfortable feeling it had to do with her. Although nothing had been said directly to her, Cath was fairly certain her moving in did not have Rennie's whole-hearted blessing. Rennie rarely came into her room, and when she did, she had little to say. She simply looked around the room with disdain, as if something had spoiled the pleasantness of her home.

Cath was right. Matt and Rennie were arguing over her—again.

"Do you know how many of your mother's friends came traipsing through my house today? You didn't tell me when you insisted that your mother move in here that my house would become a major freeway."

"Good God, Rennie, she's been sick and they're her friends. They've been concerned about her, just as we've been. I'm sure as she grows stronger, she'll be visiting some of them at their homes, but until then, try to show some compassion, will you? She's my mother."

"Well, you don't notice my mother upsetting our lives, do you?" she snipped, petulantly.

As always when Rennie mentioned her mother, Matt softened. Rennie had never gotten over her mother's untimely death. Putting his arms around her, he said, "Your mother's been gone for a long time, Rennie, and I know the pain has never left you. Honey, we can't help your mother, but we can help mine. Please, Rennie."

But Rennie was enmeshed in rage, and nothing Matt said caused her to ease up on her anger one bit. "Why do I have to move my beautiful Queen Anne bedroom suite out of that room? I had that room decorated just to fit that furniture. It's my house, and it should stay just the way it is!"

"It's our house Rennie—yours, mine, and now, Mom's."

Rennie glared at him, hating the idea that she was giving up some of the sovereignty of her home to anyone—especially to Cath.

"I want Mom to have her own bedroom furniture. For one thing, hers isn't quite so grand in scale, so she'll have more space. And her own furniture will make it more like her own place. She needs to feel that room is hers. And," he added with emphasis, "it will be hers for the rest of her life."

Rennie wondered what Matt would say if he knew that, right then, she hoped it wouldn't be a terribly long life.

"And just what do you suggest we do with the Queen Anne suite? I'm certainly not getting rid of it."

"I'm not asking you to get rid of it. I don't want that either. But we have space in the almost empty bedroom upstairs."

"But it won't look right—the colors are all wrong, and the room isn't nearly big enough," Rennie argued.

"Redecorate it then," said Matt with a sigh. "I'm going to have Mom's room redecorated as soon as she's well enough to be up. We might as well do both at the same time." With that pronouncement, he turned and left the room, weary of arguing.

Rennie watched him walk away, her unspent anger broiling. "Damn you, Matt. I swear I'll get even with you for this," she swore under her breath.

And so the deep burgundy and ivory decor in the guest room was replaced by sunny yellow and white, and the dark cherry Queen Anne suite was moved upstairs, replaced by Cath's own walnut bed, dresser, chest, and desk—furniture she and Jack had used their entire married lives.

"Oh, Matt. Doesn't it look wonderful!" Cath enthused. "Thank you so much. It makes it look like home."

"It *is* home, Mom—mine, Rennie's, and yours. Now why don't you take a rest in your bed, in your room, in your home."

Cath crawled into her freshly made bed feeling close to contented, feeling happier than she had since moving in. Perhaps living here with Matt and Rennie will work after all.

Cath grew stronger, even weathered her chemotherapy very well. Matt had set everything else aside on the days his mother was slated for treatment, scheduling his client appointments around, what he regarded, as the most important task at hand. He also accompanied her on her frequent follow-up appointments with Dr. Hazelton—except for one. When a court appearance ran far later than anticipated, he asked Rennie to take her to see the doctor in his stead. This she did, although she complained to Matt at great length that it wasn't her responsibility—Cath wasn't her mother.

Little by little, Cath began to regain her strength, and little by little, she began to feel at home in her sunny yellow bedroom in Matt and Rennie's house.

Always an early riser, she joined the two of them for breakfast as soon as she felt able. Breakfast-time was a bright moment in her sometimes-lonely day. Often, the conversations were light, covering topics no more weighty than the weather, but sometimes, she and Matt discussed important news items in the morning paper. Always well-read, Cath had kept abreast with the news and enjoyed the discussions. Occasionally, Rennie would enter the conversations, offering her opinion or viewpoint. Most often, she did not.

Daily each morning, Matt would question his mother about how she felt, whether she had rested well. As her answers continued to be positive, as Cath's health continued to improve, his questions were less fervent, his attitude less tense. His mother was getting better.

Cath resumed some semblance of a normal life. She arose on schedule most mornings, and even tidied her room as much as she was able. In the afternoons, she rested.

She was a determined woman, and part of her determination included not allowing herself to be a burden to her son and his wife, not casting a pall of sickness over their day-to-day living.

Chapter Eleven

Damn Matt! Insisting that I bring Cath to Lincoln with me. Rennie was seething as she recalled their argument that morning.

"Take Mom along," suggested Matt when he learned his wife was planning a drive to Lincoln to look for drapery fabric. "She's been a virtual prisoner in this house since we brought her home from the hospital. She needs to get out more."

"Well, it certainly isn't my fault she's finding our home a prison. It wasn't my idea to have her come here, if you recall," Rennie added, sarcastically. "If you want her to be 'out and about' so badly, why don't you take her yourself?"

"Rennie, what's come over you? This isn't like you." But even as Matt made the statement, he knew it wasn't true. This was exactly like Rennie. Like the person she had become. The spoiled child had become the totally self-centered adult. Most of the time, she seemed unable—or unwilling—to consider the needs of anyone but herself.

Matt could feel his anger rising. The color in his already ruddy face heightened, and he was about to spew out an angry retort. Then he looked hard at this beautiful woman before him, and in spite of his disgust over her growing self-centeredness, he admitted to himself how very much he still loved her.

Putting his arm around her trim waist, he drew her close to him. "C'mon, Rennie, what will it hurt? You said you were only going to stop at Vanderhover's to check out their fabric. It looks like a beautiful day—an ideal one for a drive and a change of scenery for Mom. And you're right. I should be taking her out myself. This darned case! But I need to be in Chicago to take depositions this afternoon—and for a meeting at eight tomorrow morning. I'll be back tomorrow night, and then maybe we can talk about how to get Mom out more."

"Okay, okay. I'll take her with me. I guess it won't hurt this once. But, Matt . . ."

Rennie didn't finish, but Matt caught the meaning: *Cath is your mother, you're the one who insisted she live with us, and it's up to you to take care of her—not me.*

Cath was late this morning, and they ate in strained silence. Newspaper rustled as each read a favorite section, and silver clinked against china, their breakfast devoured without comment. A bird warbled a joyous song outside the window, oblivious to the hostile silence inside.

"Sorry I'm so poky this morning," apologized Cath as she finally came into the dining room. Her face still showed the pallor of her illness, and she moved more slowly than she had before the surgery. But the light was back in her eyes; the determined Cath was beginning to shine through.

"Good morning, Mom," said Matt, getting up and giving his mother a peck on the cheek as she sat down. "Don't you look aglow this morning."

Cath had donned a colorful robe—a bright, almost iridescent blue background covered with multicolored flowers. It was a charming contrast to her snow-white hair and really did make her look "aglow." She had even added a slight touch of lipstick.

She smiled at her son's compliment as Matt poured her a large glass of water. She dutifully accepted the brimming-full glass, but not without a sigh.

"How I miss my morning coffee," she said. "It seems almost uncivilized not to begin the day with a cup of coffee."

"I know, Mom, but remember what the doctor said."

"Don't worry. I'm following the doctor's orders, but that doesn't mean I'm enjoying it. I really do miss the coffee—that wonderful aroma as you take that first sip. Mmmm." She reached for her water again. "Guess I'll settle for what I can have."

Cath ate her fruit and cereal and drank her water, joining Matt and Rennie in their silence. They appeared engrossed in reading the Blakefield Bulletin, so she decided not to disturb them with conversation. Anyhow, she was eager to read about the groundbreaking for yet another Montgomery's store that was to have taken place yesterday. She selected the local-news section of the paper and perused it for a story of the expansion of the retail empire still bearing their family's name.

While his mother was occupied with her reading, Matt looked at Rennie, trying to tell her with his eyes that now might be a good time to invite Cath to join her in her jaunt to Lincoln. But Rennie was having none of it. She simply refused to meet Matt's gaze throughout breakfast, pretending to be totally absorbed in reading the newspaper.

Finally, Matt said, "Mom, Rennie's going to drive to Lincoln this morning, and she thought you'd like to go along."

Cath missed the glare Rennie directed Matt's way, so pleased was she about the thought of a nice drive on such a beautiful morning. "Oh, I'd love that! I really do need to get out now that I'm feeling so much better. I opened my window just a wee bit this morning, and the wonderful smell of fall is in the air."

And now, looking out the window from where she sat at the dining room table, Cath could see that there wasn't a cloud in the sky. A truly beautiful day.

"I need to decide what I'm going to wear," she said with animation—the most she had shown since she was told she had bladder cancer several weeks earlier. She pushed her chair away from the table, obviously excited about the events of the day. "It seems like my attire has been gowns and robes for so long now. For much too long."

She started towards her room, then turned back, looked at her daughter-in-law, and smiled broadly. "Thanks, Rennie. You're a dear to think of me."

Rennie felt a pang of guilt as Cath walked away. "Okay, so I acted like a cad. But Matt, you're always in court or somewhere else and have no idea how trying it is to have a sick old lady around all the time."

Again, Matt flushed. He spoke softly and distinctly, carefully enunciating his words in quiet anger. "Yes, Rennie, I am gone a lot. I've already told you how sorry I am about that, and I'll try to be home more as soon as I get back from Chicago, and this current case is over.

"But remember that 'sick old lady' is my mother, and she isn't 'around all the time.' She lives here. This is her home."

With those clipped words, Matt excused himself from the table, grabbed his briefcase, and started for the door. But immediately, he had second thoughts about his abruptness. He walked back to his wife, put his hand beneath her chin, and lifted her lovely face up towards his.

"Try to have a good day, Ren. Please try. For all of us." He bent down and kissed her gently. Before she could say a word, he walked out the door to the garage, started his car, and in a moment was on his way to the airport to catch his flight to Chicago.

Chapter Twelve

Reliving this morning's conversation with Matt, Rennie drove back towards Blakefield. Her anger rekindled and destroyed any pleasant mood she had managed to acquire as the morning progressed.

Cath had actually been fairly good company on the way over. They talked and even laughed a little over lunch. But now, Rennie was weary of her. She was just so darned—well, burdensome.

She glanced quickly at Cath and saw that she was resting her head back against the seat, napping. A small dribble of drool had collected in the corner of her mouth, and she snored lightly, seemingly sound asleep.

Good, thought Rennie. *Now I at least won't need to make small talk.*

She again became lost in her thoughts. So preoccupied was she with them, in fact, that Cath's voice startled her.

"Rennie, I hate to ask you to do this, but could you please stop at that service station just ahead. I badly need to use the restroom."

"Really, Cath, I told you to go before we left the restaurant. You're worse than a child," she said with disgust.

"I know," said Cath, embarrassed. "It's just that . . ."

"Can't you wait for another half hour? We're only thirty miles from home, and I'm really anxious to see how this fabric looks in the bedroom. For a long time, I've looked hard for the perfect color and pattern for that upstairs room, and this might be it. Nothing seems to look right since we put the Queen Anne suite in there."

Cath heard the petulance in Rennie's voice as she complained, but more urgent matters demanded her attention at the moment. "I really can't wait, Rennie. I'm sorry, I know that this is an imposition, but it seems like ever since the surgery, I just can't—"

"God, am I going to have to hear about your surgery for the rest of my life? Okay, we'll stop. But hurry, will you?" Rennie ordered as she pulled her shiny black Lexus to an abrupt stop at the service station.

Cath all but ran towards the restroom, then realized she needed a key from the attendant. She went inside the station and, with key in hand, hurried to the designated door and shakily inserted it, unlocked the door, and rushed inside.

After a few minutes, Rennie looked at her watch and tapped her fingers against the dashboard impatiently. She turned the radio dial, looking for music that matched her mood. When she couldn't find anything to suit her, she angrily clicked the radio knob off and thrust out her lower lip in a childish pout. She took the mirror from her purse and checked her lipstick. And again, she looked at her watch, her anger building along with her impatience.

Rennie glanced at the station, colorful with its red roof and neon sign advertising food and drink that could be purchased inside. She surveyed the surroundings and noted there was nothing—absolutely nothing—around the station. Nothing but highway and fields.

"What a God-forsaken spot," she said aloud.

She stared towards the restroom door, but saw no Cath emerging. *This is ridiculous,* she thought. *Why am I sitting here waiting for an old woman whose company I didn't want in the first place?*

She honked the horn—loudly and long. A young station attendant ran over to her car, his long, light-brown hair hanging over his forehead almost to his hazel eyes, covering much, but not all, of his teen-age blemished face.

"May I help you?" he asked eagerly.

"No, no. I accidentally leaned against my horn," she lied. "Sorry."

The friendly and accommodating young man trotted over to another car as Rennie seethed, embarrassment added to her anger. She checked her watch one more time.

Cath was having some problems. The urgency of her situation, along with the woolen slacks she had chosen to wear on the cool fall day, resulted in an abundance of perspiration settling on her legs and abdomen, making them damp and sticky. Gliding her hose back up turned into quite a struggle. She was tugging at her clothing so hard, trying as best she could to hurry, that by the time she had accomplished her feat, she was trembling from the effort.

She felt almost faint when she was finally dressed again, but she found some humor in the situation. *I guess I understand now how little ones feel when they're sent to the bathroom alone,* she thought. *The clothes never seem to go back on as easily as they did in the first place.*

Wearing a slight smile and glad to again be fully clothed, she closed the door to the restroom, walked back into the station with the key, and handed it to the attendant. Then she headed for Rennie's car, ready for the remainder of the trip home.

Suddenly, she stopped in her tracks. She looked over to the spot where Rennie had been parked; then she scanned the rest of the lot, but saw no Rennie—no black Lexus.

In fact, there wasn't a car in sight.

It appeared Rennie had left without her.

Chapter Thirteen

At first, the shock of her situation immobilized Cath. She simply stood and stared at the spot where Rennie had been parked. She was confused—and a little bit frightened. Where did Rennie go? Why would she leave without her?

"I don't understand," she said aloud. She shook her head sadly, perhaps denying that her daughter-in-law could have been so uncaring, so unkind. She felt abandoned. And she was indeed so.

Abandoned and alone, thirty miles from home.

Realizing that feeling afraid would accomplish absolutely nothing, she sighed deeply, thrust back her shoulders, and walked inside the station with her head held high.

"Is there a phone I might use?" she asked the attendant courteously, but with the authority of someone who had taken charge.

"Outside, just around the corner, there's a pay phone," responded the young man without looking up, his attention focused on the newspaper's sports section.

Cath opened her purse and searched for coins for the phone, but found no change—nothing smaller than a fifty-dollar bill. "I guess I'll need some change. Will you break this for me, please?" she asked, handing him the bill.

"Geez, lady, don't you have anything smaller? This isn't a bank, y'know," he whined.

"No, I don't," she said with uncharacteristic sharpness, some of the fear she had felt a few moments earlier returning. Tired, she had difficulty holding herself erect—as erect as her pride preferred. "Now will you please break this for me?" Her voice quavered, a combination of anger, fear, and weariness.

"Sure, lady, sure," said the young man, recovering his manners. He had been drilled in basic customer-service skills when he was hired, but sometimes he—well, sometimes, he just forgot.

He took her bill and counted out her change. "Hey, are you okay?" he asked, noticing her hand shake as she accepted the money. "Do you want a soda or something?"

Cath smiled at the young man's thoughtfulness—and his change in demeanor. *He's just a boy,* she thought. *A boy left in charge. Probably a very nice boy, really.*

Suddenly her eyes filled with tears. She felt needy and vulnerable—grateful for a little momentary kindness from someone not much more than a child.

"Thank you, that's very kind of you. But I really need to make a phone call and be on my way," she said, attempting once more to sound self-assured and in complete control. To sound more in control than she felt.

The young man studied the elderly woman before him. He looked outside, around the station, which was situated quite far out from the closest small town and about thirty miles from the nearest city, Blakefield. He didn't see any car. There hadn't been one since the woman driving the great-looking Lexus left five minutes ago, squealing her tires as she sped away like she was being chased. Where did this woman come from, anyhow?

"But . . ." he began.

"Thanks, again," said Cath as she hurriedly went out the door.

He watched her go around the corner of the station to the phone. Just then, a car drove up. Until Joey came back from the service call, he was "it," so he hurried out to service his new customer, with just one more glance towards where Cath had disappeared.

Later, when again there were no customers, he walked around by the phone to check on her. She was a very pleasant lady—sort of pretty, in a grandmother kind of way. And she was very nicely dressed. He still wondered where she had come from, but when he checked, she was gone.

Cath had dialed home first, but hung up even before the first ring. *I'm being ridiculous. Rennie couldn't possibly be there yet, even if she went straight home—and she may not have gone directly home. Besides, if she wouldn't wait for me, she certainly isn't going to turn around and come back for me.*

She again felt frightened and very foolish, an old lady in a predicament she wasn't sure how to resolve. She picked up the receiver again to call one of her many friends in Blakefield—friends whom she knew would come get her in a heartbeat, the very many she knew well and had known most of her life. She knew their phone numbers, each and every one.

But how would I explain why I'm stranded this far from home? Certainly, no one would believe I had just gone for a stroll and found I had walked thirty miles. I can't bear to think of telling them the truth—that my own daughter-in-law abandoned me like an unwanted kitten. No, it would be too humiliating.

Cath replaced the receiver, filled with a sense of sadness, a feeling of separation. It seemed unreal to her—how she could possibly be stuck so far from home with nothing around except a gas station?

So Cath began to walk along the highway, heading towards home, certain she couldn't walk all the way, but not knowing what else she could do. Hopefully, Rennie would change her mind and come back. Maybe she was just trying in some misguided way to show Cath who was boss.

Her attempts to hold her head high collapsed as soon as she turned away from the phone. She didn't feel confident. She didn't feel self-assured. And she couldn't pretend that she did, not even to herself.

The day had turned cool, typical of a fall day. Cath hadn't dressed for the outdoors, nor was she wearing shoes really meant for walking, at least not for walking any distance. She was dressed stylishly, like a fairly well-to-do elderly lady going shopping.

Her gray wool slacks, which had been almost too warm in the comfort of Rennie's car, didn't keep out the cool breeze; they were too lightweight. Her shoes, although having a low heel, were, nonetheless, a dress shoe with thin soles and minimal support. Her jacket was a beautiful muted rose and gray plaid, a lightweight cashmere in a one-button style.

Cath turned up the collar and clutched the jacket tightly to her.

Her steps were painfully slow, not at all like the spirited gait Catherine Montgomery was known for. She walked a long way that day. Long for a woman no longer young and no longer well.

All in all, she walked about seven miles, continually keeping a hopeful eye out for Rennie's Lexus.

She was just coming to the outskirts of New Harmon, a small town twenty-three miles east of Blakefield, whose primary claim to fame was their outstanding high-school basketball team. Here, perhaps, she could find help.

By now, she could barely think, and she was incredibly cold. Her head ached, and she could scarcely feel her uncovered ears, pink with cold—a sharp contrast to the ocean pearl earrings she wore. From time to time, she held her glove-covered hands over her ears, warming them slightly.

But she found she needed her arms at her sides to steady herself—to help keep herself from staggering on to the highway. With each step, she felt that she surely could not walk another inch. Her steps minute, she dragged her feet more than actually walking. Her shoes were covered with the dust of the roadside. Through their thin soles, she could feel the small rocks and pebbles scattered along the shoulder that had become her path, and more than once she turned an ankle as her foot rolled over the rocks. She had been limping for the last four miles.

Her head was bowed, as if by watching each step, she could encourage another.

Several cars stopped along the way, but Cath refused their offers of assistance. She was totally exhausted and hardly able to think straight, but not so much that she no longer cared about her well-being.

Catherine Montgomery simply refused to be a helpless, vulnerable old woman, robbed and possibly injured by a so-called helpful citizen.

She began to totter and weave. Her weariness totally encompassed her being, and she wondered how she could keep going. New Harmon was right there within her reach. It was almost as if she could touch it, but it was just beyond her fingertips.

It seemed she couldn't make it to anywhere for help. She just wanted to lie down alongside the road and sleep. Tears fell unbidden and dropped from her face. Her nose ran as if she were an unattended child.

"I'm so tired, Jack," she said in a broken voice.

Another car slowed to a stop and pulled to the side of the road. An older man and woman got out of the car and came over to Cath. He was heavy-set, with only a fringe of gray hair showing beneath his cap and friendly gray eyes reflecting concern. The woman was large, nearly as tall as he, with short-bobbed, dark hair streaked amply with white and large dark eyes.

The man's speech had the soft inflection of one who had grown up in the Deep South. "Ma'am, can we help you?" he asked. "My name is Clay Smith, and this is my wife, Patsy." He nodded towards the woman, who had placed her hand gently on Cath's shoulder.

"No," said Cath softly, barely looking their way and attempting to continue her slow and unsteady gait.

Patsy pleaded with her. "We just can't leave you out here alone. It's cold and soon will be getting dark. Please let us take you somewhere. Please."

Cath knew she wouldn't be able to continue much longer, no matter how much perseverance she had. She simply couldn't get home without assistance.

Home to Matt.

These people seemed so genuine, she decided to accept their kindness. She simply had to; she was sure she couldn't walk many more steps without collapsing.

"Thank you. You're most kind. Now, I think I'll accept that ride," she said, trying to force a smile.

Chapter Fourteen

Clay Smith gently took Cath's elbow and guided her into his car. The warmth pleasantly engulfed her, and she shuddered as a strong current of chills swept over her. Leaning her head back, Cath relinquished herself to her weariness.

As she momentarily closed her eyes, a lone tear trickled down her cheek.

Patsy Smith took a fresh, clean handkerchief from her purse and wiped Cath's face. She patted her shoulder and said, "Just rest. You look so tired."

"No, no, I'm fine," lied Cath. "It's just that . . ." But Cath knew she couldn't tell even these strangers what really happened, no matter how kind they were. It simply would be too degrading.

"Such a foolish old woman I am," she said in a weak, faltering voice. "I drove over to Lincoln this morning, and on the way back, the car developed some strange noises, so I brought it to the service station back there." She nodded her head in the direction she came from. "I thought New Harmon was just a mile or so, and it was such a beautiful day . . ."

She abruptly halted her rambling. She couldn't think of another word to explain how she happened to be walking along the highway. In fact, momentarily, she couldn't think at all.

The Smiths looked at one another, suspecting Cath's tale wasn't exactly what had happened. But not wanting to seem as if they were interrogating her, they let it go unquestioned.

"Would you like us to bring you back to the service station?" asked Patsy.

"No," responded Cath, perhaps too hurriedly. "My car won't be ready today. Just bring me to New Harmon. I'll call my son from there, and he'll come to pick me up."

She didn't remember that Matt had left for Chicago that morning and wouldn't be home until tomorrow night

"Do you live near New Harmon, Ma'am?" asked Clay.

"No, I live in Blakefield. Have all my life," said Cath with a sad, slight smile.

"Blakefield. That's where we're headed. Let's just take you home," he said, pulling away from the side of the road.

"No, that's too much of an imposition," argued Cath, her voice faint, not really giving much substance to her argument.

The Smiths didn't heed her plea. Patsy had been head nurse in the geriatric unit of Cook County Hospital for many years, and her experience helped her recognize that Cath was an older woman in distress—that she was not just taking an afternoon stroll.

Cath leaned her head back again and let some release from her exhaustion wash over her. She was trembling, and her breath was heavy and labored.

The Smiths were worried.

"Ma'am, I really think we should make a stop at the hospital," said Clay as they came to the edge of New Harmon. "It's a mighty small town, and the hospital isn't much, but they're very friendly and helpful over there."

"No. I don't want a hospital. I just want to go home," begged Cath, her voice quavering, suggesting tears all too close to the surface.

"Clay," said Patsy, catching her husband's eye. "Do you know what I need? I'm really thirsty. Please pull into that convenience store over there and get a bottle of that great spring water for me, will you? It'll just take a minute."

"Sure," he replied, nodding knowingly. He knew his wife was aware of various danger signs in the elderly, and he remembered the many times she'd spoken of guarding against thirst and dehydration. Why hadn't he thought of that? "Y'know, honey, a nice cool drink of water sounds great to me, too."

The two women waited in the car while he quickly ran into the store, emerging soon with three chilled bottles of spring water. Cath's hand shook terribly as she took hers and, tilting her head back, drew in the cool refreshing water, drinking quickly. Some of it escaped her mouth, rolling from the corners, dripping from her chin. Cath swiped at the wet with her gloved hand.

The Smiths sipped their water, watching Cath carefully, concern evident on their faces. They were also confused and troubled. How did this woman happen to be walking along the highway? There were no signs she was hurt in any way. Her clothes were not in disarray, and she had no visible injuries.

What in the world had happened here?

Soon, Cath's water bottle was empty, and she handed it to Clay. He noticed her hand still trembled, and except for two bright pink circles on her cheeks and flushed ears, she was deathly pale.

"That was wonderful. Thank you. Now I really must be getting home," she said, with an unsuccessful attempt at determination in her voice. "I could call a cab from here. You two have been so kind," she added, with a weak, but warm, smile.

"Nonsense," said Clay and Patsy simultaneously. "We're taking you home."

Cath didn't argue. She again laid her aching head back against the seat. It lolled from side to side as they drove the remaining miles to Blakefield.

These people, so kind, must think so badly of me—a doddering old lady dragging herself along the edge of the highway. Embarrassment consumed Cath.

Twenty-five minutes later, Clay drove down the street where Matt, Rennie, and Cath lived, noting the tree-lined boulevard that spoke of affluence. He pulled up in front of the house, a large two-story brick home surrounded by flowers, fading as summer gave way to fall. The sun was low in the sky, late afternoon settling in before nightfall. It seemed to Cath that this morning was eons ago.

This morning when she had been so excited about a drive to Lincoln.

Chapter Fifteen

Rennie was in the living room at the piano when the Smith's car drove up. She wasn't playing anything in particular—just fingering chords, trying to shut out what had happened earlier in the day.

A handsome walnut baby-grand piano adorned Matt and Rennie's living room, and it wasn't unusual to hear strains of Bach or Beethoven filling the rooms of the Montgomery home in the late afternoon or early evening. Rennie played the piano effortlessly and flawlessly, with feeling and deep emotion. In her music, Rennie showed a depth of feeling, of passion, that she showed no other time—except perhaps when making love to her husband. Rennie and Matt Montgomery, for all their troubles and dissension, remained impassioned love partners.

Rennie had been restless ever since she'd arrived home. Nervous. Maybe even feeling guilty about leaving Cath. A little guilty, anyway.

But what's wrong with making her understand who was in charge? It wasn't as if Cath were a child, unable to take care of herself. She'd certainly been in worse situations. She could have waited thirty more minutes to get to a bathroom.

What babies old women are.

Rennie thought of her own mother, dead since she was in her early teens. *Why couldn't it be* my *mother living here? She was so beautiful, and so talented.*

If Mama were alive, I bet Julie would have learned to play the piano. She could have been a brilliant pianist, too, instead of a painter—playing with paints like a child. Rennie's brow furrowed with disdain. *A painter, just like her grandmother. An utterly worthless thing to do with your life.*

Thinking of her mother gone and Cath underfoot filled Rennie with self-pity—the unfairness of life. She missed her mother, needed her as much now as she had as a child.

"Freddie . . . Freddie, I can't bear life without Mama," sobbed young Rennie, clinging to her Aunt Fredricka.

Fredricka Mueller—Freddie—was several years younger than her sister Magdalen, Rennie's mother, and was one of Rennie's closest girlhood friends. They did everything together, almost like sisters. She understood Rennie's grief at her mother's death. She felt it, too. How bleak life would be without Magdi.

"Yes, you can, Ren," she said, wrapping her arms around her distraught niece, burying her own tear-stained face in Rennie's chestnut-brown locks. "I know you'll miss her. I will too. But she was suffering so." A sob choked Fredricka's voice. She had to stop a moment before she could speak again. "She needed peace, sweetie. She just couldn't hurt anymore."

With those words and the recollections of all the suffering Magdalen had endured in her battle with ovarian cancer, Fredricka broke down, and her sobs mingled with Rennie's as the two heartbroken girls wept into the night.

Rennie's grief over her mother's death seemed to know no bounds those first few days. A child who had always been blessed with good fortune, she was not prepared for the incomplete life her mother's death had left her. Although her father adored her and showered her with anything she wanted—and more—her mother had been her friend. Her friend and her teacher.

Rennie Spaulding had deeply loved her mother.

After the funeral, Rennie shed no more tears. In fact, for days she showed very little emotion about anything. She moved about the house in an almost zombie-like trance. Without her mother, she didn't think she would ever feel anything again.

Her father was so engulfed in his own grief, he seemed unaware of the depth of his daughter's despair. And he buried himself in work to help him forget. He, too, seemed lost without Magdalen.

One day, about two weeks after the funeral, Fredricka and Emma, the eldest of the Mueller sisters, stopped by to see Rennie and found her in the midst of chaos. She was sitting on the floor in the middle of the music room surrounded by sheets and books of music—systematically destroying them. Page by page, she tore them into shreds and small pieces. Stone-faced and dry-eyed, she was demolishing a link to something she had most loved about her mother. Music.

"Good God, child, what are you doing?" demanded Emma, pulling Rennie to her feet.

Rennie jerked her arm away from her aunt's grasp and said with disdain, "Well, we certainly don't need all this music without Mama around to use it." With that pronouncement, she turned on her heel, tossed her hair haughtily over her shoulder, and stomped from the room, scattering shreds of paper as she walked.

"Rennie, wait," called Fredricka as she caught up to her and laid her arm affectionately across her shoulder. An arm Rennie summarily brushed off.

"Leave me alone, Freddie!" Rennie walked away, entering her room and slamming the door behind her.

But not before Fredricka had a chance to look deeply into her niece's eyes, where she saw a flash of such intense anger, it frightened her.

Emma Mueller Schoen immediately called her brother-in-law at his office and expressed her concern over Rennie's destructive behavior. "Don't you think it might be a good idea to have a doctor take a look at her, Harold?" she suggested. "She's expressing her grief in a rather frightening way."

"What for, Emma? So a doctor can tell me my daughter's terribly upset because her mother died? I already know that." Harold sighed and added, punctuated by what was evidently his own anger, "Why don't you and Freddie just leave her alone?"

Emma did. She never went back to her dead sister's house.

Freddie, however, was not that easily kept away. Much of the time, Rennie ignored her or was extremely rude or unkind to her. But occasionally, the spark of the life-long friendship between the two girls would ignite, and they could be seen talking at great length—and even laughing together.

Rennie's spirits seemed best lifted when she was away from her house. Harold began to schedule trips for her—anything to distance his daughter from the painful reminders of her loss. Sometimes, he accompanied her on these journeys away from the past. Other times, he sent her with others.

Rennie generally was in high spirits when she came home. For a while. She even began playing the piano again. Much of the music she had destroyed was replaced. Discretely, Harold purchased the replacements without ever making any reference to the incident.

But Rennie's periods of contentment were short-lived. Each time she came back home, it was only a matter of days before her outbursts of temper reappeared.

Harold was concerned. As much as he hated to admit it, perhaps Emma had been right. Maybe he should bring her to see a doctor.

Instead, he decided to move. If away from this house was what she needed, then that's what she'd get. He flew to a small city in Nebraska where he purchased a business and a home—all within less than a week.

When he came back to Chicago, he sold his share of the business there to his brother, put his home up for sale, and with his daughter, headed for Blakefield, Nebraska.

The Spauldings were starting over. *This will be so good for Rennie,* thought her father. *I just know it.*

It had been good for Rennie. She met Matt, and he loved her—thought she was the most wonderful person in the world. And she loved him. They had a good life—until Cath invaded their home. *How I wish she would just disappear,* she thought as she lightly fingered the piano keys.

Worry gnawed at Rennie, though—worry at what Matt would say or do if he came home, and his mother wasn't there. *Should I drive back to get her?* Rennie was asking herself when she heard a car door slam.

My God, not Matt! It's too early for Matt to be back! She felt panic as she ran to the window. He wasn't due back until tomorrow night.

A newer model, nondescript white car had stopped in the driveway. A man she didn't recognize was opening the back door of the car, assisting an older woman as she slowly exited the back seat.

Cath.

Rennie stepped back into the shadows of the draperies and watched unseen as the man took Cath's elbow and helped her until she had both feet firmly on the ground. He kept his hand on her arm for some time, as if he feared she'd fall if left to stand on her own.

In fact, that's exactly what he feared.

"I can't thank you enough, Clay," mumbled Cath in a voice so low Clay could scarcely hear her. "Patsy, too. You've both been wonderful. I don't know what would have happened to me if you hadn't come along when you did."

"It was our pleasure, Ma'am. Here, let me to walk to the door with you," said Clay, taking a step beside her, his hand still supporting her arm.

Cath just shook her head and again forced a smile. "No, I can manage it alone. I'm fine, really. I'm—I'm here. Home."

She waved her hand slightly at Patsy, still in the car, and ambled slowly up the walk to the house. She weaved from side to side as she approached the door.

Patsy held her breath. She felt certain Cath would never make it. Clay remained outside the car until Cath opened the door to the house and stepped inside, ready to race forward and catch her if she collapsed. He was not a doctor, but he could see this woman was not well. Not well at all.

"There's more to this story than we've been told, Patsy," he said as they drove away, adding emphatically, "and I don't like it."

"I know, Clay. But I don't think we'll ever know just what really happened."

Cath leaned against the door as she closed it, weariness surrounding her like a heavy fog.

"Well, I hope you're satisfied," said Rennie as she stepped away from the window where she'd been spying on Cath's arrival. Her voice was tinged with a bit of fear. Cath looked terrible! "You could have waited thirty more minutes, you know. Then we'd have been home. Just who were those people, and what did you tell them?"

Cath made no attempt to answer either question. She looked at Rennie and didn't like what she saw. A self-centered woman who had so little love left after her own self-indulgence that she had none to give to anyone else—most certainly none to give her mother-in-law.

And right now she was just too weary to care.

"I'm tired," declared Cath weakly. "I'm going to lie down." As she slowly and unsteadily wended her way to her room, she walked in front of Rennie, ignoring her, concentrating only on putting one foot in front of the other, on reaching the haven of her own room, her own bed.

"If you tell Matt about this, you'll be sorry," Rennie called after her. "You'll be sorry," she repeated, shouting shrilly.

Finally reaching the safety of her room, Cath was hardly aware of removing her clothes. She carelessly laid her jacket across a chair and stepped from her now-worn shoes. Her slacks she let lie where they dropped on the floor, and she took off her soiled under-garments and placed them in the clothes hamper.

So weary was she, she didn't notice they were stained with blood—something that had been common immediately following her surgery, but hadn't happened for quite some time now.

When she had donned her nightgown, she climbed into bed, barely garnering enough strength to pull back the comforter and blankets. She stretched out the length of the bed and pulled the welcome covers up to her chin. How cool the sheets felt against her skin.

Sleep was instant the moment she closed her eyes, and her intense weariness gave way to deep slumber.

Chapter Sixteen

Rennie didn't see Cath the following morning—hadn't even thought about her since she had watched her painfully make her way to her room yesterday, feeling sure her mother-in-law was too beaten down to ignore her warning about reporting her abandonment to Matt. After downing a quick cup of coffee, she dressed in her favorite suit, a scarlet wool flannel with a matching cashmere jacket. The ensemble heightened her beauty, and she knew it.

Rennie was glad for the cool snap, the first of the fall. She would be comfortable in her outfit of the finest wool. It had cost several hundred dollars, but it was worth it. Even Matt agreed. But of course, Matt was never one to oppose Rennie's extravagant taste in clothes.

She was pleased with her appearance as she gave herself one last glance in the full-length, solid-cherry-framed Cheval mirror before she left for a Bridge luncheon at the Blakefield Country Club. She'd be home in plenty of time to prepare lamb chops with mint jelly and twice-baked potatoes, Matt's favorite meal. She didn't give a second thought to Cath, lying sleeping in her out-of-the-way bedroom at the back of the house.

Cath had slept deeply for close to six hours. As it had been about six in the evening when she crawled between the cool sheets and pulled her warm down comforter over her weary shivering body and instantly fell into deep sleep, it was close to midnight when she awoke.

Yes, it had been midnight, because she had heard the grandfather clock strike twelve. The booming but beautiful gong seemed distant at first, as she heard it through deep slumber. But by the twelfth gong, she was awake and aware of it.

She was also aware that she was hot. Extremely hot. She rolled out of bed and stumbled to her bathroom, clinging to furniture as she struggled through the dark. She ran cool water over her wrists, then soaked a cloth and laid its wet coolness against her face.

She was trembling terribly, and realizing her legs felt barely strong enough to support her, she knew she had to return to her bed or collapse on the bathroom floor. Dampening the cloth again, she clutched it in her hand as she slowly made her way back to bed. Once more, she crawled between the sheets and lowered her head slowly on to the pillow. Then, she closed her burning eyes, and laying the wet cloth across her forehead, she again fell asleep.

Sleeping fitfully for several more hours, her body alternated between burning heat and teeth-chattering cold. Sleep came and went.

In mid-afternoon, Rennie drove her Lexus back into the garage. How she loved that car. Matt had presented it to her on her last birthday, and she showed it with the same pride that some mothers show their children.

She had an enjoyable day at the Club—played great Bridge and received several compliments on her astute bidding.

Glancing at the clock, she thought, *Good, I have lots of time before Matt's due home. I'll fix a great dinner.* She barely gave a thought to Cath, hoping only that she would stay out of her way and allow her to pretend her home was hers alone once more.

In spite of Rennie's preoccupation with herself, she really did care about her husband. She had decided Matt Montgomery would be hers the first time she laid eyes on him, and her determination to possess him had never wavered.

She changed from her wool ensemble to something more casual, yet equally stunning, and spent the next couple of hours preparing dinner. She enjoyed cooking—as long as she had the best cuts of meat, the freshest fruits and vegetables, and the newest and best cookware money could buy.

When she was a young girl and her mother was still alive, Magdalen had insisted her daughter learn to cook. Rennie not only learned, she really liked it, then and now. Perhaps because it was a piece of her mother—like playing the piano.

And Rennie hung tightly to those things that had been a part of Magdalen Spaulding.

As promised, Matt was home in time for dinner. Rennie heard the garage door open at just past six o'clock.

"Can you believe it," he announced as he walked in the door, "the flight was actually on time. Mmm, smells good in here. What's the occasion?"

"Since when do I need an occasion to cook your favorite meal, Matt?" questioned Rennie, feigning hurt.

Matt smiled and gave her a hug and small peck on the check. "Whatever the reason, Rennie, I appreciate it. I'm starved, and I'm beat. I hate this commuting crap. But the meeting went well, and we're finally ready to bring this case to trial."

As he loosened his tie and grabbed a handful of vegetables from the relish tray, he asked, "Where's Mom?"

"In her room, I guess," said Rennie, suddenly feeling as nervous as a teenager coming home past curfew. "She wasn't up yet when I went to the Club, and I haven't seen her since I came home. She's probably reading or watching television."

"I think I'll go back and say 'hi,'" he said, heading down the hall to Cath's room.

"Mom," he called softly as he tapped on the door. When there was no answer, he called again, a bit louder this time.

There was still no answer, and not sure exactly why, a wave of anxiety swept over him. He turned the knob, grateful it wasn't locked. Though the door had a lock and key, he had begged Cath not to keep it locked.

"We'll always respect your privacy, Mom," he had promised. "All you have to do is close the door if you want to be alone."

That promise made him a bit reluctant now as he slowly edged the door open.

"Mom?" he repeated.

As soon as he entered the room, he knew something was wrong. Cath was lying in bed, her face deathly pale.

"Matt?" Cath's voice was barely audible.

"Mom, what's wrong?" asked Matt anxiously as his hand rested on her hot cheek. "My God, you're burning up!"

He raced back to the bedroom doorway. "Rennie, call Jason," he shouted down the hall. "Or better yet, I'll call him myself," he said with panic in his voice as he rushed over and picked up the phone by his mother's bedside.

An instant later, Rennie came into the room.

"How long has she been like this, Rennie?" he demanded, holding his hand over the mouthpiece, the phone ringing repeatedly at the home of his physician and lifelong friend, Dr. Jason Miller.

"I don't know, Matt. She was fine when—"

"Hello, Jason. This is Matt. Jason, my mother is sick. Possibly very sick. Could you come over, please? I don't know. I just got in from Chicago, but she was fine yesterday morning. I just don't . . ."

Jason Miller had known Matt Montgomery too long not to recognize the panic in his friend's voice. And he knew immediately that, although he never made house calls, he would be making one tonight. Right away. He had also known Cath Montgomery all his life, spending countless hours at the Montgomery house when he was a boy, as Matt spent an equal amount of time at the Millers.

Cath and his mother had often discussed their boys over coffee, sharing the joys and woes of their sons' teen-age years. And when Jason's mother died ten days before his high-school graduation, Cath and Jack Montgomery stepped in to lend support for Matt's best friend and his grief-stricken father.

Oh, yes, he would be making a house call tonight.

"I'll be right there, Matt. Stay by her until I get there. And I'm calling an ambulance to be ready, just in case."

Jason made the usual twenty-minute drive in less than fifteen, and soon Rennie was ushering him into Cath's room, where a worried Matt sat next to her bed, his hand holding her cold, clammy one.

"Jason, I'm so glad you're here. Thanks so much for coming. I just can't figure this out," he said, running his fingers back through his thinning hair.

"Why don't you step out a second, Matt. Let me examine her and maybe I can tell what's going on. Grab a cup of coffee or something, and I'll be with you in a minute."

As Matt started for the door, Jason asked, "Has she been awake at all?"

"Not really. She spoke my name once, but that's about it."

Jason nodded and turned his attention to his patient.

Matt went to the kitchen where Rennie was sitting at the counter sipping coffee. He poured a cup for himself, his hand trembling, spilling coffee on the counter. "Rennie, what happened? Mother was doing so well. She was downright chipper when I left yesterday."

"Nothing happened," she replied. "We drove over to Lincoln yesterday morning. You knew we were doing that. You were the one who insisted I take Cath along," she added. "We came home, had an early supper, and Cath—uh—Cath said she was tired and went right to her room afterward," she lied.

Matt looked at her, mistaking the fear he heard in her voice as concern. He put his arm around her shoulders and hugged her. "She'll be okay, hon. I just know she'll be okay."

A statement of hope more than certainty.

Jason came into the kitchen, stuck his hands in his pockets, and looked at them—a worried expression covering his face. "We'd better get her to the hospital, Matt. The ambulance will be here in ten minutes. I've also called her oncologist. I think it's pneumonia, but I want Dr. Hazelton to check her out, too. It just hasn't been that long since he gave her a clean bill of health on the cancer, and we need to be sure."

He walked towards the door. "I'll meet you there," he said, adding. "Please try not to worry," knowing full well that his advice wouldn't be heeded. "Cath wouldn't want that."

Rennie grabbed Jason's arm. "Did she say anything? I mean, did she tell you how she felt, or how come she felt that way. I mean . . ."

"She briefly opened her eyes, but, no, she didn't say a word." Jason looked at Rennie as he answered her question, noting desperation in her voice.

But then, he shouldn't be surprised by anything Rennie said. Rennie Montgomery was not one of Dr. Jason Miller's favorite people, although he and his wife, Paula, socialized with Matt and Rennie often. But he did it for Matt. Matt was his dearest friend.

There had been a time when he competed with Matt for Rennie Spaulding's attention. But it soon became clear to a young Jason Miller that Rennie, with the almond-shaped brown eyes and chestnut-brown ponytail that swished back and forth as she bounced through the halls of Blakefield High, only had eyes for Matt.

His feelings that he had lost a prize to his best friend changed over the years, replaced by feelings that he had been lucky. In Jason's eyes, Rennie Spaulding Montgomery was one of the most selfish, uncaring human beings he had ever met. And somehow, he had the very uncomfortable feeling that she knew more about Cath's current state of health than she was telling. But he'd be damned if he could guess what it would be.

"I'll go back and wait with her until the ambulance gets here," said Matt. "Then, we'll see you at the hospital."

"Good," said Jason. He studied Rennie intently as she accompanied him. She appeared placid, considering her mother-in-law was deathly ill—and she looked as beautiful as ever.

His eyes met hers. Her stunning brown eyes were as cold as stone and gave away nothing. A good reader of people, Dr. Jason Miller could not read Rennie Montgomery.

Chapter Seventeen

Jason was right. Cath had pneumonia. Her long walk in the chilly fall air proved too much for a body not yet fully recovered from the trauma of cancer surgery.

Matt stood outside his mother's hospital room and spoke with Jason. "How is she?"

"Doc Hazelton has assured us this is in no way related to your mother's cancer, Matt, except that whole ordeal did weaken her resistance and leave her vulnerable to things like pneumonia."

"It just happened so suddenly. My God, I never would have asked Rennie to take her to Lincoln with her yesterday if I hadn't thought she was really feeling well."

Jason looked quickly at Matt. "Cath and Rennie went to Lincoln yesterday?"

"Yes, yes, I encouraged it. I had no idea she was feeling sick. She'd been doing so well. At least I thought she was, but obviously, I was wrong. I never should have asked Rennie to take Mom with her." Matt buried his face in his hands, distraught and fearful for his mother.

"Matt, this isn't your fault. Your mother got sick, period. It just happened—probably couldn't have been avoided." After a brief pause, he asked, "Did Rennie say anything about how Cath seemed to feel on the drive? Did she give any indication she wasn't feeling well?"

"I asked her, but she said Cath was just fine," responded Matt without much assurance.

"I just don't know, Matt. I just don't know," he repeated. Jason slowly shook his head as he spoke. Together they walked into Cath's room.

Matt looked at his mother lying in her bed, with tubes in her body and surrounded by machines meant to keep death at bay. She looked so helpless and frail. "It's bad isn't it, Jason."

"I won't lie to you, Matt. It's very bad. Cath is no longer a young woman, and her strength was already seriously compromised by cancer, surgery, chemo—all of it. It may take all the fight she can muster to pull through this one, buddy."

Jason squeezed his friend's shoulder. "We're doing all we can for her, you know. The rest is up to God—and to Cath herself. Are you going to call Julie?"

"I already have. She's taking the first flight out of Minneapolis."

"Then I guess all you can do is wait. Wait and pray." Dr. Miller gently squeezed his friend's shoulder again and walked away.

Matt sat down by his mother's bedside—to wait and pray, just as Jason had suggested. He sat with his elbows on his knees, his head resting in his hands, a pose repeated from such a short time ago. Remembering his mother's other recent hospital stay increased his anxiety. And his sadness.

Such a short time ago—and now, here he was at her hospital bedside again, hoping and praying for his mother's life.

For several days, Matt stayed close by Cath's side, relieved only by Julie. He knew that when—or if—she really awoke, she'd want to see one or the other of them.

The day Julie arrived, father and daughter sat together, hand-in-hand. Rennie stayed in the background.

"It seems like we just did this, Dad," said Julie, choking on her tears. "Grandma Cath has had to deal with so much. Too much. It just isn't fair." Julie buried her face in Matt's shoulder, giving way to nearly silent sobs.

"I agree, honey. It's not fair. But she pulled through before, and we just have to believe she'll do it again," he said, soothing his distraught daughter.

Cath awoke when not one, but both, were by her bedside. Still connected by tubes to life-sustaining equipment, she couldn't speak, but she reached out her small, frail hand. Matt and Julie quickly enfolded it in theirs. With a smile on her lips, Cath fell back to sleep.

Each day, Cath was awake a little while longer, and her smile was a bit broader. When her respirator was removed, she said in a small, raspy voice, "Hello, you two."

Neither Matt nor Julie could contain their tears of joy.

Remarkably, Cath recovered. But her recovery took quite some time. She was hospitalized for three weeks and required nursing care for some time after she came home.

Julie returned home to Minnesota once she was assured her grandmother truly was going to pull through yet another time. It was a sad good-bye for both, but Julie assured Cath she'd be back soon.

Whenever Matt was with Cath, Rennie hovered near by. At least after Cath was awake and alert—after she was again conversational and might possibly tell Matt her tale of abandonment.

At times, Rennie would find Cath watching her and look fully into her eyes. Rennie tried to stare her down, wishing she could know what was going on in her mind, wondering if Cath would ever tell Matt what his wife had done. Matt would never forgive her for abandoning Cath so far from home.

He would leave her without ever looking back.

Matt misunderstood his wife's constant presence in Cath's sick room and reacted warmly to her perceived caring. "We were lucky, hon," he said with his arm around her waist. "Jason says we were just a hair's breadth away from losing her."

Rennie hugged him back, in apparent gratitude that her mother-in-law had been spared.

Chapter Eighteen

When Cath came home this time, recovering, but weak, Matt hired Miranda Rowan, a distant cousin of his, to be an around-the-clock nurse. Rennie resented terribly having another female encamped in her home, but realizing the alternative was that she nurse Cath back to health herself—a possibility unthinkable to Rennie—she kept quiet about her resentment.

Miranda, or Randy, as she had been dubbed early in life by her three brothers, was a typical Rowan. She was an intense woman with a dry sense of humor who approached her profession with boundless passion. Matt couldn't have found a better nurse and companion for his mother, and it wasn't long before Cath's throaty laughter could be heard from her bedroom, mixed with Randy's resounding guffaws, trademark of the humor of the Rowan clan.

How Rennie resented the joy and camaraderie she heard emanating from Cath's bedroom. She had long forgotten that she was responsible for Cath's illness and instead, saw herself as a martyr caring for a sick old lady in her home.

The laughter became the norm as Cath continued to mend, and Randy continued to enjoy caring for her. Soon, they were spending their idle hours playing two-handed Solitaire or Cribbage.

And each day, Cath seemed to get a little stronger.

The week before Thanksgiving, Blakefield was blanketed with a pristine coating of snow. Cath, now allowed up some each day, stepped gingerly from her bed, pulled back the curtains, and "aahed" at the sight.

"How I love the first snow. It just seems so God-like. It also makes me nostalgic for the old place, the place where I grew up in the country—untouched, sort of uncontaminated, by civilization."

Randy smiled. "I know what you mean. My folks' place is the same. When I first went to work at Omaha Memorial, I thought I'd die of loneliness, of 'city-ness.' Especially this time of the year."

She crossed the room to enjoy the view with Cath. "I roomed

with other student nurses in a building right next to the hospital. I'd look out the windows at night and watch the traffic slither and slide, snow shooting up from the tires, making a dirty mess of the streets. How I longed for the country. Still do, much of the time."

"Sometimes, I long for it too, Randy. Although mostly I long for my own home—for the days when Jack was alive," Cath added with a sigh. "In fact, I'm finding I really regret selling my home. I miss it so much, I can't even stand to drive by. But having cancer scared me, and I thought maybe I shouldn't be alone. I know Matt didn't think I should." A small tear tracked down her cheek.

"I know it's hard, honey. It especially has to be hard when you've been so sick. But you have your son. And his wife," she added with some hesitation.

Miranda Rowan could see the tension between Cath and Rennie, but no amount of probing had encouraged Cath to shed any light on why. Randy decided it was just normal tension between a wife and her mother-in-law—probably no more than jealousy over attention from a husband who just happened to be an only child. But Miranda had to admit—to herself, of course—she did not like Rennie Montgomery.

"Yes, I do have Matt and Rennie," said Cath, a note of resignation in her voice. "I've been thinking, though, Randy, maybe I should find a place of my own when I'm on my feet—something small, something I can easily manage. It wouldn't be the old place, but it would be mine, and . . ." Cath let her sentence dangle, unfinished, sadness obvious in her voice.

"Talk it over with Matt, Cath. Just don't make any decision too soon. You've been terribly sick."

"I know."

Not willing to allow her patient to be sad for long, Randy said, "I'd like to look at your photo album again, Catherine. We only made it halfway through the other day. What a great collection of memories you have!"

Cath ran her hand tenderly over the cover of the album, now worn threadbare, the yellow roses so faded, it was difficult to recognize they were flowers.

"This is my most prized possession, Randy. As you said, it's a wonderful collection of memories."

Cath perked up instantly when she opened the album to its halfway mark, where she and Randy had stopped their reminiscing a couple days earlier. For the remainder of the morning, they looked and laughed and shared their common bonds as Rowans.

Randy left at the end of the week, just before Thanksgiving. Cath no longer needed round-the-clock nursing, and she began to join Matt and Rennie again for most meals and was able to attend to her own needs almost as well as before.

Randy's parting was tearful. She had been a link to Cath's past. In many ways, Randy reminded Cath of Spence—and a little bit of her Aunt Molly, her father's younger sister. She had that same Rowan determination and wry, contagious sense of humor.

Cath felt alone without Randy.

Very alone and very, very vulnerable.

Cath never did garner the courage to talk to Matt about moving into a place of her own. It just sounded so ungrateful after all he had done for her—bringing in her bedroom furniture, redecorating her room—always asking her how she felt. She was certain her show of ingratitude would hurt her son tremendously. And she really couldn't bear to do that.

Chapter Nineteen

The three Montgomerys—Cath, Matt, and Rennie—observed Thanksgiving quietly. Rennie prepared one of her always excellent holiday dinners, filling the house with wonderful, mouth-watering fragrances. When Rennie announced that dinner was ready, Matt and Cath joined her at the dining room table, elegantly appointed with crystal and silver, a silver cornucopia teeming with brightly polished fresh fruits and vegetables in the center flanked by russet-toned tapers in silver candleholders.

With an ivory-handled carving knife, another of Rennie's heirlooms, Matt attacked the turkey, roasted to a golden brown, enhanced with a mouthwatering apple and walnut dressing, a recipe once belonging to Rennie's mother.

"Honey, that was a fantastic meal," said Matt, as he forked the last morsel of pumpkin pie into his mouth. "Lady, you really know how to cook," he continued with a mock bow.

"It was delicious, Rennie. I agree with Matt," said Cath kindly, "you are indeed a wonderful cook."

Rennie seemed pleased by the compliments, smiling and fluttering her eyelashes, just as she did when she was a girl.

Following dinner, the trio napped, read, and watched television, much like millions of others observing this first of the winter holidays. To add to the laziness of the day, a steady, cold November rain beat against the windows all day long, washing away the beauty of the snowfall the week before and giving the day a sullen, non-festive face.

But all three Montgomerys were feeling especially thankful this year. Matt and Cath, because Cath was regaining her health and strength. Rennie was thankful her cruel act towards Cath had gone undetected by her husband.

"That delicious dinner has left me dreadfully sleepy. I guess it's about time for a nap," said Cath later with a yawn as she headed for her room.

"Rest well, Mom," called Matt as he briefly glanced away from the football game.

Rennie was in the kitchen, directing the woman she had hired to clean up after the dinner. When all instructions had been explained to her satisfaction, Rennie joined Matt in the family room, curled up on the sofa with a book, and promptly fell asleep.

In her room, Cath picked up her album and, propping up her pillows behind her, leaned back to page through it a bit before closing her eyes. She thought of how, just a few days ago, she and Randy had looked at the photographs and reminisced together. Cath sighed.

How I miss Randy. She reminds me so much of Spence—dear Spence, gone now for so many years. My brother was a mainstay of my life growing up, and my dearest friend later on. Whatever would I have done without Spence?

Thinking about him now, a pang of emptiness stabbed her. She smiled as she looked at a photo of Spence as a boy, the perennial overalls, his hair bleached white from the sun and hanging in his eyes, a serious expression clouding his young face.

So serious you were Spence—a man before your time. I wish I had known Daddy, but all he ever was to me was a photograph. You were my dad, really, at least you acted like it much of the time. You surely acted like it when I introduced Jack to you. The way you looked him up and down, I think you scared Jack half to death. I'm surprised Jack didn't turn around and run instead of asking me to marry him.

Glancing through several photos of Spence, Cath came to one of him taken shortly before his death. He was sitting on the front porch of the farmhouse he had so loved, and with him were the Bakers.

The farmhouse had been a landmark, known just as "the Rowan place." If someone asked directions in town, they might be told to drive past the Rowan place and take a right—or a left. Or a spot might be identified as being "so many miles from the Rowan place."

Spence loved the farm—the house, the land, the creek that ran across the far side of the property. Spence loved everything about the place that was the Rowan home.

The house had always been yellow. Whenever a new paint-job was in order, swatches of other colors in an array of possibilities were laid out on the kitchen table, and callers, as well as family, would offer an opinion. The rainbow of choices ranged from pure white to sky blue, apple-blossom pink to slate gray. But always yellow reigned.

Even in the last photograph ever taken of him, Spence Rowan carried the same rugged handsomeness he had when Jack and Cath were married. He was tall, slender, and sun-tanned. His hair had long been bleached white from the sun, so it appeared unchanged with age. His only concession to the years flitting by was his eyeglasses. Just like his mother, Spence wore small wire-framed glasses with thick lenses.

When in his mid-sixties, Spencer Rowan began to slow down appreciably. He no longer was able to work the farm alone and finally consented to sharing the old farmhouse with a young couple he hired to help with the upkeep of the family place. The two, Annie and Ralph Baker, were a delight. Ralph was tall and lean—so lean that in profile he resembled the insect known to children as the walking stick. But his energy was incredible. Rarely did he stop moving. His deeply tanned weathered face could be seen everywhere on the farm.

His countenance always appeared serious and stern. That is, until he smiled. When Ralph smiled, his gray eyes seemed to flash light and warmth. Although he was a quiet man, his voice, with the soft brogue of the hills of West Virginia from which he hailed, invited trust and friendship.

Annie was a small and round woman, and as boisterous as Ralph was quiet. She reminded Spence and Cath of their Aunt Molly— fun loving and carefree. She shared Molly's housekeeping abilities, as well. Molly couldn't seem to dust without breaking something, cook without turning the kitchen into a disaster, or make a bed that wasn't full of lumps.

No one would ever claim that Annie Baker was the world's great-est housekeeper, either. Little dust bunnies continued to inhabit their hiding places under the beds, just as they had ever since Spence first lived alone, and the windows continued to appear only semi-translucent—as if they hadn't been thoroughly scrubbed since Sarah died.

But her cooking was sheer magic. Spence was served meals he hadn't even thought of since his mother's death. Roast chicken stuffed with the most divine herb dressing; fried chick-en and gravy with hot melt-in-your-mouth biscuits on the side. Every vegetable imaginable, prepared in new and delectable ways; asparagus dripping with melted butter and lemon; car-rots floating in a cream sauce; and squash deep-fried to a rich golden brown.

Sunday dinner was again the time for homemade pies. Never just one kind, but at least two, and sometimes three. Fresh apple pie with the smell of cinnamon and nutmeg beckoning the taste buds; lemon piled so high with meringue that a normal-sized mouth couldn't possibly open wide enough to accommodate it; and cherry just tart enough to bite a bit, but sweet enough to make you smile.

The Bakers added a good dimension to Spence's life. The life of the farm would go on, but he could pull away from the most stren-uous parts of it. He could relax—as much as Spence Rowan would ever relax.

He worked beside Ralph every day, but little by little, he let Ralph be the leader and he, the assistant. Now he was freer to visit Cath or Julie when he wanted to without having to worry about getting back to his work. And that he did. Often. Spence appeared to be happy, but somewhat restless much of the time. And often, very tired.

More tired than he ever revealed to anyone.

Three years after Annie and Ralph moved in, Spence suffered a heart attack, killing him instantly.

"God, I miss him," said Cath aloud, her eyes brimming with tears as she looked at the last photograph she had of her brother. "He was such a good man."

* * *

The days following Thanksgiving brought a return of the snow. It also brought the heightened activity that nearly always accompanies the weeks before Christmas. Rennie was gone during the day much of the time—shopping or attending the many social functions that highlighted the season. Matt and Rennie attended an equal number of holiday social events in the evenings.

One night, as they were bedecked in their holiday finery—Matt formally attired in a custom-tailored dinner jacket, and Rennie in black velvet, accented by her diamonds and a stunning emerald bracelet Matt had presented to her on their last wedding anniversary—Cath smiled at them and expressed her admiration.

"I doubt if anyone will hold a candle to you two. My, but you look grand. Both of you," she said with enthusiasm.

Matt smiled sheepishly and said, "I feel a bit like a store-window mannequin, Mom. But thanks for the compliment."

Even Rennie appeared flattered at Cath's comments and smiled at her—the first time she had smiled at Cath in a very long time.

Perhaps, thought Cath, *this wonderful, joy-filled season will heal what's happened between Rennie and me. I'll just let the past remain past, and we can start anew.*

Cath's life during the hectic days before Christmas, in contrast to Matt and Rennie's, was extremely inactive. Sometimes, it left her feeling lonely and disassociated from the holiday season. Other times, she was overcome with remarkably strong feelings of peace.

And the rest and quiet allowed her body to mend.

Matt and Rennie did take her shopping early one evening—very briefly, but long enough for her to feel a part of the season and absorb the air of Christmas present everywhere in Blakefield. She was grateful for the outing. She liked to select her own gifts, especially this year. There would be some very special guests in the house for the holidays.

Cath was so excited, she could hardly contain herself.

Chapter Twenty

Julie, Kenneth, Hal, and Jack were coming to Blakefield for Christmas—something the Matsons hadn't done since the twins were born. Other years, Julie had argued that it was just too difficult to haul two little boys and all their paraphernalia through snowy country. Consequently, her visits to Blakefield with the twins were always in the summer. That way, she reasoned, she could be outdoors with them as much as possible.

They came when the days were hot. Julie would sit by the pool and watch her two young sons as they played with delight in the water, enveloped in their bright orange life jackets, bouncing up and down like buoys in the bay. Or she'd join them in the pool, patiently teaching them the rudiments of swimming. Little faces with sunburned noses dipped in the water, blowing bubbles as they breathed out, small arms flailing and feet flapping as they "swam."

Often, they'd pack a picnic lunch and walk to the closest Blakefield park. Julie watched her sons play, just as she had in the same park years before; they'd run and romp, building up an enormous appetite for such small bodies. The delicacies of the picnic basket would then be laid out on the colorful plaid picnic blanket and devoured in no time.

Sometimes even Rennie could be persuaded to accompany them on the outings, and always, Grandma Cath. Long naps for all generally followed their excursions.

Jack and Hal had spent many a summer day in Blakefield, but never before had they spent a Christmas Day there. Julie loved Christmas at her own home in Minnesota. Kenneth and the boys would string lights on their deck overhanging the lake. At night, they could look out the windows and delight in the twinkling colors reflected off the ice that covered the expansive body of water. The effect was spectacular. It always thrilled Julie to see the expression on the faces of her sons when they watched their surroundings transformed into a colorful sparkling fairyland.

Kenneth's mother and father, Henry and Gen Matson, lived on

several acres in the country, not far from the Twin Cities. Although they didn't farm, they kept many animals just for the pleasure of having them around; they were avid outdoor folks. Visiting Grandma and Grandpa Matson, which they did regularly, was always an exciting pleasure-filled experience for the twins. There they rode ponies, fed the ducks on the pond, and ran for hours in the surrounding fields with M'Lady, the Matson's Collie. M'Lady kept a close eye on the boys, and when they were younger, more than once dragged one or the other of them back toward the house when she felt they were straying too far.

Kenneth's father had taken early retirement from the Montclair Equipment Company, where he had been Chief Operating Officer for many years. After his retirement, he wanted to get as far as he could from the hustle and bustle of the corporate world, but still be accessible to the benefits of the Twin Cities. Kenneth's mother, Gen, after raising three boys, opened a gift shop, where she sold hand-crafted items—many of them her own creations. She and Julie had great times together, each appreciating the artistic bent of the other, and when Cath came to visit, the three had an artistic holiday.

Julie and Kenneth decided to forego their usual country Christmas in Minnesota this year, however, and planned to arrive in Blakefield two days before Christmas. The boys hated the idea of giving up their Christmas sleigh ride at Grandpa Matson's, helping to hitch up the horses, decorating the sleigh with green-ery—all the traditions that they had come to associate with this special day.

"But, Mom," argued Hal, "who'll help Grandpa hitch up the sleigh? I've helped him do it ever since I was a little kid," boasted the eight-year-old proudly.

"And Grandpa says I'm the best sleigh decorator there is!" exclaimed Jack with dismay, tears about to fall. "Grandpa and Grandma will just be too lonesome without us for Christmas."

"I know guys—you're both Grandpa Matson's best helpers," agreed their mother. "The very best. But Grandma and Grandpa promised they'd try really hard to get along without your help—just this once. And you haven't been with your Grandma and Grandpa Montgomery on Christmas Day ever. Or with Grandma Cath. Daddy and I thought it'd be great fun for all of us to go to Blakefield this year."

Hopefully, she added, "You know what? You'll be waking up Christmas morning in the same house I did when I was your age."

When their mother explained that they'd be seeing Grandma Cath, whom they both adored, and when she added that Santa knew his way to Grandma and Grandpa Montgomery's house in Blakefield, they were suddenly very excited about the approaching holiday—excited as only little boys can be a few days before Christmas. The acquiescence relieved Julie, who had flown to Blakefield when Cath was in the hospital—both times—and she wasn't willing to let Christmas go by this year without being with her. She had thought she'd lose her dear grandmother before the holiday season came around, and grateful she hadn't, vowed they'd be together.

"And it will be nice to spend Christmas with Mom and Dad, too," said Julie when she laid out her plans to Kenneth.

"Of course, Julie. We haven't spent Christmas in Blakefield for nine years—not since the year before you were pregnant with the twins. It's about time. Anyhow, I'm eager to see Cath, too," he added, knowing very well the reason Julie wanted to make this holiday journey. Kenneth Matson was very fond of Julie's grandmother, and he marveled at the bond between grandmother and granddaughter. Although separated by a generation, they viewed the world much alike.

So on December twenty-third, the four Matsons arrived, stomping snow off their boots in the foyer of Matt and Rennie's spacious and elegant home. Something Julie was certain hadn't occurred since she was a schoolgirl.

"Grandma!" shouted the boys together as Rennie greeted them with a hug.

Julie had thoroughly briefed the twins regarding expected behavior at this grandma's house at Christmas time, and she prayed they wouldn't fail her. Eight-year-old little boys could sometimes be terribly unpredictable.

"Where's Grandpa, and where's Grandma Cath?" asked Hal, the bolder of the two.

"Your grandfather will be home in about two hours, and . . ."

Not waiting for an answer regarding Cath's whereabouts, Jack and Hal took off down the hall toward their great-grandmother's room. They'd had had many a great story-telling session there during their last visit and remembered it well.

"Hi, Mom," said Julie, giving her mother a kiss on the cheek. "I guess they'll find Grandma Cath, ready or not," she said with a shrug. "I think I'll go in to say 'hi' to her as well."

"Of course, Julie," said Rennie. "But I hope you don't plan to spend your entire visit in Cath's room. She's been sick, you know," she added, with a detectable note of sarcasm.

Julie knew she would have to put up with her mother's old jealousy of the relationship between her and Cath, and had decided in advance she wouldn't let it get to her this time.

"I know she's been sick, Mom," she said patiently. "Which is exactly why I need to go in there," she added with a smile. "I need to rescue her from those two."

Julie hurried down the hall before Rennie could offer any more comments regarding her grandmother.

"Julie," called Cath, as she saw her stick her head in the doorway. She stretched out her arms, and soon Julie was in them.

"It's so good to see you, Grandma Cath." As Julie released herself from her grandmother's clasp, she stepped back and looked closely at her grandmother's face. Cath's eyes sparkled, and she had color in her cheeks, very different than when she had been here a couple months ago and so feared that Cath was dying.

"Are these two driving you crazy yet?" asked Julie as she fondly tousled Jack's hair, then Hal's.

"No. And they've just persuaded me to join the rest of you in the living room. So let's go."

Cath took the hand of one of the boys, and Julie, the other.

"Julie," said Cath, turning towards the granddaughter she loved so dearly. "I'm so happy you decided to spend Christmas with us. I've been just counting the days until today. This is going to be such a wonderful time."

Chapter Twenty-one

That night, with two days yet to go before Christmas, the Montgomery household bustled with activity. Although Rennie always had her packages wrapped in the stores where she purchased her gifts, and her perfectly wrapped silver and gold selections were already carefully stacked beneath the tree, the other family members were behind closed doors. One could hear the rustle of paper as all put the finishing touches on their creative packaging.

The twins asked Cath to help them. Each clasping one of her hands in theirs, they led her into the guest bedroom that had been designated for them and pulled their suitcases out of the closet. Each dug in the bottom for gifts made by little hands, secretly stored beneath underwear, socks, and pajamas, away from their parents' eyes.

"Do you think Mom and Dad will like this?" asked Jack, holding out a hand-made frame crafted of cardboard and felt surrounding his school photograph. In his photo, Jack looked so much like his mother and his deceased grandfather, her Jack, it gave Cath's heart a tug.

"Oh, Jack, it's perfect! They'll love it."

"I stuck my picture in an ornament," said Hal, placing his gift for his parents carefully in Cath's hands.

She held the ornament made of Styrofoam and glitter—copious amounts of glitter—displaying the mischievous smile of her other great-grandson. "It's beautiful, Hal. Your mom and dad will be so delighted and surprised. Now let's get these wrapped."

A short time later, the three emerged from the bedroom with packages colorfully wrapped by small hands—ribbons askew and paper crinkled at the corners. Beautiful packages, thought the boys. Cath thought so, too.

Other packages had been added during their stay in the bedroom, and the boys and Cath "oohed" and "aahed" at the sight of them all stacked beneath the huge Christmas tree.

The twins studied the tree. It was very pretty, although not as pretty as the one they had at home, back in Minnesota. Theirs was decorated in lots of different colored ornaments. Many they had made themselves—even some when they were really little boys in kindergarten.

Grandma and Grandpa Montgomery's tree was all blue and white. Every ornament on it was either blue or white. Even the tree was white—like it had been out in a snowstorm.

"How come your tree isn't green, Grandma?" Hal asked. "I thought all trees were green."

"Couldn't you find any green and red decorations? We could have brought you some," Jack offered with a smile. "We have lots."

"Grandma decorates her tree to match the living room, guys," explained their mother. "Isn't it beautiful?" she added diplomatically.

"Yes, it's pretty," they responded in unison—much to the relief of their mother.

Excused from the after-dinner ritual, Jack and Hal crept into the living room to again admire the tree and the bounty of packages around it as the grown-ups lingered over their after-dinner coffee and conversation. Weariness overtook them both, and they snuggled up to packages bearing their names and soon drifted off. They were discovered by their parents and grandparents when the adults finally left the dining room, having exhausted the first round of reminiscing and story-telling.

"Kenneth, you take one of these weary guys upstairs, and I'll take the other," directed Matt quietly, gently lifting one of the boys.

"Thanks, Dad," said Julie. "And I'll be right behind you to tuck them into pajamas and bed."

"Just a minute before you pick them up," whispered Cath. "Let me get the camera. Such a great picture."

The others waited, smiling at the scene before them as Cath went to her room for her camera.

The photo was the first of many taken that Christmas.

Around noon on the day of Christmas Eve, snow began to fall.

By mid-afternoon, the ground was covered with a new layer of white, and although it was not a great day for driving, it was a superb day for playing in the snow.

Kenneth and the boys were just finishing what they thought to be a grand snowman when Julie bounded out the door, her arms laden with treasures to add to their creation to make it really special. She carried a plaid scarf, big black buttons for eyes, a top hat that had been used in a centerpiece for "theater night," and a big rubber nose, formerly part of a Halloween mask. The boys rolled in the snow with laughter after Julie added the nose, the final touch.

"Where d'ya find it, Mom? It's just perfect!"

"Oh, I have my stash. I was a kid once, too, you know. Right here in this house."

"Okay, it's 'pose time,'" said her father, who had been snapping pictures as the foursome completed their snow sculpture. "All four of you—in front of Mr. Snowman," he directed. "That's great! Mom will love adding this to her album."

The snow had abated by the time the family left for church. The stars were out in abundance, and an almost full moon cast such bright light dancing on the snow, it scarcely seemed like night.

The Montgomerys belonged to a large church in downtown Blakefield, a spectacular architectural masterpiece. But tonight they were attending Christmas Eve services at a small historic church far out in the country, towards the Rowan farm. The church where Cath and Jack Montgomery were married many years before.

Rennie was most unhappy about their decision to spend Christmas Eve in the little country church—and to miss the festive and far more elegant service at the church they usually attended.

"What! Why would you want to go to church in the country when we have a church here in Blakefield—a church where all our friends are?"

"Just this once, Rennie," argued Matt. He thought the idea,

proposed by Julie, a wonderful one. Nostalgic. Very "family."

"Please, Mom," begged Julie. "I really want to do this. I want the boys to get some feeling for their roots."

"Well, there's certainly more to their roots than the country," said Rennie as she walked away in a huff.

Cath said nothing. She thought the idea was great, but surely both Matt and Julie knew how she felt. There was nothing to gain by voicing her opinion and angering Rennie even more.

But this time, Rennie was outnumbered. Everyone except her thought the idea perfect for a most memorable Christmas.

So the three Montgomerys and four Matsons filed into the overflowing little church just as the strains of *Joy to the World* were filling the crisp winter air. An usher seated them in the only space available for seven—the front row—right beneath the huge fir, splendidly decorated with green and red ornaments and teeming with multi-colored lights.

Cath was so moved by the surroundings, rich with countless memories, she had to fight to keep her tears from escaping. The lights on the tree shimmered as she viewed them through misty eyes. *Oh, Jack, how I wish you were here. How you would have loved this night.*

Rennie was quiet on the drive back home, but as the others were not, no one seemed to notice.

No one, that is, but Cath. Cath was very finely tuned to Rennie's moods—had been ever since that day Rennie abandoned her at the service station.

When they arrived home, the excitement of children and Christmas Eve took over, and after enjoying an elegant buffet Rennie had prepared, they opened gifts. Paper rustled, and "I love it," and "It's just what I wanted," were declared by all. Bulbs flashed as smiles were captured to be remembered another day.

Even Rennie seemed to be having an enjoyable time, her mood of earlier in the evening forgotten.

"Okay boys, time to hang your stockings for Santa and call it a day," said Kenneth.

"Oh, Dad," they both moaned.

"No arguing. It's been a busy day, and tomorrow promises to be another," said their mother. "Let's go."

They dutifully kissed each of the grownups and went with their mother to beds awaiting two very sleepy little boys. But first they hung two bright-colored Christmas stockings on the fireplace mantle—one with the name "Hal" embroidered across the top, and the other, "Jack."

"I'm going to call it a day, too, everyone," said Cath. "I think I'm as weary as the boys."

Cath gave in to sleep easily on this memorable Christmas Eve. Her dreams were filled with laughing little boys and an old church beautifully decorated to honor the birth of the Christ Child.

Chapter Twenty-two

Jack and Hal were up bright and early Christmas Day—and what a bright one it was. A sky unblemished by a single cloud heralded the day, and the sun was blinding on the fresh, white snow of yesterday.

Soon the house was filled with the sounds of the family awakening as, one by one, they joined the eager and excited little boys. Rennie was the first adult to join the young, less than enthusiastic about the clamor and noise they were bringing to her usually quiet and serene household.

"Boys," their grandmother lectured, "there will be some people here for dinner that you don't know. Good friends of mine. I'll want you to play quietly and . . ."

"I'm not sure they know the meaning of the words 'play quietly,' Mom," said Julie, joining her two sons and mother in the kitchen.

After a quick good-morning and Merry Christmas kiss, the twins ran back to the living room, the site of their goodies from Santa. Julie picked up a slice of Christmas bread from the counter. "Mmm, this is delicious. I'll be sure they behave. They're really good kids, Mother."

"I wasn't implying they weren't, Julie. I was only letting them know about our guests."

Julie wondered if her mother would ever cease trying to impress the upper social strata in Blakefield. No, she decided. It would never happen. Rennie would always be drawn to what she regarded as high society.

Not wanting to press the issue, she simply ignored it and instead asked, "I heard you tell the boys someone's coming for dinner. Who, Mom? Anyone I know?"

"The Pritchards and Devlins, and Amanda Taylor. This is her first Christmas since Melvin's death, and I really thought she should be with friends."

"That's sweet, Mom," said Julie, knowing that Rennie had always despised Amanda, and wondering why this sudden caring. "I promise I'll keep the boys in tow."

"And your grandmother, too. Honestly, sometimes she looks so tacky these days, I wish she'd just stay in her room." With that declaration, Rennie walked away.

Julie was speechless. She knew her mother could be thoughtless at times; Rennie was known for her cutting remarks. Heaven only knows she had been the target of many herself. But she had never before heard her say anything as unkind as those words about Cath.

She was sitting pensively picking at the crumbs remaining from her slice of Christmas bread when Kenneth walked in, tying the sash of his new burgundy velour robe, a present from his in-laws.

"Sometimes I forget how loud your kids can be," he declared. "Was that a short night, or is it just me?" He noticed the sad, serious look on Julie's face. "Hey, honey, what's wrong? This is supposed to be a happy day, remember?"

Julie got up, and wrapping her arms around his neck, she buried her face in the soft, warm fabric of his robe and sighed. "It's nothing, Kenneth. Nothing new, that is. Just something Mom said."

"Look at me, Julie." Kenneth gently placed his hand beneath her chin, raising her face to look at him. "You can't go through your life letting your mother hurt you—or trouble you—by the things she says. She's just being Rennie, and I doubt very much if she'll ever change. Sometimes I think she does it just because she sees it hurts you. It gives her some kind of a feeling of power over you."

Julie hugged him again. "I know you're right. It's just that she said something so mean about Grandma Cath, I can hardly . . . . But you're right," she repeated with a deep sigh, letting her explanation trail, unfinished. I have to work on not letting her hurt me—somehow. I'm not really sure it's hurt that I feel. It's just that she makes me so damned mad sometimes!"

She tweaked him teasingly on the chin as the boys came running back into the kitchen. "Now, what is this about my kids being loud. You have part ownership in those two, if I recall."

"Mom—Dad. Come see what Santa left in our stockings."

Each of the twins grabbed a parent's hand, and Julie and Kenneth joined the boys in front of the living-room fireplace to examine their Santa treasures, soon forgetting Rennie's remark. It was, as Kenneth had reasoned, not at all unusual for Rennie to say unkind things, particularly about Cath. Particularly to Julie. Rennie's jealousy over the close relationship between the two had long been a problem.

As a child, Julie Anne Montgomery was somewhat of an enigma. She wanted for nothing, more spoiled than her mother, Rennie.

But it had a different effect on Julie. She shied away from those who responded to her every whim, those who presented her with gifts on every occasion—and for no occasion. She was more drawn to people who gave her their time instead of things.

People like her great-Uncle Spence, people like her Grandma Cath. Julie was never away from Cath's side when they were together. It seemed as if she were more of a Rowan than a Montgomery—and most certainly more of a Rowan than a Spaulding.

This annoyed Rennie immensely, although there didn't seem to be a thing she could do about it. Julie drifted towards Cath like a magnet whenever they were in the same room. It wasn't because Cath showered her with gifts, that's for sure. In fact, sometimes it seemed to Rennie that Jack and Cath gave Julie very little.

For her eighth birthday, Grandma and Grandpa Montgomery's gift to Julie was a paint set with an easel—a smaller version of the one Cath used. Rennie's father presented her with a pony. And what was Julie's favorite gift? The paint set.

Julie dutifully thanked her Grandpa Spaulding for the pony, which she named Ben, and she rode him immediately, as she was certain was expected of her. Her Uncle Spence had taught her to ride when she was a mere five years old. And she loved to ride. She really did.

But she loved to paint more.

Julie's love for painting began even before she entered school.

Cath had shown her how to grip a palette, how to hold a paint brush when her small chubby hands still wanted to clutch it with all four fingers—even how to mix paints.

"Cath, what are you thinking of—have you lost your mind?" screamed Rennie, running out to the patio where Cath was helping the young protégé artist try out her new skills. "I have enough trouble keeping her clean without her being covered with paint."

"It's water paint, Rennie, and washes out beautifully. Anyhow, she's pretty well covered with the smock," said Cath, referring to the old shirt she had buttoned backwards on Julie's little body, the shirttail dragging on the ground.

"She looks like a ragamuffin, and just look at her hands," complained Rennie as she swept her daughter up in her arms. "If it isn't you and your paints, it's that brother of yours and his farm. My God, you should see her when she comes home from visiting him! I don't even want her out there. My daughter isn't going to be a farmhand, and she isn't going to be a painter!" She slammed the door, going back into the house, a screaming Julie in her arms.

"Grandma Cath, Grandma Cath! I want Grandma Cath," she cried.

Cath didn't offer Julie any more painting instruction for a few years after that—not until Matt asked her to do so.

Julie began piano lessons when she entered first grade. Rennie's dream for her only child was that she be a pianist—a brilliant pianist. But Julie balked every step of the way. "I hate playing the piano," she declared, "and I won't practice, even if you make me sit here on this stupid piano bench all day—all week. You can't make me touch the keys."

Her mother begged her, coached her, and screamed at her headstrong daughter, but nothing Rennie said could persuade Julie to practice doing something she didn't like—and for which she appeared to have little talent. Matt decided he'd better intervene.

"Honey, I'll tell you what. I'll make a deal with you. If you'll practice every day like your mom wants you to, I'll buy you some paints."

"Really? Oh, Daddy, I love you," she said bounding into his arms and giving him a strong, little-girl hug. "I'm going to call Grandma Cath right now and tell her," she announced as she tore down the hall to the telephone.

"Just a minute, young lady. You need to promise me first that you'll practice, and if you break that promise, the paints will be taken away."

Julie stopped in her tracks and walked back to her father. "I promise, Daddy, I'll practice the dumb piano," she said, wrinkling her nose with distaste.

She tried—or at least, she appeared to—but she hadn't inherited her mother or maternal grandmother's exceptional ability to express herself through the compositions of the masters. Her playing was expressionless and laborious. Julie was very relieved when, at the age of twelve, her mother finally relented and deemed her daughter, "hopelessly without artistic talent," and the lessons were dropped.

Of course, by that time, Julie was devoted to painting—thoroughly enjoyed it and displayed remarkable talent.

She especially enjoyed painting with her grandmother, Cath.

"Grandma Cath, why doesn't mine looks like yours?" questioned Julie, critiquing her painting of the oak tree behind the Rowan farmhouse, comparing it to her grandmother's. "Yours is much better," she said with dismay.

"It's not better, Julie. It's only different. You see, honey, we really paint with our minds, our eyes. Our hands only do what our minds tell them to do. And my eyes can no longer look at that big old oak and see what you see. I could once, when I was eight years old like you. Now I can only see it through the eyes of an older woman, of a grandmother. When you're older, yours will look more like mine. Not quite the same, though, because each person sees the world differently, Julie. Each sees it differently, and each paints it differently."

Julie had listened to her grandmother's explanation and its hidden philosophy with wide eyes, and soon her dismayed frown was replaced by a happy smile. She hugged her grandmother, paint-covered smock and all.

"You're a good little artist, Julie. I think the day will come when we'll have to find a spot in the gallery for the works of Julie Anne Montgomery."

"Really, Grandma Cath? Do you really think so?" asked Julie excitedly.

"I really think so," reassured her grandmother.

Cath accurately predicted the career of Julie Montgomery Matson—much to her mother's chagrin. Rennie didn't have the respect for painting that she did for music. She regarded painting as child's play. So when her own daughter, her only child, latched on to painting as her chosen career field, Rennie was livid.

And she blamed Cath.

It was ridiculous, of course, to blame anyone for the remarkable artistic talent displayed by Julie, even as a child. Perhaps the gift was inherent in Julie, just as Rennie's mastery of music was, surely, in part, inherited from her mother. But other than what had passed to Julie through her Rowan genes, Cath had done nothing to encourage Julie's career choice. Julie decided at a very early age that she would be an artist—like her Grandma Cath.

It was the "like her Grandma Cath" that grated on Rennie. This made it very easy for Rennie to blame Cath for the poor relationship between her and her daughter. But Cath really had nothing to do with that volatile relationship. Their contentious struggles began during Julie's toddler days and followed through her high-school years.

The strange thing was, Julie was seen by many to be a model child. An excellent student, her teachers sang her praises year after year. Her father found her to be unbelievably cooperative—although he had to admit, she was very strong willed.

Julie was the progeny of two remarkable great-grandmothers, Sarah Rowan and Magdalen Spaulding. For her not to be willful would have been an anomaly. But her strong will made it impossible for her mother to manipulate her; they battled daily. Rennie wanted Julie to be the daughter of her dreams, and Julie firmly vowed to be just who she was—a bright, affectionate child, quick to laugh, a tomboy who loved the outdoors—especially the Rowan farm.

Vivacious and assertive, Julie stole her mother's show for many years, and Rennie really wasn't able to cope with that. She had too long been the center of attention. So Julie turned to her grandmother for her maternal bonding—and bond they did. Even to the point of selecting the same profession. As her grandmother had predicted, Julie became a really noteworthy artist, surpassing Cath by far in both talent and fame.

And her mother begrudged her success every step of the way.

Rennie's anger over Julie's talent and Cath's alleged responsibility for her pursuit of an artist's career even invaded the joyous atmosphere of Christmas Day.

Chapter Twenty-three

In spite of Rennie's upsetting comments of the early morning, the events of Christmas Day rolled along as planned. By mid-morning, the living room had been put back in perfect order, and there was little evidence of two small boys having celebrated Santa's arrival there.

Now all energies were focused on dinner.

Rennie frequently had help come in to assist with her dinner parties, but when it came to Christmas dinner, she preferred to do it alone. She was, after all, an excellent cook, and rather enjoyed having the opportunity to show it—and adored the praise that invariably followed.

Julie planned to help her mother however she could with the dinner preparations. "Okay, Mom, I'm ready," she said, tying the Christmas apron Rennie had handed to her around her waist.

The two women would have the house to themselves while they worked. "I'm taking the boys out for a walk in the snow," Kenneth had said.

"And I'm going along," announced Matt.

Cath remained in her room for the morning. The heavy activity the previous day and evening had left her extremely weary.

Weary, but happy.

With no distractions from the rest of the family, Rennie and Julie worked diligently preparing such an assortment of food that Julie thought her mother was mistaken about having invited only five guests. Surely there was enough for fifty.

They worked quietly, side by side, their silence broken only occasionally by a new directive from Rennie. The clatter of pots, pan, dishes, and silverware sometimes drowned out the soft, lyrical strains of Christmas hymns and carols playing on the radio on the counter.

Soon platters and bowls resplendent with foods filled every space in the kitchen, the visual appeal matched only by the delicious aroma that wafted throughout the house. A standing rib roast, it's succulent juices already sizzling in the pan, was in the oven; the "crown" which was to top the culinary master-piece sat on the counter, ready to add its regal touch to the roast when ready. For those guests who might prefer an alter-native to roast beef, two pheasants were roasting in the oven, and Rennie was gathering the ingredients for the cream sauce to pour over the birds.

Roasted small potatoes and wild rice were readied to accom-pany the meat and fowl, and Julie and Rennie prepared an array of colorful vegetables to brighten the plates of the diners. By the time the two had finished adding the last pickled crab apple to the relish tray, the kitchen counter looked like a catering estab-lishment.

"Mom, you're really something. What a spread!"

"It does look good, doesn't it," Rennie confirmed, satisfied with the morning's efforts.

The outdoorsmen came back in, their ruddy cheeks a testimony to the brisk winter day, and Cath joined her family, refreshed from rest and ready for more celebration. The guests soon arrived, laden with colorfully-wrapped gifts for their host and hostess, and after the customary handshakes, hugs, and words of good will, they joined the Montgomerys and Matsons around the dining-room table to partake of the magnificent holiday feast prepared by Rennie and Julie.

As expected, Christmas dinner was superb. The table décor, a crystal Christmas tree edged in gold and surrounded by small crys-tal candleholders with tiny white tapers, was elegant, and the food cooked to perfection.

"Rennie, as always, your dinner is a delight to behold. It's so pic-ture perfect, it almost seems a shame to eat it," said Amanda Taylor. "And those cream puffs," she added nodding towards the buffet where tens of tiny cream puffs were piled to form a Christmas tree. "I don't know anyone who's as artistic with food as you."

The other guests spoke in agreement; Rennie smiled demurely, absorbing the compliments with obvious pleasure.

Amanda's right, thought Julie, *Mom's a true artist with food. Dear God, I hope no one calls her an artist—it'd ruin her day for sure.*

Dick Pritchard and Carl Devlin graciously toasted their host and hostess, and the conversation flowed freely.

Except from the Matsons—or from Cath.

The Christmas magic of last night was gone, evaporated. To Julie, the festivities now seemed as shallow as cardboard, and she was suddenly very eager to go home, to go back to Minnesota.

Early in the afternoon, she, Cath and the boys stole back to Cath's room to look at the photo album. For Julie, it was the high point of the day.

"Mom, look at you," said young Jack, giggling. "You were so skinny."

Julie looked at the photo taken when she was twelve, skinny and gawky, grinning as she clutched her kitten. "Just you wait, kiddo," she said, tickling him and wrestling on Cath's bed. "You'll be twelve some day, too."

The boys wanted to look at every photo of their mother—and of their grandfather, especially when he was a little boy. Their favorites were of a birthday party when he was four years old.

Cath remembered that party so well, it seemed almost impossible that so many years had gone by since her son was celebrating his fourth birthday, impossible that he now was a grandfather.

Chapter Twenty-four

The day of Matt's fourth birthday was hectic from beginning to end—hectic and wonderful.

"Will you please sit down a minute, Matt," urged Cath. "Mommy'll never have your party ready if you don't stop tearing around. Here." She lifted her small son onto a chair and scooted it up to the table. "Lick this frosting bowl clean. That ought to take you a minute or so."

"Oh boy," said Matt, liking this day more every minute. Bright colored balloons tied with string drifted over the back of a chair, and crepe-paper streamers of every color in the rainbow waved from the ceiling.

"Now for the finishing touches to this cake." Cath turned back to the circus-decorated creation and carefully placed four bright red candles at evenly spaced intervals. "There," she said proudly, stepping back to admire her handiwork. "That's a great circus cake if ever I've seen one."

"That's a great cake," echoed Matt.

Cath turned to him and smiled. "And you look like a cake yourself, birthday boy. Didn't you get any of the frosting in your mouth? Or did you just decide to wear it on your face."

Matt giggled, wiping his hand across his already frosting-covered countenance.

"Hey, here comes the 'Bath Master.' Jack, how would you like to guide this aging young man through his bath? His guests will be here in about an hour."

"Sure," agreed Jack. "Just don't touch anything," he admonished Matt, "including me, ol' sticky fingers."

As Jack guided their excited young son down the hall to the awaiting bath, Cath smiled. How she loved those two. She couldn't imagine anyone having a better life than they did. Jack, a successful retailer, following in his father's footsteps. Matt, a sweet, intelligent, healthy little boy.

Cath was almost as excited at Matt over this party, his first real birthday party. For the preceding three, there had been grandmas and grandpa, aunts, uncles, and countless other relatives stopping by for cake and ice cream. But this year they had invited twelve of his little friends, and a real clown was coming to entertain them—complete with red shaggy wig, polka-dot suit, and a performing poodle.

Almost as much planning and anticipation had gone into the party as opening night of a Broadway show.

The day, as promised, was as one might expect with a large gathering of excited four-year-olds—loud, hectic, and exhausting. As the last little one left, his hand in that of his mother, giving Cath, Jack, and Matt a shy "thank-you" in response to the prompting whispered in his ear, Cath plopped down in the closest chair.

"Don't expect me to move until he's five," she told Jack.

"Mo-o-ommy. That's gonna be too long," moaned Matt.

"She's only kidding, son. Why don't you start hauling your gifts to your bedroom? I'll be in to help you in just a minute."

"Come here, honey," said Cath, extending her arms. "Of course, I was kidding. I'm just going to relax one minute. Then Daddy and I'll come and help you put away your toys. Okay?" she asked, hugging him tightly.

"Okay," said Matt, pulling away and dashing towards his dozen-plus new gifts. He piled his arms with as many as he could possibly manage and ambled off to his room, looking much like an elf commissioned to help Santa prepare toys for delivery on Christmas Eve.

Jack sat down beside Cath and pulled her towards him. She laid her head on his shoulder and sighed. "I really do think I'll recover by the time he's five. It was a good party though, wasn't it."

She wasn't asking a question, simply making a statement she knew was true. A dozen smiling faces, wide-eyed with wonder at the antics of Ralph Aston, "Chuckles the Clown," was all the affirmation she needed.

"Let's go help our little guy. He won't get all that stuff put away before he's ready to graduate from high school," she said, pulling herself to her feet.

Jack and Cath walked arm-in-arm into Matt's bedroom where they found him curled up in the middle of his bed, clutching a new toy tractor, his very special gift from his Uncle Spence.

"Let me get the camera. I have one shot left," whispered Jack, as Cath gently laid a blanket across their weary four-year-old.

"We'll have some great photos to remember today," said Cath, softly, so as not to wake their son.

"Was that a real clown Grandpa had at his birthday party?" asked Jack, sounding doubtful.

"Yes, a real clown," assured Cath. "His name was Chuckles, and the kids thought he was just great."

Cath, Julie, and the twins laughed and played and paged through the album for a long time, enjoying the stories Cath told to accompany every photograph. All too soon, they noticed it was nearing dusk. Christmas Day was nearly over.

"Grandma Cath, we didn't mean to steal your entire afternoon. You should have rested some. Didn't Dad say the doctor ordered daily rest? I'm so sorry."

"Julie, having you here has invigorated me more than any rest could begin to do. It's been wonderful. Now, why don't you rejoin the others, and the boys and I will spend a little quiet time."

Julie took her husband's hand in hers as she sat down beside him, having guided the boys to their own room to play a quiet game. "I'm sorry to have abandoned you," she whispered. "Are you surviving?" she asked softly, so no one but Kenneth could hear.

"Barely," he whispered. He squeezed her hand, then put his arm around her, and together they feigned interest in conversations in which they had no interest, laughed when appropriate, and agreed when agreement seemed called for.

The guests departed as the lights outside the house came on, signaling the approach of evening. The holiday-weary family was left with recollections of the day, more raving about the fantastic dinner, and two very, very tired children.

Christmas Day drew to a close.

The Matsons left for home the next morning.

Chapter Twenty-five

"'Bye, Mom, 'bye, Dad," said Julie, the last to make the round of hugs and good-byes. "'Bye, Grandma Cath," she said, as she hugged her tightly and long. "Please stay well."

As they drove away, Julie said, "Something's wrong, Kenneth, and I can't figure out what it is."

"Wrong? What do you mean?"

"Grandma Cath seemed afraid of Mom—and Mom seemed afraid of her. Sort of. Oh, I don't know. Something just didn't seem right."

"Afraid? Honey, that makes no sense. I don't think I've ever seen Cath afraid of anyone—and most certainly not Rennie."

"I know it makes no sense, Kenneth. I can't even put my finger on anything in particular. It was just a feeling, the way they avoided each other, and it disturbs me."

Kenneth Matson glanced quickly at his wife. He knew what a levelheaded woman she was—not prone to fears and fabrications. Cath had seemed unduly quiet at times. But my God, she had had a very recent brush with death.

And Rennie? Well, Rennie was just Rennie. Who could ever know what was going inside his mother-in-law's head. Certainly not him.

He reached over and stroked Julie's hand as it lay clenched in her lap. "Don't worry about Cath, honey. She looks wonderful when you consider all she's been through."

"I'm sure I'm just being silly, Kenneth. You're probably right. I just wish I could shake this feeling."

Months later, Julie and Kenneth recalled this conversation, deeply regretting they hadn't acted on Julie's concerns.

Many photos were snapped that Christmas—photos of little boys sitting cross-legged under the tree, of Julie and Kenneth. Of the entire family, of Rennie and Matt with the Matsons, of Cath flanked by Jack and Hal, absorbed in the Christmas story she was reading them, the beautifully decorated tree in the background casting its silver-blue glow over their shoulders. After the holidays were past, long after Julie, Kenneth, and the boys had embarked on the snowy trek back to Minnesota and the dark, dreary days of January set in, Cath mounted the Christmas photos in her album. Carefully, she placed them one by one, adding to her cache of memories.

"This is a great one of you and the boys, Mom," said Matt as he held up a photo of Cath and the twins in front of the Christmas tree.

"I like that one, too; it's certainly one to treasure. Aren't those two something?"

"They're great little boys, all right," said their grandfather proudly. "It was a wonderful Christmas. One we'll remember for a long time."

That night, after spending the entire evening going through her album yet again, feeling the joy and the pain of her memories, those she loved marched through her dreams—her mother, her brother Spence, Julie and her family, Matt, and even Rennie.

And especially, her dear Jack.

Chapter Twenty-six

January was brutal that year, in Nebraska as well as points further north. The winter seemed endless Everyone's spirits sagged, and Cath was no exception. She spent hours alone in her room, often poring over the pictures in her album, trying to recall the joy of the times they depicted and the love of the people now gone.

Matt's case load was exceptionally heavy again, and he was gone for full days, long cold winter days. He left home early in the morning and returned late in the evening. Many nights, he came home so weary—depleted, really—that he had little energy left for anything other than dinner and just sitting, trying to relax. And often, he didn't even take the time to relax. Some evenings, he would finish dinner, grab his briefcase, and retire to his office-at-home to prepare for the following day.

Rennie resented it terribly and felt neglected. And she hated the fact that so much of the conversation during the brief time she did have with her husband these days was centered on Cath.

One evening, when Cath had gone directly to her own room after dinner and Matt had not as yet become involved in the multiple pages loading down his briefcase, Rennie attacked him with an angry tirade regarding their table conversation that evening.

"Do you have any idea how damned sick and tired I am of hearing about how your mother feels? It's all we talk about anymore!" she shouted.

"Rennie, pipe down. Mom'll hear you."

"Let her. I really don't care what she hears—or how she feels. 'How are you, Mom,'" she mimicked, snidely. "'Fine, son.' 'Are you sure, Mom?'"

Her words of mockery cut Matt deeply. "She's my mother, and I care how she feels."

"Well, I repeat. I don't care. And furthermore, need I remind you that she is *your* mother, but she most certainly isn't *mine.*" Angrily,

Rennie stomped up the stairs and into their bedroom, slamming the door loudly behind her.

Matt sat down at the dining room table, the remains of their dinner congealing unpleasantly on the dishes still there. He ran his fingers through his graying hair, a habit he had adopted from his father, and shook his head, muttering, "What can I do to make Rennie understand that it really can work out fine—Mom living here?"

He tried to think of the reasons Rennie resented Cath so. Mom really seemed to be quite pleasant to her. She helped when she could, asked about Rennie's social activities, complimented her on the way she looked. She wasn't Rennie's mother, but Rennie could think of her more as her mother if only she'd try. She'd just really never gotten over her mother's death. But that certainly wasn't Matt's fault—or Cath's.

But still, I need to do whatever I can to keep Rennie happy. I love her, and I do neglect her too much—just have to learn to leave office matters at the office, I guess.

He sat for a time, trying to resolve his dilemma: How could he be a good son and a good husband—and a good attorney?

With no real resolution in mind, but vowing to focus more on Rennie's needs, he went upstairs to make promises to his wife that he hoped to keep.

Everything went more smoothly for a while, Rennie mollified for the time being by Matt's avowed attention. Even the weather brightened for three or four days, and the optimists spoke of an impending January thaw.

But by the end of the week, another blizzard raged, followed by depressing steel-gray skies and relentless wind. The interminable cold weather added to Rennie's self-pity. She felt as if Mother Nature had teamed with Cath to make her life miserable. Her disposition, rarely great these days unless everything was going her way, totally eroded. She was unpleasant to everyone, including Matt, as he was again bringing work home from the office.

She was especially unpleasant to Cath.

"My God, Rennie, leave Mom alone! I haven't heard you say anything nice to her for so long, I'm beginning to wonder if you ever did," declared Matt after Rennie had again criticized Cath for some little encroachment on what she continued to regard as her domain.

"How would you know what I say to her? You're rarely here, and when you are you're behind closed doors with that damned briefcase."

Cath, sorry that something she had done had presented yet another reason for hostility between her son and his wife, went back to her room and quietly read until sleepiness overtook her aging eyes and she turned in for the night.

That was last night. At breakfast, Rennie and Matt appeared to have resolved their anger, and although the conversation was not spirited, it was at least civil.

"I'll try, Rennie, I'll really try to get away early, and maybe we can have an enjoyable evening for a change."

Rennie didn't respond, simply gave him an "I'll believe when I see it" look.

Cath returned to her room after breakfast and after Matt had left for the day. It would be another bitter day, the clear sky and the promise of sunshine belying the bitter cold, as a steady wind whistled through bare tree branches, a day that called for warm clothing. Cath was standing in front of her closet, trying to decide what to wear, when she heard a distinct click, sounding much like the doorknob turning—or like the key turning in the lock.

"Rennie, is that you? Come in."

There was no response.

"Come in, Rennie," she repeated.

Cath went to the door to open it and invite her in. She turned the knob and pulled gently, but without success. It wouldn't open.

The door was locked.

Cath was confused. Why in the world would someone lock her door? Panic filled her.

"Rennie?" she called with some desperation in her voice, turning the knob and pulling on the door—hard this time. "Is someone there? Rennie?" she called loudly.

But no one answered her calls.

Even the thought of confinement had always frightened Cath, and fear was overtaking her thinking now. Her heart was pounding. She leaned her forehead against the door and closed her eyes tightly. She could almost hear her heart racing, and she was breathing rapidly; she felt dizzy.

For a few minutes, Cath stood with her head resting against the door, her hand resting on the knob fruitlessly. Then she realized how pointless her fear was.

"You old fool," she said aloud, softly talking to herself. "What are you afraid of? Calm down. I know it was Rennie who locked the door. It just had to be Rennie. But I can't imagine why she'd do such a thing. I know she can be unkind—very unkind, even vindictive at times. But why in the world would she lock me in my room?"

Cath thought about how it would be if she were locked in the room all day until Matt came home, and again she felt some panic. She reached for the phone at her bedside.

I'll just call Grace—or maybe Emily. They're good friends, they'll come. But what will I say to them? What will I ask them to do—come over here and demand that Rennie unlock the door?

No, I can't do that. How ridiculous I would look. I could never bear to look them in the eyes again if I called, whining, asking them to come and rescue me.

Cath had always been quite claustrophobic and wasn't fond of closed doors that she couldn't open. She walked over to her bed and lay down, knowing she needed to control her fears. Her heart was still pounding, and her brow was beaded with sweat. The wispy white curls surrounding her face stuck unpleasantly to her forehead and damp cheeks.

She looked around her bedroom. This was her room. Her lovely room. The room that Matt had redone just for her when he brought her here to live. The room she had learned to like—to enjoy.

It was home. All was familiar. The sunny, pale yellow walls, matched perfectly to the color of a yellow rose. Snowy white curtains, crisp and clean.

Her bed, the wonderful walnut bed she and Jack had shared for so many years, and folded neatly at the foot, the quilt her mother had made for her the year before she died. The quilt with pieces from clothing familiar to her as a child—clothing she could still recall to this day.

Cath sat up. She ran her hand down the bedpost, delighting in the smooth feeling of the beautifully turned wood. She tenderly stroked the quilt.

"Oh, Mama, Oh, Jack," she whispered, tears gathering in her eyes. "How I wish you were here with me now."

She looked at the sampler hanging on her wall over her desk. The same sampler that had hung in the kitchen of the Rowan family farmhouse years ago. The cloth was see-through threadbare in spots, and many of the stitches had disappeared, the embroidery thread disintegrating with age. In the alphabet running around the edge, the "B" appeared as a "P," and "Q" and "S" were completely gone. "Home Sweet Home" now read, "Home Sw-et Hom-."

"I will not have that old piece of junk hanging in my house," Rennie had ranted when Cath showed her the treasured memento. But Cath had been adamant about keeping one of the links to her past as a Rowan on full display, and Matt had supported her stance. He remembered when his grandmother had given the sampler to his mother, and he knew how much it meant to her.

Cath sat down in the chair by the window, laid her head back, and concentrated on relaxing.

I know it won't do to allow loneliness and despair to engulf me now. It's going to be a long day, and if I allow myself to feel desperate, it's going to be a hopelessly long one. Surely, there are things I can do, activities to keep me occupied and my mind free from thinking about being under lock and key.

My books. Yes, there's the book I started last night. Great story. Even my television is here to keep me company if I want a change from reading.

Her bathroom with its clean white tile and yellow-rosebud wallpaper adjoined the bedroom. All she needed for the day was right here.

Yes, I'll be just fine, she told herself. *Just fine.*

Her panic eased, her racing heart quieted down, and she relaxed—somewhat.

If only I knew what Rennie was up to. She's probably angry with me again. She seems to be angry with me most of the time of late, Cath thought, sighing. *Why, I've spent many a morning alone in my room without even thinking about leaving, This will be no different.*

She went into the bathroom and washed her face, enjoying the feeling of the warm water and soft cloth on her skin. She looked through her closet and selected what she would wear for the day. Gray-blue slacks with a matching sweater. She'd be comfortable and warm, and look nice too. The gray-blue was very flattering with her white hair and fair skin.

I may not see anyone at all today, but at least I'll look nice to please myself.

She dressed slowly and deliberately, using up as much time as possible. When she was done, she checked herself in the mirror and was satisfied with what she saw. She willed herself to smile at her reflection and was uplifted by the smiling face, even though it was her own.

She made her bed, taking great care to make it smooth and neat. She refolded the quilt, and as she did so, briefly buried her face in its folds. Even now, she could feel the presence of her mother.

She hung her bathrobe and placed her slippers in the closet. She looked over her attractive room and smiled. *I'll be just fine.*

Picking up the book she'd been reading, she sat in her favorite chair by the window. For a while, she merely watched the birds flitting by, stopping to rest on the wind-whipped branches in the tree overhead, gathering their winter nourishment from the bird feeder just outside the window. The bright red of the Cardinal's feathers was made brighter still by the contrast with the brilliant white snow and cloudless blue sky.

It's a lovely day. Cold, but lovely. Cath opened her book and soon was lost in the pages. Always an avid reader, she had become a voracious one since Jack's death. She regarded her books as her very good friends.

Before she knew it, the morning was nearly gone. She stood up and thought, *Perhaps the door is unlocked now. I haven't heard anything, but then I have really been engrossed in my book.*

Her hand sweated and trembled as she tried the door.

It was still locked.

Cath held her ear to the door, but she heard no sound. Of course, Matt and Rennie's home was very large, and she rarely heard sounds from the rest of the house when she was in her room. Perhaps someone would hear her if she called out again?

Not likely, she reasoned.

Again, she felt the panic rise in her throat, and again, she told herself to calm down and wait. She turned on television and watched a popular daytime show, but it held her interest only briefly.

Starting to feel hungry, Cath wondered if there was a possibility she had anything to eat in the room. Even as she searched the drawers of her nightstand, she thought it was probably fruitless. She rarely brought food to her room.

She finally did find two cellophane-wrapped crackers. The crackers and a glass of water were her lunch. She ate slowly, hoping it would help the hunger pangs she was experiencing.

Crackers and water. My goodness, just like a prisoner.

She shuddered. *A prisoner. That's what I am. A prisoner in my own room—in my son's home.*

A tear rolled down her cheek and an overpowering sadness filled her, a sadness as great as any she had ever experienced. She felt so alone. So terribly, terribly alone.

Cath sat immobile for quite some time, wrapped in her sadness. She didn't even feel the warmth of the sun, now pouring in her window as it crept from east to west.

I won't let this defeat me. I just won't! Maybe Rennie will tell me what it is I do that makes her so angry. I'll ask her. Yes, that's what I'll do. So I just have to get through today. I can do that.

She sighed a great sigh, walked to her desk, picked up her photo album, and returned to the chair by the window.

Cath paged through the album and relived each and every event pictured there, photo by photo, until darkness began to replace daylight. At one point she dozed slightly, the book clutched closely, giving her comfort as a child might find consolation in a favorite teddy bear or a well-worn blanket. The grayness of early dusk encompassed her as she alternated between half-asleep and half-awake.

She didn't hear the key turn in the lock. Nor did she hear the garage door go up as Matt drove in. She wasn't aware of the time—wasn't aware that it was now early evening, dinnertime. She wasn't even aware that her day of forced isolation was over.

Chapter Twenty-seven

"Hi, hon," said Matt, as he kissed Rennie. "How was your day?"

"It was perfect," she replied. "Madge and I went out for lunch, then to Dana's for a couple hands of Bridge. A good, relaxing day."

"Great," said Matt with enthusiasm, hugging his contented wife, pleased that her day had gone well. "Where's Mom?"

"In her room, I suppose. You know she stays in there much of the time. I've hardly seen her all day."

"Guess I'll stick my head in the door and wish her a good evening. Man, I'm beat," he said as he walked down to the hall to his mother's room.

He knocked softly on the closed door. "Mom?"

Cath didn't answer immediately. She was still partially dozing, hungry, and a bit disoriented.

"Mom?" Matt knocked louder a second time.

"Matt?" Cath's reply sounded faint and tentative.

"Yes, it's Matt. Mom, may I come in?" he asked, feeling somewhat anxious, recalling the time not too long ago when he came to her room and found her nearly comatose.

"Of course," she replied, wondering if the door was now unlocked. She turned on her bedside lamp just as the door opened.

"Mom, are you all right?" Matt had seen the light come on as he entered and knew she had been sitting in the dark. It was nearly seven o'clock. Cath was not one to be sitting alone in the dark in the early evening.

"I'm fine," she said with forced conviction and an equally forced smile.

"Are you sure? You look pale."

"Do I? Well, I'm just feeling a bit tired. I've been resting."

Slowly, Cath stood up, hoping the dizziness she felt wouldn't be obvious. As she brushed her hair back from her face, her hand trembled.

Matt noticed. "Mom, I don't think you're fine at all. I'm going to call Jason."

The last thing Cath wanted was a doctor and an outsider at this point. Not even Jason Miller. She had a problem. A family problem, and only family could help.

How she longed to tell Matt. Tell him that his wife was so eager to have her gone, she had locked her in her room—kept her in isolation all day. But she couldn't. At least not yet. Not until after she had the opportunity to talk to Rennie, to try to correct what it was that made Rennie so angry with her.

Maybe Matt knew what it was. "Matt," she began, but then decided against saying anything to her son. It wasn't fair not to speak to Rennie first.

"Yes?"

"Never mind. It wasn't important—just a thought that crossed my mind."

Cath knew that Matt was aware of Rennie's selfish ways. He became aware of his wife's fixation on herself shortly after they met as teenagers. But he loved her so, he really didn't care.

In spite of her self-centeredness, Rennie was Matt's wife, and he loved her—Cath could see that. And with Julie so far away, who would Matt have without Rennie?

No, I can't tell Matt that, in addition to being selfish, his wife can be cruel.

"Son, you worry about me too much," she said, with an attempt at flippancy. "You're going to have to accept the fact that I'm an old woman who sometimes just doesn't look 'fine.' Now run along, and I'll be out for dinner in a minute."

"Okay. If you're sure you're all right. Don't try to be the stoic now. Even the Irish are allowed to not feel well once in a while."

Cath laughed lightly. "I know. Now be off and let me freshen up a bit." Matt reluctantly left Cath's room, still not fully convinced all was well with her.

Cath moved across the room slowly. Her legs felt as if they might collapse beneath her. She felt dizzy and fearful she might fall. She almost called Matt back to help her.

But she decided against it. She was determined to forget that today's nightmare had ever happened.

The attractive ensemble she had selected to wear this morning had served her well. In spite of the fact that she had been lounging in it all day, it looked nearly as fresh and unwrinkled as when she had put it on in the morning. She again washed her face and combed her hair, pinched her cheeks to heighten their color. When she was satisfied that she didn't look drained or ill, she left her room, making a great point of leaving her door open.

Wide open.

When she appeared in the dining room, she really did look quite refreshed. Matt watched his mother and was pleased that she seemed considerably better than she had just moments before.

Cath looked squarely at Rennie, and Rennie didn't look away. Cath saw the mockery in her eyes, and she was sure she would be a prisoner in her room again. Some of the fear she had felt earlier in the day returned, and her hand trembled as she brought her fork to her mouth, partly from panic and partly from hunger.

The food was delicious, as always. At first, Cath feared she was eating too rapidly. *Mustn't draw attention to the fact that I'm starved.*

But then she found she could eat only very little after all. Her tension and nervous exhaustion took over the moment her immediate hunger was satisfied.

The conversation was as normal as any other day in the Montgomery household. Rennie elaborated on her social activities of the day, and Matt shared the high points of his day at the office. Matt and Rennie had always enjoyed sharing their day over dinner. Ordinarily, Cath joined right in. But tonight, she was silent.

Matt was aware of her silence and watched her out of the corner of his eye. The concern he had felt returned. Something was wrong with his mother tonight. But what was it? So as not to anger Rennie, he didn't ask again if she was all right. He had, after all, just inquired about how she felt when he was in her room.

She said she was fine. Maybe she's right. Maybe I just worry about her too much.

Incredibly weary from the tension of the day, Cath still didn't care to return to the room where she had been imprisoned. So she lingered this evening. She even joined Rennie and Matt as they watched television—something she rarely did.

She put off returning to her room as long as possible. Her room with the sunny west exposure decorated just the way she liked it. Warm and bright. The room that had been her haven since she had come to live with Matt and Rennie.

Until now.

Chapter Twenty-eight

It was three days before Cath had the opportunity to confront Rennie. She was nervous, her hands perspiring profusely, her mouth dry. *This is ridiculous,* she thought, critical of her own reluctance to talk with a member of her own family. *This is my daughter-in-law. What am I afraid of?*

"Rennie, can we talk a minute?"

Rennie looked at her, both surprise and impatience evident. Cath and she had had few one-on-one conversations since Cath moved in.

"I guess so," she said, glancing at her watch, letting Cath know she had her attention for a limited time.

"Why did you lock my door Monday morning?"

"What in the world are you talking about, Cath? Why would I lock your door?"

"That's what I'm asking you, Rennie. Why did you lock my door?"

"I didn't," she lied. "Now if you had trouble opening it, I can understand. That door has always had a problem sticking from time to time. If it's sticking again, talk to Matt about it, just don't be accusing me of something I didn't do."

"Rennie, I . . . I—" Cath stammered.

Is that what happened—my door stuck? And I've made Rennie angry by accusing her.

"I'm so sorry, I never thought about the door sticking. I tugged and tugged—it just wouldn't open. I'm really sorry."

"Tell Matt to fix it," said Rennie as she walked away, not willing to discuss it further. As she turned away from Cath, she smiled the self-satisfied smile of someone who had just won something—a smile of triumph.

"Matt, my bedroom door's been sticking," said Cath that night at dinner. "Do you think you have a minute to take a look at it? Of course, it could be that I'm just getting weak in my old age," she added, an attempt to lighten the embarrassment she felt over questioning Rennie.

"A spunky 'old lady' like you? I doubt it. Sure, I'll take a look at it after dinner."

"Hmm, it seems okay," he said later as he turned the knob and swung the door back and forth. "Must have been an especially humid day. I'll spray a bit of lubricant on the hinges and around the knob."

Finished, he added, "I hope it didn't inconvenience you too much, Mom. I'm really sorry."

"No, it was fine, really. It was only sticking a little bit," she said, still mortified that she had actually suspected her daughter-in-law of locking her in her room.

A week later, while she was making her bed, Cath again heard the distinct click of the lock. She knew as she walked to the door that it wouldn't open. She knew then that Rennie had lied, that she had indeed locked her in—and would do so again.

She was sick at heart. This isn't what she had expected when she moved in. She was family—Matt was her only child. Why did Rennie resent her so?

I've tried very hard not too interfere with their lives? Have I so totally failed that I've made my daughter-in-law despise me? But what have I done?

Cath tried once more, about two weeks later, to talk to Rennie about being locked in her room. They were in the kitchen early in the morning; Matt had just driven away.

"Rennie, I hate to bring this up again, but I feel I must. You are locking the door—I hear the click of the lock. It has to be you Rennie, there's no one else in the house. Please tell me why."

Rennie stood still, facing Cath, until she was done speaking. She looked her straight in the eyes for a moment, and then without a word, turned and walked away.

It became a game, with Cath and Rennie the only players. Cath would linger outside her room, in the kitchen as long as possible in the morning after Matt left for his office. Or she would hurriedly dress and return to the living room before he left.

Often she wouldn't go into her own room until afternoon. She didn't care so much if she was locked in for the afternoon. She frequently spent that time there anyway, reading or writing letters. On many days, she'd steal a small nap after lunch. The doctors had advised that she do that daily.

But I'd like to choose whether or not I want to spend time alone in my room, especially in the morning. I'd like to do as I wish in the morning—feel free to go for a walk, if I want. Even feel free to get cleaning supplies or the vacuum cleaner from the hall closet to clean my own room.

Cath also liked to assist with cleaning the rest of the house. Rennie had professional cleaning help weekly, but Cath wanted to do her part with the day-to-day care of their home. It helped her feel useful. She had started taking part as soon as she was able to after moving in. She enjoyed it and had thought Rennie enjoyed having her help. But recently, Rennie had been finding fault with any effort she made, and to keep peace, Cath started doing less and less.

Cath loved going outside in the mornings, when the weather permitted it. Long strolls invigorated her, and she enjoyed the change of seasons. All of them.

Neighbors accustomed to regularly seeing her out walking on beautiful days were relieved when they saw her amble by after an unexplained lengthy absence. Although her absences hadn't alarmed them, they were somewhat concerned. They knew Cath had been very ill on a couple of occasions.

Surely, they had no reason for alarm. After all, Cath was the widow of the president of the Montgomery stores, the mother of Matt Montgomery—who was making quite a name for himself in the legalities of corporate mergers.

Catherine Montgomery most certainly was receiving the best of care.

This they thought—and believed—when they saw Cath stroll by.

Her gait was slow but steady, and her shoulders were somewhat stooped. But her step was sure and deliberate. The neighbors had no idea they were watching a woman celebrate brief periods of treasured freedom.

She smiled and greeted the neighbors she had come to know, and they greeted her in return, giving her an opportunity to tell one of them of her plight—to ask for assistance, if she desired. Cath had considered it, but only once and only briefly.

How could I? What in the world who they think of me—what would they think of Matt? Oh, I couldn't possibly say anything that would reflect badly on my son. He's a good man. I just have to solve this problem myself. If only I knew what to do.

When the days were warmer and sunny, Cath would try to get out early, before Matt left the house. She knew if she didn't do it then, she might not get out at all that day. And she hated missing a walk on a sunny day.

"Mom, why don't you wait until mid-morning for your daily stroll?" asked Matt one day as Cath walked out the door just as he was leaving. "It's still a bit brisk this early in the day."

She longed to tell him that the walks were no longer daily, that they were instead, "whenever she could avoid being locked in her room." And she was sure she should tell him that many days she had nothing to eat from breakfast to dinner, when he got home. But she just could not bring herself to share her nightmare existence with her son. Instead, she gave weak explanations for her actions.

"You know how much I love mornings, Matt. Always have. I really enjoy these early walks."

"Okay. Just don't overdo it," he advised.

Matt thought his mother looked very tired of late, and she appeared to be losing weight. *I need to have Jason give her another once over,* he decided as he drove away, always fearful of the return of his mother's cancer.

Many thoughts went through Cath's head as she walked throughout the neighborhood on these beautiful mornings. Pleasant thoughts. Memories of walking with Jack, hand-in-hand, arm-in-arm. Laughing at small meaningless things, enjoying totally each other's company.

Walks along this same street with Julie when she was a small child, her tiny hand clutched warmly and safely in her grandmother's. She recalled Julie's little-girl laugh—tinkly, like tiny bells. She remembered how warm and pleasant the small chubby hand had felt in hers.

Julie. How she missed Julie. Should she tell Julie about her episodes of imprisonment? She would help. Cath knew she would.

But how could she bring herself to tell Julie? Cath knew how much it would upset her. Julie dearly loved her grandmother, but she loved her mother, too, in spite of their longtime stormy relationship. She'd be asking her granddaughter to make a choice between her and her own mother, and that she couldn't do—wouldn't do. It would be too unfair.

So Cath did nothing. She simply didn't know where to seek help.

She had spent her entire life in the area. Her husband's family, as well as hers, had been pillars of the community for decades. Their department store, although no longer owned by a Montgomery, still bore the name.

She was a well-known artist—not only in Blakefield but throughout the entire region. Only the very young in Blakefield had not heard of Catherine Montgomery.

And yet she had no one to turn to. Not without making a tremendous sacrifice.

It's not easy to admit to someone you've known all your life that you are a victim at the hands of your own family. The total loss of pride and dignity, Cath mused one day as she walked along. She would appear to be a pathetic old woman and become the object of intense sympathy.

Could she bring herself to admit to anyone what was happening? She honestly couldn't imagine how.

Chapter Twenty-nine

Each day Cath eagerly anticipated Matt's coming home for the evening. It was the only time of day—no matter that it was brief—when she had any semblance of relaxation. When she could set aside her fear and anxiety.

Often during the day she'd pick up her album and look at the photos of her son. It was so exciting, that first day when she and Jack brought him home from the hospital. And Jack did a wonderful job of capturing their joy with his camera.

Looking at Matt's first baby picture, Cath recalled with delight that day—and the days of her pregnancy leading up to it.

"Ugh. I'm uncomfortable," said Cath as she changed her position for yet another time. "Are you sure I haven't been pregnant forever? I feel like an elephant, and I understand they're pregnant for years."

Jack sat down on the sofa next to her, the burgundy mohair cushions still stiff with their newness. They were furnishing their new home little by little, hoping to work their way to the coming baby's room before his or her arrival.

The living room had been their most recent endeavor, the sofa complementing the blue and gray striped chair that had been their first new-home purchase, back when the end tables had been upended fruit crates. Rummage-sale lamps had precariously teetered on top of the crates—lamps that Jack had dubbed the "ugliest in the universe."

The crates had been replaced with fine mahogany tables, and the ugliest-in-the-universe lamps by attractive brass ones, which shed soft light across the room where the young couple sat. A sturdy wooden rocking chair filled the corner, completing their living-room decor.

"I've never seen an elephant with red curly hair," teased Jack, putting his arm around Cath and drawing her close. "Anyhow, don't criticize the mother of my child. She's wonderful and beautiful—even if a little on the plump side these days."

"Ha! Plump—I'm massive!"

"Shush. You're beautiful, Cath. Always have been. The first time I laid eyes on you, I thought, I'm going to marry that beautiful girl with the red curls and snappy blue eyes. You'll always be beautiful, honey, inside and out. And just think, very soon you'll be holding our beautiful baby, right here in our very own living room, in our very own house."

The young couple sat for a while, her head on his shoulder and his hand resting lightly on her swollen abdomen where their unborn child lay. Both were lost in thoughts of their soon-to-be-born baby and the challenging days ahead. Both were excited about their approaching parenthood; both were apprehensive, as well. Having a baby was a tremendous responsibility.

Jack had a good position with the department store his father founded and still ran. It would be his to manage some day, but he was very much in the learning stage right now—learning about everything.

John Montgomery, Sr., had built a solid retail establishment from an old-time country store, and he was determined it would remain a solid retail establishment long after he took his place on the hillside in the Eternal Rest Cemetery just north of town. He knew his son and namesake had a flair for retail and was dedicated to the business. But he also knew that young Jack had a lot to learn about the fine points of running the area's major department store.

Jack was a willing and eager learner. He just wondered, sometimes, if he'd ever get it all right and be successful—successful as well as being a good father and a good husband. It was a great deal to worry about, and worry he did.

Then there was all that talk about what was going on in Europe. Was it really possible that there would be another war? If there was, would the United States be involved? It sure sounded like it, to hear the older guys talk.

Will I go to war? he wondered. *And if I do and am not here with Cath and the baby, how can I be a good father?*

Jack was struggling with the same questions as thousands of other young men throughout the country in that period before the United

States' involvement in World War II: *How do I put my life on hold?*

As it turned out, Jack never did have to put his concerns about going to war to a test. He didn't pass his physical. The doctors didn't like the sound of a strong heart murmur—which Jack hadn't even been aware he had.

Cath's worries were more singular. She knew she would be a good mother. After all, she had had Sarah as a role model.

No, her worries were of one thing and one thing only. Her constant prayer was that her baby would be perfect—five fingers on each hand, five toes on each foot. All the parts, and in all the right places. The usual worries for a very pregnant young woman thinking about the impending birth of her first child.

Within the month, seven-pound-eight-ounce Matthew John Montgomery was born. He had ten fingers and ten toes, as well as all his other parts—and they were all in the right places.

Just as his father said he would be, he was beautiful. He looked very much like his mother, except at first, he didn't have the curls. Those came later.

Cath wrapped the soft blue blanket around his feet, so tiny she still couldn't believe they were real. His small hands were balled into fists, as if he were ready to take on the world. His head, which by his first birthday would be covered with curls so blonde they were almost white, now looked hairless. But when Cath rubbed her hand ever so gently across his head, she could feel the softness of the fine down-like baby hair.

"Sit here, hon, in the rocker," said Jack.

Cath sat as directed, carefully, so as not to wake their sleeping son. She tucked the blanket beneath his chin, away from his face. She wanted all his little face to show in the photograph. The luminous glow of the setting sun seeped through the curtains, gently spotlighting the pair.

"Ready?" asked Jack, the camera poised.

"Ready." Cath smiled down at her son.

The bright flash of the camera startled her, and the baby winced in his sleep. But his eyes remained closed as his slumber continued.

"He's so wonderful, Jack. I knew he would be, but I didn't know how very wonderful he'd be. I've never felt anything like this in my entire life."

Jack's eyes misted as he watched her looking adoringly at their son. He felt if he could capture this moment forever, he'd never ask for more.

"Yes, he is, Cath. Our son. We have some great years ahead of us, watching him grow, teaching him, loving him. And we'll always have the photographs to remember this great day when we brought our son home—our first-born."

"They'll go in the album, Jack. Right after our wedding pictures. We'll have them to look at as long as we live."

Chapter Thirty

Matt did bring his mother to see Dr. Miller. At first she refused to go, arguing, "Matt, it's just plain silly to see a doctor when I feel well."

But his persistence wore her down, and she feared her continued refusal would only arouse his suspicion that something surely was amiss.

"I'm fine, Jason. You just tell that buddy of yours that he's being overly anxious about his mother growing old."

It disturbed Jason that Cath was losing weight, and he shared Matt's concern that something didn't seem quite right with her. But none of her tests revealed any problems, and she claimed to feel just fine.

Still, Jason pondered, something was out of sync. But what?

So reluctantly—and tentatively—Dr. Miller gave Cath a clean bill of health and did as she requested. He told her son to quit worrying about his mother growing old.

"Cath might not be telling the whole truth, Matt. She might not be feeling as fine as she claims to be feeling. But I can't find any medical reasons to substantiate my hunches. Except that she has lost weight. Keep an eye on her. You know how spunky your mom is. It may be nothing, but she just doesn't seem to have the spark I'm used to seeing in Cath. And prepare yourself, too, old buddy. It may just be what she says—that she's growing old. Enjoy her—she's a remarkable woman."

"I know she is, Jason." Matt sighed deeply. "You're probably right. I'm not allowing for Mom's age. It's just that sometimes she really doesn't seem quite with it, and other times, she's as sharp as she's always been. Do you suppose it could be some kind of dementia?"

"I don't know, Matt. Possibly. I'm not seeing much evidence of that right now, though. That's why I want you to keep your eye on her for a while, and let me know of any really unusual behavior."

The friends shook hands, and Jason put a reassuring arm around Matt's shoulders. Then, he returned to his other patients, and Matt took his mother home.

Home, where things continued as they had been.

There were days when Cath wouldn't go into her own room, and there were days when she wasn't free to leave it.

Cath and Rennie continued to be locked in a game of cleverness and will. Cath knew that Rennie wouldn't dare even think about locking her in her bedroom when Matt was around, and she made a concerted effort to stay out of her room when he wasn't. This frustrated Rennie tremendously, and her anger grew. What she had hoped to accomplish by locking Cath in her room was to keep Cath away from her.

In actuality, what really happened was that she had her underfoot more than ever.

This cat and mouse game went on for several weeks. Some days, Cath would not so much as walk back into her room to retrieve a book. Other days, Rennie would have Cath locked in before she knew it was happening.

Chapter Thirty-one

Cath hadn't even dressed this morning. Most days she strived to look her best, even though her own eyes seeing her reflection in her mirror might be the only eyes viewing her that day. But it gave her a lift to see that she looked nice, that her eyes still sometimes twinkled, her spirit not totally crushed by the sadness of her situation.

This morning, however, there was no light in the eyes that looked back at Cath as she stared in the mirror. She saw eyes almost opaque in their deadness, straggly, uncombed white curls, wrinkled and pale skin—except beneath her dark, dead-looking eyes. Beneath her eyes were circles of grayish purple.

She hadn't slept well last night. And she hadn't made it out her bedroom door before Matt left for work, before it was locked. It was barely dawn, but Matt had a breakfast appointment with a client and left more than an hour earlier than usual.

There would be no freedom for Cath today.

She slipped on her bathrobe. It was such a pretty robe. Pink and soft and fuzzy. Julie and Kenneth had given it to her for Christmas. That wonderful Christmas Cath could sometimes scarcely recall, even though it was only a couple of months past.

Cath thrust her hands in the pockets and pulled out a square of toast. Yesterday's toast. She had pocketed it during the previous morning's breakfast. Why, she wasn't sure. Rennie had seemed very angry all through breakfast, and it had upset Cath. Made her feel terribly uneasy.

Then the toast had been warm and fragrant, tasty with the melting butter and tart plum jam. Now it was soggy and cold, the jam sticky, pink fuzzy lint adhering to its stickiness. The pocket of her pretty pink robe was filled with crumbs and stained with melted butter and gooey red jam.

Cath licked the sweet stickiness from her fingers and lay down on her bed. She closed her eyes and savored the sweet tartness of the

jam. She thought about another time she had so enjoyed plum jam.
Another long-ago time.

"Cath, honey, I think you have about enough of that jam on your
bread, don't you?"

"But Auntie Irene, it's soooo good!"

"I'm glad you like it, hon, but you're going to have a tough time
eating without getting . . . . Oh, what difference does it make. If you
end out with more on you than in you, I'll just dunk you in the
washtub, clothes and all," said Irene laughing, her double chins
shaking as she leaned over and planted a kiss in the middle of Cath's
jam-covered cheek.

"Really, Mama?" asked five-year-old Elmer, his eyes wide as he
imagined his cousin of the same age with water dripping from her
hair, face, and clothes, all over the spacious kitchen of their large old
farmhouse. "Won't that make Aunt Sarah mad?"

Little Cath, much less serious than her cousin, just giggled as she
savored the sweet splendor of her Aunt Irene's homemade delicacy.

"She's just fooling, Elmie. I know she's just fooling."

And so she was.

The elderly Cath's mouth curled in a smile as she remembered
that day so well—that day many years ago when she was surrounded by so much love—so very much love and caring.

Different from now.

The following week, Cath again brought some of her breakfast
back to her room—this time a bit more successfully.

"My, aren't we hungry this morning," said Rennie, noting how
fast the plate of muffins had disappeared.

"They're just so delicious, Rennie, I've had twice as many as
usual," said Cath, who had actually pocketed two of the tasty apple
muffins, her favorite, when Rennie's back was turned and Matt had
his nose buried in the morning paper.

Cath took great care to slip away to her room quickly, so no one
would notice her bulging pockets. *I feel like a thief, like a child on*

the streets of London in a Dickens novel. What is happening to me? she thought with distress.

She did, however, enjoy the muffins later in the day, even though by then they were crushed and crumbled. She turned the robe pockets inside out over the bathroom sink and carefully brushed out every single crumb, washing them down the drain—destroying the evidence.

From time to time, Cath would have success in bringing at least part of her breakfast back to her room, but not often. And each time she did, she was filled with remorse, overwhelmed with feelings of guilt because what she was doing felt like stealing.

Stealth and subversiveness had never been components of the personality of Catherine Rowan Montgomery.

Chapter Thirty-Two

Towards the end of the brutal winter, Matt's hectic schedule and the demands of life as an attorney-in-demand caught up with him. He came down with a serious case of the flu. One that kept him home—first, flat on his back wrestling with high fevers and aches that left him totally spent, followed by a lengthy recuperation period. Respite from the life of a maybe-too-successful attorney.

And a respite for Cath.

Cath was deeply concerned about Matt's illness, as was Rennie. Even as a child, Matt had rarely been ill enough to be confined to bed, and when he was, he was never ill enough to accept his fate.

This was different. Matt simply wanted to sleep, as if to regain a lifetime of hours spent struggling with the problems of others.

"He's beat, Rennie," explained Dr. Miller when he stopped by to see his best friend. "He was a perfect target for this flu that's going around. Those damned little bugs were just waiting for someone weak and weary to attack. He'll be okay, but he's not going to be his old rambunctious legal-eagle self for a least a couple of weeks."

Matt wasn't Dr. Miller's only concern. He was also worried that Cath might catch this harsh winter attacker. Many of the community's victims of this year's bug were its elderly residents, and there had already been one death as a result, seventy-nine-year-old Harold Wheeler.

Before Jason left, he drew Cath aside and admonished her to keep her distance from her son. "After your round with pneumonia, you'd be an easy candidate for a bad case of this stuff, Cath. I know you're concerned about Matt, but until he's better, much better, you let Rennie take care of him. You just worry about taking care of yourself."

"But Jason, I'm fine these days. Just fine. I'd like to help nurse him, after all, he is my son, and—"

"Dammit, Cath! No! Do you think it's going to help Matt get

well if he's worrying about you? You stay clear of that room. Understand?"

Jason didn't feel quite right about talking to Cath this way, but he still wasn't convinced she was in great shape and was fairly certain that a bad case of anything could easily kill her. And he wasn't about to let that happen.

He put his arm around her shoulders gently. "He'll be all right, Cath. I promise. If I didn't think so, I'd have him bedded at the hospital pronto. You just watch out for yourself right now. Okay?"

"Okay," agreed Cath reluctantly.

Cath spent most of the next week in her own room—with the door open. But Rennie was too busy with Matt to bother with Cath, too busy to lock her in.

To Rennie's credit, she took good care of Matt, although complaining frequently, by phone, to her friends.

"Sick men are such babies," she griped after the first five days, when Matt's fever had broken and worries about complications had lessened.

At the end of the week, when Jason again stopped by for the fourth time to check on Matt, he gave him the all-clear to get out of bed and work at regaining his strength. And without question, he had strength to regain. He felt terrible, and he looked dreadful. His face was covered with stubble trying to give the appearance of a beard—a very straggly and pathetic looking beard. His skin had a gray pallor, and he had lost a considerable amount of weight.

"Well, I guess I won't have to harp at you any more to lose that spare tire around your middle, old buddy. It appears to be long gone."

"I'm as weak as a babe, Jason. God, what a week this has been. Although it seems longer than a week. I sure hope Mom and Rennie haven't caught this bug."

"No sign of it yet. I've kept a close eye on both of them. I did ask Cath to stay out of here—ordered her to, in fact. I don't think that frail body of hers could handle this nasty stuff."

"Thanks, Jason. I don't think it could either. She's been through just about enough for this year. Maybe in a few days, after I've a chance to air this room out a bit—not to mention me."

"You do look like a good stand-in for any derelict I've ever seen," said Jason with good humor. "Now, you take it easy for a few more days. Up just a little at a time. Everyone's been having serious trouble with relapses, and you had enough trouble with the first round."

"Okay, boss. Thanks for checking on me—and Mom and Rennie. I guess I'm finally resolved to rejoining the land of the living."

Each day the following week, Matt stayed up longer, and by the end of the second week, he began to look like a new, thinner version of his old self.

Except for her worry about Matt, the two weeks had been like a vacation for Cath. She had not closed her door at all, not even at night.

Cath and Rennie had shared their meals. Quiet meals.

"What can I do to help, Rennie?" Cath had asked the first day as the two of them sat down for a late supper. Rennie had just finished helping Matt with his soup, tasty vegetable soup that had been simmering on the stove all afternoon, its appetizing aroma filling the kitchen. Cath could see Rennie was exhausted, and she felt sorry for her. She really did want to make the days ahead easier for her daughter-in-law.

Rennie was tired, her shoulders slumped, her clothing wrinkled. She did not relish her nursing duties—had it been anyone but Matt, she would have refused. But she really was worried about him and was trying.

Her spoon was halfway to her mouth when Cath asked what she might do, and she halted it there, looked at Cath and said, sharply, in a low voice, "Just stay out of my way," and resumed her eating.

Cath was shocked at such abruptness and rudeness—even from Rennie. She continued eating, but now the delectable warm soup, so perfect at the end of the bitter cold winter day, had lost its appeal.

Cath excused herself and went to her room where she sat staring out the dark window until it was time for her to go to bed.

The next day, and all those following, Cath would ask how Matt was doing, and Rennie would give her an updated report on his progress that day—nothing more. Cath did not again offer to help; she feared too much a repeat of the rebuff she'd received at her first attempt.

Once, in an effort to extend their conversation about Matt, Cath began to tell Rennie what Matt was like as a boy the few times he was sick. "He was so organized, it was quite funny. His toys piled neatly on one side of his bed, a written schedule on his bedside table. He had a slate, and he would list . . ."

Suddenly, Cath's voice was drowned out by the radio as Rennie reached over and turned up the volume. She apparently preferred loud music to listening to Cath.

Cath's face reddened with embarrassment. She did not again try to engage Rennie in any conversation during their meals. She only inquired after Matt's health. That much Rennie would give her.

Cath found release from her loneliness in her walks. Every day— except one that was too cold and snowy, winter hanging on with its last hurrah—Cath would take her walk. She waited until afternoon, when the temperatures reached as high as they were going to, and a possible sunshine warmed the day.

She felt free and invigorated each day as she walked back in the door, her face ruddy from the winter winds and her eyes teary from their sharpness. But she felt good. Better than she had in some time.

Matt also noticed—after he exited from the confinement of his sick room. His mother seemed more alert and looked healthier than she had for the past several weeks.

He shook his head in bewilderment one evening as she beat him resoundly at a game of Scrabble. *This woman is a wonder,* he mused. *Sometimes she seems so old, downright muddled and confused, and other times she seems to be more on the ball than I am.*

Rennie often looked daggers at Cath, even when Matt was up and in the same room with them. But Matt didn't appear to notice. Or if he did notice, he wasn't willing to break the peace that he so treasured in his home.

Matt returned to work, although to a slower schedule, at least initially—orders from his doctor and his own body. The cold began to diminish, and occasionally, the ever-present winds would carry a hint of the approaching spring.

Life in the Montgomery household returned to normal. And on days when she couldn't outsmart Rennie, Cath was again locked in her room.

Chapter Thirty-three

One April night during dinner, Matt said, "Rennie, I need to go to Chicago for two or three days next week." He had, little by little, added to his hours of work, his illness of a couple of months earlier and his vows not to be strapped to the demands of his profession forgotten. This would be the first out-of-town trip since before his illness, however, and he had told Rennie the jaunt would be coming up—hoping by warning her in advance, he'd defuse the scene he expected, but definitely didn't want.

His preliminary planning apparently worked; she didn't react in the least to his announcement.

"Oh, fine," she said, looking at Cath.

Cath met her gaze. Rennie's eyes seemed filled with triumph. *You're not going to win this contest y'know, old lady,* her look said. *Definitely not.*

Cath was very quiet during the rest of the dinner hour. Matt noticed that she appeared to be in deep thought. "You seem unduly quiet tonight, Mom. Are you okay?"

"Of course I'm okay, Matt. Just a bit tired. I think I'll turn in early."

Cath went to her room right after dinner. She closed the door and dialed Julie.

"Grandma Cath, what a surprise! I haven't talked to you in ages."

"I know. I figured it's about time to contact my favorite granddaughter. How are you, Kenneth, and the boys?"

"We're just fine. How about you?"

"Fine here, too. In fact, so fine, I'm thinking I'd like to do some traveling—like going to visit my favorite young family."

"That's wonderful! When, Grandma Cath? I can hardly wait."

"How about tomorrow?" asked Cath hurriedly, with urgency obvious in her voice.

Julie caught the urgency, and it both confused and troubled her. But after only a split-second hesitation, she said, "Tomorrow would be perfect. When does your flight arrive—what time should I meet you at the airport?"

"I don't know yet. I still have to make reservations. I just needed to check with you first to be certain now was an 'okay' time for a visit."

"Grandma Cath, anytime is an okay time for you to visit. You know that."

"Then I'll call you back as soon as I know the time. See you soon, Julie."

Julie turned to Kenneth after hanging up the phone and said, "Grandma Cath's coming for a visit tomorrow."

"That's great, hon. Isn't it?" he asked, noticing her troubled look.

"Sure it's great. But she sounded so . . . so . . ."

"She sounded so what, Julie?"

"Urgent. Desperate. Something didn't sound right."

Kenneth thought of the concern Julie had expressed after their Christmas visit. Then, too, she had sensed something was just not right.

"What do you mean?"

"I'm not sure I know what I mean. But all the many times I've talked to her, I've never heard her like this before. She sounded almost frantic."

"Frantic? What in the world would make Cath frantic? Do you think you should call your mom or dad to find out if something's wrong?"

"No, I'll wait. Grandma Cath is going to call right back with her flight information. Anyhow, I talked to Dad this afternoon, and he didn't mention any problems."

Cath went in search of Matt. She needed to ask about riding with him to the airport in the morning. She finally found him in his workshop.

Matt's workshop was a collection of the finest tools, most of them gifts from Cath or his dad, pieces of wood of every size, shape, and description, and an accumulation of unfinished projects. The workshop's purpose wasn't to turn out artistic creations in wood; its purpose was to provide Matt with a place free from the stress-laden life of the corporate attorney.

Two unmatched chairs in differing stages of completion hung from hooks on the wall. A wooden train for the twins to ride—planned and started before the twins were too big to ride a toy train—lay unfinished in one corner, and a three-legged table sat in another.

Cath smiled as she came through the door and looked around at her son's partly finished projects. She recognized the creativity, that certain piece of himself that he put into each and every piece. She also recognized that he had no great need to finish any of them—only to put his heart into what he made with his own hands.

Matt was absorbed in what he was doing and didn't see her come in. Rarely did his mother come into his workshop. Rennie—hating the "mess," as she called it—never did.

"What are you making, Matt?"

Startled, Matt glanced up, surprised to see her. "Hi, Mom. Nothing in particular. Just puttering. I thought you were turning in early."

"I am. I just had a brainstorm I wanted to run by you first. I'd like to ride to the airport with you tomorrow morning. I'm flying to Minneapolis to visit Julie. I could take a taxi of course, but since you're going there, too, I thought I might as well see if I couldn't ride with you." Cath spoke hurriedly, laying out her plan quickly—almost as if she feared her son would reject the idea. Urgency—the same tone of urgency Julie had recognized—was also apparent.

Matt looked at his mother. She hadn't traveled alone in quite some time. She hadn't been well enough. "Sure. But it's a bit sudden, isn't it?"

Cath looked down, not wanting to meet his gaze.

"Mom, what is it? Is something wrong?"

"No, nothing's wrong. I just need a ride to the airport in the morning, that's all. And I'm tired. I already told you I was tired." Cath sounded close to tears.

"Of course, Mom. Just be ready bright and early. Okay?"

"Thanks, Matt. I'll be ready. First, I guess I'd better call the airlines and get a ticket," she added as she walked away.

Matt watched her go. *What is going on? Mother always made plans weeks in advance to go visit Julie. And she sounded like it was so very important. I know nothing's going on at Julie's, at least I don't think so. I just talked to her this afternoon.*

Matt sighed, suddenly feeling very weary himself. *Maybe I'm just trying to find trouble where there isn't any. So my mother's getting a bit eccentric. Older people sometimes do, that's all.*

Cath went back to her room and called the airlines. In luck, she was able to get a seat on the early flight. She then called Julie to give her the flight time and number, packed a bag, set her alarm for an early hour, and went to bed.

She slept a restless, haunted sleep.

"I was surprised to hear Mom's going to visit Julie," said Matt as he and Rennie were getting ready for bed.

"She's going to what?" Rennie was obviously surprised when she heard of Cath's plans. "When is she planning to do this?"

"Tomorrow. I'm taking her with me to the airport in the morning."

"How about that," said Rennie, not really intending to say it aloud.

Matt looked at her, confused by her comment. "Rennie, is Mom okay? I mean, have you noticed anything? Doesn't this sudden trip seem a bit strange to you?"

"Lots of things your mother does seem strange to me, Matt. You just refuse to see it. She's a strange old lady," she added derisively.

"No, Rennie, I don't see it. And I venture to guess that neither does Julie, or Kenneth, or any of the many others that know her. You seem to be the only one with this special gift of vision," he added angrily.

"Never mind. You always did refuse to listen to reason where your mother's involved."

Matt sighed. They were again getting dangerously close to issues he didn't want to address—refused to address. Issues having to do with Cath's living with them. As far as he was concerned, it was working well. To hear Rennie talk sometimes, you'd think it was a total disaster.

"Rennie, let's not quarrel," he said, coming up behind her and drawing her close to him. "I'll be gone a couple days, and I don't want there to be hard feelings between us. You'll have some free days to just do as you please."

Weary of talking about Cath, Rennie turned and hugged Matt tightly. "I'll miss you, y'know."

"Me too," he said.

The discussion about Cath, if not forgotten, was avoided. Matt shoved his concerns about his mother to the back of his mind—unspoken and for the time being, forgotten.

Cath was up bright and early. It promised to be a beautiful day, and she felt the excitement of seeing Julie, Kenneth, and the boys. She donned a pale rose suit and tied a bright-colored floral scarf around her neck. She clipped on her earrings, patted her hair one last time, and walked into the dining room for breakfast.

Matt looked up and smiled when he saw his mother. She looked so—so together. His questions and concerns of the night before totally dissolved.

"Good morning, Mom. The traveler ready?"

"She sure is," said Cath brightly.

Rennie eyed them both. She had to admit that Cath looked good—well ready for a short vacation. Although she couldn't help but wonder if the pink in Cath's cheeks wasn't partly because she had gained the upper hand in this situation. Cath had accomplished what she wanted. She wouldn't be in the house alone with her. Rennie's pleasure at having a few days without Cath around was somewhat tempered by the knowledge that Cath had outsmarted her.

As they drove to the airport, Matt glanced at his mother, again wondering about the suddenness of her trip and the urgency in her behavior last night. But she certainly didn't have that air of urgency about her this morning. She seemed quite relaxed.

"Was Julie surprised you were coming?" he asked.

"I don't know if she was or not. She didn't say. She seemed very pleased, though."

"Of course she was pleased," said Matt, smiling. "You two have had this wonderful relationship since the day you laid eyes on one another. You always seemed to understand her. You 'arty types' aren't always so easy to understand, you know," he teased.

"Your father would have agreed with you there. He was a saint, that man," commented Cath, shaking her head as if in disbelief.

They laughed together, recalling Jack Montgomery as only wife and son could do.

"You really surprised me last night, Mom. I've never known you to be impetuous before," he said, conversing as he parked the car and carried her suitcase into the airline terminal, obviously referring to her quick decision to visit Julie.

"Maybe it's about time, Matt. I simply know I want to visit Julie today. I'm really excited about seeing her."

"Well, you have a great time. And give those grandsons of mine a big hug."

With a hug of his own and after checking her luggage, Matt set out to catch his own flight.

Cath's parting words to him were, "Now you're sure you'll be back Wednesday night? Positive?" When he nodded, assuring her of his return one more time, she said, "Okay, then I'll plan on returning Thursday. You can pick me up, can't you?"

"Sure, Mom. See you Thursday."

As he walked away, he was puzzled anew by his mother's behavior. He had never known her to be "clinging" before. But this is what she was doing. Cath was clinging to him, her son.

Chapter Thirty-four

Cath had a similar thought as she gazed out the window at the cotton-like clouds so close she knew she could touch them if the window were open. *I'm afraid not to be with my son. I'm afraid to be without him when I'm in Blakefield.*

That admission of reality startled Cath. She had been afraid only a few times in her entire life.

She remembered the first time—at least it was the first time she could recall. She must have been about five—maybe six. Not in school yet.

Spence had brought Cath along with him and his good friend, Marty, to explore the caves overlooking the riverbank not far from their parents' adjoining farms. Boys in the area had been exploring these caves for ages—a ready-made site of entertainment for children of the not-very-prosperous families that dotted the banks of the river.

It was an excruciatingly hot day. The heat sizzled up from the prairie fields, with not even a breeze to ease its relentless fury. Spence and Marty were dressed nearly alike in overalls and worn shirts, the standard attire of boys growing up in rural Nebraska in those days. Their clothes were flecked with hay and dirt, and their hands, callused from their labor.

Both boys had spent their mornings doing chores. Spence's were those of the man of the farm. Marty helped his dad, getting by with as little work as possible. Marty was a fun-loving boy, and work wasn't one of his favorite pastimes.

Spence had worked exceptionally hard and fast this morning in spite of the heat. He and Marty had made plans to go through the caves this afternoon—something they both thought was great fun.

And Spence invited Cath to come along.

"Geez, Spence, do we have to drag that little kid along with us?" objected Marty.

Spence looked at his little sister—her faded sundress spotlessly clean when she had dressed in the morning, now covered with stains from her morning play. Her little browned toes peeked through her open-toed sandals.

"She's okay, Marty. Really, she's hardly any trouble at all. I told her about how cool the caves are, and it's so doggoned hot today." With his sleeve, Spence mopped the sweat rolling down his sun-tanned face. "Besides, she begged me," he added with a crooked grin and downcast eyes. Sometimes, Spence was embarrassed that Cath managed to always get her way with him.

"Oh, all right, I guess," said Marty skeptically, eyeing Cath with disdain. Marty Collins was an only child and couldn't understand his friend's patience with this talkative little tag-along who always seemed to be underfoot.

Cath stood, looking down at her brown toes, as the boys talked about her as if she wasn't even there, and she tugged at Spence's shirttail to remind him that she was. Marty made her mad.

I don't care if Marty doesn't want me along, Spence said I could come. Marty's just an old meanie. I think I'll call him Mean Marty. Maybe not today, though. Another day, when I'm not going along. He might get really mean and yell at me—or tell me to go home. I don't want to go home; I want to be with Spence.

So Cath followed the boys along the river. The trio kept their distance from the sometimes swiftly flowing river, even though today it wasn't much more than a trickle. The river, too, appeared to be hot.

Marty led the way with the long legs of a tall-for-his-age lanky boy, a shock of dark hair falling over his near-sighted brown eyes, bobbing up and down with each step as he set a pace that challenged Spence to match—and really challenged Cath. Cath brought up the rear, running more than walking, her little legs pumping to keep up, but she was determined not to fall behind.

She trembled with excitement over the great adventure. She'd not had the opportunity for an adventure quite like this before—little girls rarely do. Being included in her brother's escapade made her feel so important, even though the trek was making her so very hot.

I sure hope Spence is telling the truth—that the caves will be nice and cool, she thought as she mopped her perspiring little face with the hem of her dress.

Soon, they were climbing up the path that led to the mouth of the caves. Spence grabbed Cath's hand as they climbed, partly so she wouldn't fall, partly so she'd keep up with him and Marty.

Marty reached the cave several minutes before the two Rowans. He shook his head in disgust as he watched his friend patiently wending his way up the path with his curly-headed little sister in tow.

"Now, we're going to need our flashlights," Spence explained to Cath. Each of the boys turned on his flashlight—Spence's bright red, Marty's silver-colored—proud possessions of the budding spelunkers.

"Okay, Cath," directed Spence. "You hang onto this piece of rope tied to my belt. These caves aren't very deep, but they're still pretty dark, and I don't want to lose you."

With the thought of getting lost, Cath eyes got wide, and she looked as if she might cry.

"Are you afraid, Cath? Don't be afraid," comforted her brother. "You'll be right next to me."

Cath first nodded "yes" in response to the "are you afraid" question. Then thinking better of it, she shook her head with determination, trying to let both boys know she wasn't afraid of anything. In actuality, her little heart was pounding. She was afraid. Very much afraid.

Marty knew the caves better than Spence. His older cousin had guided him through their obscure nooks and niches when he wasn't much older than Cath. He knew of some openings that would bring them much deeper into the hills, much deeper than he and Spence had ever explored before. It had been a few years since he and his cousin, who knew all there was to know about these caves, had explored here together, but Marty knew the way. Of that he was sure.

"Just follow me, Spence. I'm going to show you some trails in here you've never even seen," he announced with pride in a mysterious voice.

"I don't know, Marty. I think we should probably just go the places where we usually do. You know, around that bend to the right and circle back here. It's really cool back there where it's darkest, but not too black for long. I don't want Cath to be scared."

"Geez, Spence. Don't be such a baby. And you said she'd be no trouble. Just follow me," Marty ordered authoritatively.

"Okay," said Spence with hesitation, unsure that following Marty without knowing where he was going was the smart thing to do. Especially with Cath along. But he really didn't want to argue with his friend. So he directed his flashlight at his friend's feet and followed him, step by step, with his little sister behind him.

Soon they reached a familiar spot at the back of the cave, a spot they always walked by on their full circle back to the entrance.

Marty said, "Okay, stop. Here you hafta lie down flat and crawl through this little opening."

"Marty, are you sure this is smart? Do you really know where you're going?"

Marty didn't answer. He just lay down flat on the floor of the cave and proceeded to wriggle through the opening. Spence, not wanting to seem cowardly, decided to follow.

"Cath, you crawl ahead of me," he said, gently pushing her in front of him.

"No, Spencie. I'm scared. It's too dark, and what if I get stuck?"

"You said you weren't afraid. Now go. I'll be right behind you."

Cath began to sniffle, and Spence knew she was crying. But she lay down and wriggled through the opening like a little worm, and Spence followed.

"See," he said with more cheer than he felt. "We did it. I told you there was nothing to be afraid of."

"I scraped my knee on those rocks. I think it's bleeding. I want to go home, Spencie," she said, crying openly now as she felt the warm trickle of fresh blood dripping down her leg from her stinging knee.

"I told you, Spence. I told you. You and this big brother thing," mumbled Marty. "Well, you'll just have to follow me. We're taking the long way out whether you like it or not."

"Can't we just crawl back through the way we came?" asked Spence, shining his flashlight on the wall of rocks but unable to find where they had entered just moments before.

"No, doggone it. I was looking forward to showing you this neat path, and I'm gonna do it," said Marty as he stomped on ahead.

Spence knew Marty was angry. Maybe it was a dumb thing to do—bringing Cath along. Marty was his best friend, and they really had had lots of fun with their exploring. He wanted to be sure they'd do it again. He was beginning to regret bringing Cath.

"Dammit, Cath, now stop that crying. You're okay. You wanted to come along, so now be a big girl and hang onto the rope and follow me," Spence ordered, and he again handed her the end of the rope tied to his belt loops.

"You said a bad word, Spencie."

"I know, Cath. I know. But you said you wanted to come, and I can't see what you're crying about. Now c'mon."

The three of them wended their way through the dark, their lights and shadows bouncing off the cave walls. Cath said nothing more, but from time to time Spence could hear her sniffles above their footsteps, and he'd reach back and pat her head or shoulder.

"See, it's cool just like I promised. No sweating in here."

"It feels good, but I'm so scared. What if we can't get out? What if I won't ever see Mama again? You didn't tell me it would be so dark, and my knee hurts, really hurts."

Cath's tears ran down her face, and her little shoulders shook with swallowed sobs. She hiccupped with her held-back sobs, and the sound echoed in the hollowness of the cave.

"It's okay, Cath, we'll be out soon," comforted Spence, continuing to reach back at pat her red curls.

The patting felt good, but Cath wished there was room for Spence to hold her. She almost asked him to do it once, but she was afraid to—afraid to make mean Marty angrier than he already was.

After they had walked for what seemed like an awfully long time to Cath, Spence asked, "Marty, should it take this long? I need to get home in time to do my chores, and so do you."

"We should see the entrance real soon now," said Marty, his voice much less sure than when they had begun their crawl through the opening.

Marty made that same statement three times before they actually did spot a glimmer of light ahead—light fading as the midday sun was sinking lower in the sky. Their early afternoon excursion had taken most of the day. They had been wandering through the cave for hours, all three dragging with weariness—especially little Cath.

And she was not the only one who had been afraid.

The three were silent as they walked towards home, covered with the dirt from the floor of the cave, caked to the sweat from earlier in the day.

Marty said, "So long," as he turned towards the Collins farm, and Spence and Cath, hand-in-hand, continued on towards their place. Cath's knee was skinned, with dried blood caked on the dirty wound. The faded color of her dress was no longer recognizable. Her face, dirty and tear-stained, looked up at her brother.

"That wasn't fun, Spence. I was scared."

"I know, Cath. I'm sorry." Spence sounded as if he might cry—something he had almost never done in his life, and certainly not since becoming a teen-ager.

As they approached their house, they saw Uncle Elmer's truck parked in front.

"Great," said Spence under his breath. He knew his mother was going to be less than happy with him, and he'd just as soon his uncle didn't witness the trouble he was sure he was about to face. He had told Sarah that Cath wanted to come with him and Marty, and said they'd be back in an hour or so—two hours at the latest. They had been gone more than six hours.

Cath ran on ahead as soon as they were close to the house, limping somewhat, favoring the skinned knee. Spence followed slowly, taking as much time as he could.

He walked into the kitchen and saw his mother with Cath on

her lap, carefully sponging the blood from her knee. His mother looked terribly tired, her face drawn with worry so deep that not even seeing her children were safe could make it evaporate immediately.

Aunt Irene was there, too, also looking worried and also caring for the knee as if it were a major amputation. Aunt Irene didn't smile at Spence like she nearly always did. She didn't even look at him. Just at that darned knee of Cath's.

Spence felt a dull thud in the pit of his stomach.

"I was so scared, Mommy," confessed Cath, who usually boasted that she wasn't afraid of anything.

"Spence, do you have any idea how frantic I've been? You took her on what you said would be an hour's walk through the cave, and you were gone for hours. Spence, it's not like you to be so irresponsible."

"Let me explain, Ma. We didn't—"

Spence didn't get a chance to finish his sentence. Uncle Elmer, whose face didn't reflect worry but fury, grabbed him by the arm and, almost lifting him off his feet, marched him outside, where he could be heard yelling at the top of his lungs at his penitent nephew.

Cath wasn't sure what all Uncle Elmer had said during his twenty-minute lecture, but Spence was quiet and as white as the overhead clouds had been earlier that day when he came back in the house to tell Cath and his mother, once more, he was sorry.

Then he went, belatedly, to tend to his chores.

Cath couldn't remember if much was said about the incident after that. She just remembered that she admitted to being afraid, and for quite some time, she clung to her mother.

Just like she was clinging to Matt now.

Chapter Thirty-Five

Julie scanned the crowd disembarking the plane. There was a mob, as there so often was at this busy terminal. So many people rushing by, eager to get somewhere else. Businessmen carrying briefcases hurried past those meeting loved ones, their eyes not making contact, their minds only on the tasks at hand—or those soon to be.

A small girl, her tiny round face framed by a halo of dark curls, leapt into the arms of a grandfatherly looking man, knocking his glasses askew. It didn't seem to matter to him, as he tightly hugged the child, his glasses hanging precariously from one ear.

A group of giggling teenagers with sleek shiny hair and tight-fitting jeans gathered around a young man with a clipboard—apparently an organizer or guide for some sort of a youth outing.

I don't envy him, thought Julie.

As she watched a harried-looking young mother chase her toddler through the legs of the waiting airline patrons, she felt relief that her own were carefully ensconced in the classroom. They had begged to miss school this morning to meet their Grandma Cath at the airport, but Julie felt that would be unwise.

She wanted to see her grandmother alone for a while. She needed to see if there was any substance to this apprehension of hers regarding the desperation she had heard in Cath's voice—what she thought she had heard in her voice. And anyhow, the boys would see her as soon as they came home from school.

Ah, there she is. Julie waved to catch Cath's eye. Cath saw her and waved back eagerly, her face brightening with a broad smile.

She looks happy enough, thought Julie. *Maybe I was just imagining the urgency thing last night. She's sure thin, though.* Her observation was confirmed as she and Cath hugged, and she felt her grandmother's slight frame.

"It's so great to see you, Grandma Cath. Did you have a good flight?"

"It was fine. I'm always glad to get my feet back on the ground, though. Are the boys in school?" she asked, noticing that Julie appeared to be alone.

"Mm-hmmm. We don't need to be home until about three. Let's have a grown-up lunch. How does Dayton's Skyroom sound?"

"It sounds wonderful. I'm starved."

Julie refrained from saying that she looked like it.

They had a wonderful lunch—two women removed from one another by a generation, but bound by common interests and a great amount of love. They talked animatedly between bites of scrumptious chicken salad and hard crusty rolls, topped off with hot apple pie.

Most of the conversation on Cath's side consisted of questions about the twins, Kenneth, and Julie's painting. A series of questions with little opportunity for Julie to ask any in return. Cath said nothing about herself—about what she had been doing.

Only later did Julie realize how closed her grandmother had been about herself.

Julie did favorably note her appetite, though, and decided there was certainly nothing wrong with Cath in the food arena. And she knew her mother was a great cook, so Cath had to be getting excellent meals at home. So why was so thin; why did she seem so frail?

Maybe it's just taking her longer to conquer the leftover ramifications of her two serious bouts with illness this past year, she thought. *Or maybe it's just that my grandmother is getting old.*

Whatever was behind Cath's obvious weight loss and the dark purple circles under her eyes, as well as a pallor that wasn't there at Christmas time, nothing seemed to have dampened Cath's spirits.

"Honey, you don't know how glad I am to be here," she said with great enthusiasm as she clasped Julie's hand on their way back to the car. "I miss you so much."

Julie was certain she saw tears glistening in Cath's eyes as she spoke. And she couldn't deny the ones burning in hers.

"I miss you too, Grandma Cath," she said, gently squeezing the small, frail hand clasped in hers.

*   *   *

The two women were quiet on the drive home. Cath watched the scenery change from the tall buildings of the Minneapolis skyline to tree-lined roads as they approached the lake. The air smelled fresh, and a cool breeze crept through the small opening in the windows. She was thinking how wonderful it would be to live closer to Julie, to be able to see her regularly, as she did when Julie was a child. Two of her friends even lived with their grandchildren.

What would that be like? To see that charming face at the beginning and end of every day. She glanced at her granddaughter, who was concentrating on maneuvering the car down the winding roads surrounding the lake.

But first, I'd have to admit that there are problems with my living with her mother and dad. What would I say? The truth would hurt her too much. No, telling her is a bad idea, and thinking of living with her might be a worse one. She has her career, Kenneth has his, and they have the boys. They don't need an old lady like me invading their privacy. I love her too much for that.

Anyhow, when Millie Caspian moved in with her granddaughter Jenny, it really ruined their relationship. Jenny started to resent her grandmother when she became incontinent—just after the baby was born. Too much to cope with, she said, and packed Millie off to a nursing home.

It would absolutely kill me if Julie ever grew to resent me.

"Is it too cool for you, Grandma Cath?" asked Julie, breaking Cath's reverie. "I could close the windows." She reached for the window controls.

"No, please don't. The air here is wonderful. In the middle of the winter I sometimes wonder why you and Kenneth love it up here in the north so much, but right now, I doubt if there's a prettier place on earth."

"It is gorgeous, isn't it? Spring is great here, and we're so ready for it by the time it finally arrives. Sometimes I think fall is by far my favorite time of the year. Of course then the first snows come, and I'm sure winter must be. It's just so beautiful when the snow is new and so brilliantly white—though I must admit that I sometimes get cabin fever right along with the rest of the Minnesotans. Then when the crocuses and tulips poke their colorful heads up like they did last week, I get excited about a new season all over again. And you know how much I love summers on the lake. I like them all. Each is my favorite."

She laughed delightedly. "Do you think there's any hope for me, Grandma Cath?"

"Absolutely none," Cath replied, joining Julie's laughter. "You are a hopeless romantic—a wonderful and hopeless romantic."

They arrived home a little past two, and Julie carried Cath's luggage into the guest room.

"Why don't you unpack, and I'll quickly slip some cookies into the oven before the two small hurricanes arrive home from school."

At exactly three o'clock, the yellow school bus pulled up at the corner. Two little boys bounded out the bus door and dashed to their house.

"Is she here, Mom? Is she here?" asked Hal, breathless from the race with Jack, which he won. Daily the twins raced the one-half block from the bus stop to their door.

"Is who here, Hal? And 'hi' to you too," teased Julie.

"Am I the one you're looking for?" asked Cath as she came around the corner, opening her arms to Hal and Jack.

"Grandma Cath!" they shouted simultaneously.

Cath received her second very warm welcome of the day. Everyone talked at once, as the four sat around the kitchen table devouring warm cookies and milk. Cath's head was swimming with tales of school, activities, and friends.

It was a wonderful day for Catherine Montgomery.

Her welcome from Kenneth that evening was equally warm and wonderful, and Cath went to bed that night feeling loved and whole again. Her sleep was restful and untroubled. She had made an excellent decision to come for this visit—to run away from the nightmare she was living in Blakefield.

Chapter Thirty-six

Cath crawled out of bed the next morning enveloped in a feeling of contentment. She donned the warm robe she had brought with her—the lovely pink robe Julie and Kenneth had given her for Christmas—and tied it tightly around her. Then she quietly crept out the patio door that led to the deck overlooking the lake.

She didn't recall the morning not too long ago when the pockets of this same robe were filled with day-old toast and sticky jelly. The robe had been laundered since then.

Cath frequently had no recollection of the happenings surrounding her periods of abuse and the subsequent effect they had on her. Days of hunger and isolation. Periods where she couldn't think or remember.

She curled up on the wicker loveseat, tucking her feet up under her for warmth. She covered herself with an afghan Julie had left on the patio—an afghan so colorful it appeared that yarn of every hue in the rainbow was incorporated into its creation.

Cath stared dreamily at the lake, watching the waters of Lake Minnetonka lap up on the shoreline. The day was early, and the colors of dawn—gray and lavender-pink—covered the horizon. The breeze blew softly and was quite cool. Cath shivered slightly and gathered the afghan more tightly around her. The only sounds were the quiet whoosh, shoosh of the lapping water and the tinkling of the wind chimes as the breeze tossed them ever so gently about.

She gazed at the sunrise as the brightness of the coming day encroached on the gray-lavender of the dawn, mesmerized by the combination of peaceful sights and sounds. Her life in Blakefield seemed light years away. She didn't think about it—wouldn't allow herself to think about it. It was as if she had entered another galaxy, another civilization.

"So this is where you are! What on earth are you doing out here so early? Aren't you cold? The sun isn't even up yet."

"But it's working at it, Julie. Is anything quite so lovely as a sunrise over the lake?"

"Nope. Not unless it's a sunset," responded Julie, sitting down beside her grandmother, crawling under the edge of the afghan and tucking it snugly around her. She nestled close to Cath.

"Sunrises are better, though. Sunrises are beginnings. Sunsets are endings," said Cath, with a hint of sadness in her voice.

Detecting the sadness, Julie looked at Cath with concern. "Are you all right, Grandma Cath? I mean, are you sick again or anything? When you decided to come so suddenly, I . . ."

Cath took Julie's hand and held it tightly. Julie was treading somewhere Cath wasn't willing to walk.

"I'm fine, honey, really I am. I've been given a clean bill of health, and I'm spending a perfectly gorgeous morning watching the sun rise—and I'm spending it with someone I love very much."

"Oh, Grandma Cath," said Julie, as she laid her head on her grandmother's shoulder—just as she had so often done as a child. Cath's words didn't completely reassure her, but they helped. She couldn't really determine why she felt uneasy about her grandmother. It was something she just sensed—sensed, but couldn't identify.

"You know what I'd like, Julie? A nice, steaming hot cup of coffee. I'm only allowed one each day, so I make it something special. And this is certainly a something special setting."

"Sure. In fact, let's get the rest of this crew up, and we'll have breakfast out here."

"That sounds like a great idea! I'll wake the boys, and you get Kenneth."

"It's kind of cold, but we can dress warm. Certainly warmer than we are now," said Julie, glancing down at her own pajamas, robe, and toe-less slippers—attire that seemed plenty warm and cozy indoors, but not quite adequate out in the morning coolness. "You, too, Grandma Cath. I never should have let you stay out here. You're going to catch your death in just a bathrobe. C'mon in. We'll warm up and get the rest of the family going."

So the five of them, snugly wrapped in sweaters and caps, shared the first-breakfast-of-the-spring-on-the-deck as the chill of early

April blew in softly from the lake. The pleasant fragrance of warm muffins and hot chocolate and coffee drifted on the breeze.

A paradise morning.

Every day during Cath's visit was sunny except one. Wednesday morning, they awoke to the steady drumming of rain, a typical April rain drenching the entire Twin Cities area. As Cath watched the downpour out the window, she marveled at the soothing effect the falling rain had on her—directly opposite of the confined and dreary feelings similar days at home in Blakefield brought about.

The difference isn't the weather, she thought. *The difference is the people. The people and the love.* Her eyes misted over, but she quickly brushed the gathering tears away before they caused a redness someone might notice.

She went into the kitchen where the boys, donned in their bright yellow slickers, were ready to leave for school. Julie was giving them a ride today.

"I know I spoil them, but I just hate to have them sit in the classroom wet all day," she explained. "Some days, we just sit in the car and wait for the bus, but it's raining so hard today, I thought I'd take them right to the school. Will you be okay while we're gone?"

"Of course, honey. I am capable of taking care of myself, you know," Cath added with a smile. "I don't blame you for taking them. From in here the rain is quite pleasant. But it's likely to feel pretty cold and wet out there in the elements. I know how I hate to get soaked."

"But we like it, Grandma Cath," argued Jack.

"And we can just jump over the puddles," added Hal.

"More like in them," said their mother. "I don't think I've ever seen either of you go over or around a puddle. Now say good-bye to Grandma Cath, and we'll be on our way."

Cath gave each a hug and said, "Have a great day at school, boys. I'll see you afterwards, and maybe we can finish that puzzle we started last night."

The rain lasted most of the day, and Julie and Cath spent it quietly indoors. They talked endlessly about everything and nothing.

Cath laughed, as she hadn't laughed in weeks, the sound laugh full and warm as she listened to Julie tell about the twins' part in their school's spring pageant. They sat in the kitchen, sipping their cups of hot tea, oblivious to the rain, which had diminished considerably, now no more than a steady drizzle, leaving tiny ripples in the puddles left from the morning's downpour.

Julie told her grandmother about the spring pageant at the boys' school last week, laughing so hard in the telling she could scarcely finish the story.

"Hal was really upset when he was assigned the part of a butterfly—try to imagine Hal as a butterfly, Grandma Cath. He tried very hard to persuade Jack to trade, and Jack almost gave in, although he was pretty excited about being an earthworm."

Julie wrinkled her nose. "But Jack gives in to Hal too much. Sometimes, he's just too easygoing. So Kenneth took over with a major entomology lesson, found a picture of the ugliest looking caterpillar he could and told Hal that's what he really was—a really ugly worm—before, like a magician, he changed himself into a butterfly."

"Did it work?" asked Cath, impressed with her grandson-in-law's child psychology.

"Sure. Almost too well. Jack was so captivated by the story of the butterfly, he was sorry he was only a lowly earthworm. So father-turned-scientist told Hal how absolutely necessary the earthworm was to the gardens, the soil. It turned out they both felt important. And they all lived happily ever after. End of story."

Cath smiled, pleased. *They are happy. Theirs is truly a happy family.* The thought filled her with great pleasure—and great sadness. This family was a complete unit. Although it was good to be with them, she could never allow herself to be an appendage, to invade what they had. It wouldn't be right.

I can't allow myself to even think about asking to live here with them.

Wary of her thoughts, fearing they might be revealed on her face, Cath quickly wiped them away. If Julie was aware of any change in Cath's expression, of any sadness, it was so fleeting, it didn't register.

Just as they were finishing their tea, the door swung open, and two very wet little boys sloshed in, dripping water everywhere.

"Halt right there, you two. Let's see if we can't confine this mess. Off to the mudroom with you."

A small room was situated just off the kitchen, designed for coats, boots, umbrellas, and all the other necessities for a climate that was, for so many months of the year, messy, particularly when it involved small boys. A bench where they could sit to remove wet and muddy boots, long enough to accommodate all four Matsons, lined one wall; multiple hooks covered the other.

When the boys walked back into the kitchen, their great-grandmother glanced down at their pants, covered from the knees down in dripping, muddy water.

"This morning, I thought you said you jumped over the puddles. It doesn't look like that to me," she said teasingly.

"We do jump over them, Grandma Cath," said Hal.

"Most of the time," added Jack, smiling sheepishly.

"Change your clothes, guys. I'll stir up some hot cocoa for you. Now, shoo."

"Okay, Mom."

Julie shook her head and smiled as she watched them bound down the hall. "Double trouble."

"And double joy," said Cath.

Julie nodded her head in agreement.

It was a fun and happy time for Cath, her short visit to Minnesota. But she was intent on returning home before the weekend, just as she had planned.

"Please don't go back so soon," Julie pleaded as Cath packed her bags that evening, having completed the puzzle with the boys as promised.

"Honey, it's been a wonderful visit for me. You know it has. But it's time for me to get back—time to let you get back to your everyday living here."

Thursday was again bright and sunny as Julie and Cath drove to the airport. The air was warm and fragrant, thoroughly cleansed by the full day of rain. Good-byes had been said to Kenneth and the twins that morning, with each extracting her promise to return for another visit soon.

"Please come again very soon, Grandma Cath. Having you here has been just great." Julie gave her grandmother a final hug, and Cath prepared to board the plane.

"I will, Julie. I promise. And thank you for these past few days. Thank you so much."

Cath walked through the door to the plane. She was returning to Blakefield. To what, she wasn't exactly sure, but thinking about it made her heart flutter with something akin to fear.

Matt had all but forgotten his concern for his mother's well being when he met her Thursday afternoon. He was preoccupied with the large and rather complex case he was working on and more than a little bit agitated that Cath absolutely insisted he be the one to pick her up. Rennie could just as well have done so. But when Cath called Wednesday evening with her arrival time, she had been adamant that he and only he meet her.

So here he was.

Cath really was pleased to see Matt and hugged him tightly, as if it had been a long time since they'd said their good-byes instead of less than a week. She talked non-stop about her visit with Julie and her family as soon as they began their drive home, telling Matt in detail about the pageant at the boys' school, Kenneth's struggle to convince Hal and Jack how great their parts were. "And they both have the same penchant for mud puddles you had at that age."

Matt got caught up in her enthusiasm and was amused by the tales of the twins' antics. By the time they pulled up in their own driveway, he was feeling relaxed and pleased that he had interrupted his stressful schedule to meet Cath's plane. The stories of Julie and her gang had been a real tonic for him, too. Cath had much to tell, and seemed absolutely animated in her telling of it.

That is, until they turned on to Baker Boulevard, their street, less than a mile from home.

Then, she became quiet. When Matt pulled up in the driveway, stopped the car and looked at his mother, he saw how tense she was. Almost rigid. And completely silent.

"Mom? Mom, we're home."

Cath, who had seemed momentarily lost in a distant world, brought her attention back to the present. "So we are," she said, forcing a smile and stepping out of the car.

Matt carried Cath's luggage into her room and left again for his office. The house was empty, except for Cath.

Rennie had gone to Amanda's for the afternoon, Matt had said. So again, she relaxed. After unpacking, she went out on the patio with a book she had begun some time ago. Back when she read often. Her trip to Julie's had given her a new energy.

Cath had been on the patio enjoying the warm afternoon sun for about an hour when Rennie came home. Rennie opened the door to the patio, walked over to Cath, and planted herself directly in front of her.

Cath looked up, noting again what a remarkably attractive woman her daughter-in-law was. Rennie was wearing a lemon-yellow dress of a soft flowing fabric that wrapped gently around her legs as she walked. It gave her an air of soft femininity—a softness in direct contradiction to the hardness in her dark eyes.

"How's Julie?" asked Rennie in her demanding tone of voice.

Cath met Rennie's eyes before replying. She knew very well what Rennie was really asking. She wanted to know if Cath had told Julie that her mother was tormenting her.

"Julie's just fine, Rennie," said Cath, still looking steadily at her. "So are the boys and Kenneth."

Rennie lowered her eyes first. Lowered her eyes, turned, and walked back into the house.

Cath remained on the patio, reading her book until Matt came home for dinner.

Chapter Thirty-seven

Cath rattled on about Julie for several days after returning to Blakefield. Remembering how good it felt to be around her—to talk together, to laugh together—lifted her spirits tremendously.

She looked at Julie's photos often, keeping alive the joy of her presence. Sitting in her room, the spring late-afternoon sunlight streaming through her window, or in the evening, before retiring, Cath would take the album on her lap and enjoy once again the photographs of Julie—and, as an only grandchild, there were many.

Cath recalled clearly when her granddaughter was born. Julie Anne Montgomery was born prematurely, and remembering then the loss of her own baby daughter, she was terrified.

Sadly, Cath thought of her little girl, Cassie Sarah Jane Montgomery. Too small and born too soon, she had lived only four hours.

There were no photos of Cassie in the album.

"Please God, don't let it happen again," she had prayed.

Cath's prayers and the prayers of all the others who wanted so much for this little girl to live were answered. Julie not only lived, she flourished almost immediately. Although very small, the baby ate just as heartily and cried just as lustily as one twice her size. She did so well, in fact, she was able to go home from the hospital long before expected.

Home to a nursery bedecked with the most expensive baby furnishings available in the Midwest. Home to stuffed animals ten times her size and toys enough for the first three years of her life. Tiny Julie Montgomery was adored by all her grandparents, and the treasures bestowed upon her by her Grandfather Spaulding were non-stop.

She became an integral part of Cath and Jack's life; they could not imagine their lives without Julie.

"I'm so glad Matt and Rennie decided to stay in Blakefield," said

Cath to Jack one day when their granddaughter was just a young child. Placing the latest of Julie's photos in the album, she added, "How I would have hated to miss seeing Julie often."

Cath was referring to an offer Matt received from a law firm in Omaha. He had seriously considered it; it would have been a wonderful career opportunity for a young attorney. But his hometown roots tugged hard, and he decided to stay where he had grown up, where all Julie's grandparents lived.

Jack had silently wished Matt would accept the offer. Over time, some of Matt's innate independence had eroded. Rennie was accustomed to having what she wanted right now, and if her husband couldn't give it to her, her father could—and did.

Jack was seriously concerned about his son. He had once, and only once, approached Matt about the dangers of giving in to Rennie's every whim.

"Matt, marriage is a partnership. Both of your wants need to be considered. I'm not sure it's wise—or healthy for your relationship with your wife—to just continuously give in to whatever she says she needs."

Jack couldn't help but notice a rising flush on his son's face, but he daringly plowed ahead nonetheless. "We love Rennie, your mother and I—she's intelligent, talented—and my God, she's beautiful. But, Matt, use your head!"

"Dad, I love you as much as any son could possibly love his father. You're not only my dad, you're one of my best friends—right up there with Jason. But my relationship with Rennie is my business. She's had a tough life—never really gotten over her mother's death. I'm just trying to make it up to her. So, butt out, okay?"

Jack did. Although he continued to be concerned about his daughter-in-law being treated like a spoiled child, he never again approached the subject with his son.

He did share Cath's joy in seeing little Julie two or three times a week, however. She was indeed a treasure. Chestnut brown hair like her mother's, although curly like her father's and grandmother's. Huge green eyes, from whom, nobody was certain. Probably from an earlier generation of Rowans, Julie's great-Uncle Spence suggested.

Spence's relationship with Julie had been rare and unique. They were enamored with one another. It was not unusual to see a small, pony-tailed girl sitting next to Spence in his battered old blue truck as he bumped down the country road headed for town to pick up supplies. Or on the tractor beside him as he rode the fields, her small arm stretched across his back, her hand clutching the fabric of his shirt. Spence's tiny niece seemed to take the place of the child he had never had.

If anyone had asked Spence Rowan, he would say his life was now complete.

Julie was only eight when Spence died—old enough to be told he was gone, but not old enough to understand. She was a very distraught little girl when told she wouldn't be seeing her dear Uncle Spence again.

Photographs of a little girl finally graced the photo album.

Julie's baptism, her long dress of white satin and lace, a tiny version of her mother's wedding gown, cascaded over Matt's arm as he held his baby daughter. Her birthdays—a one-year-old's face smeared with icing, as she gleefully attacked the sticky confection on her four-layer cake. A laughing three-year-old astride a white horse on the carousel purchased for the occasion of his granddaughter's third birthday by Grandpa Spaulding, and set up in the back yard of Matt and Rennie's lavish home.

There were delightful photos. Christmas shots of Julie in red velvet or green satin, matching her emerald-colored eyes; Julie buried by a stack of packages piled so high you could barely see the child; Julie perched on Santa's knee.

And soon, photographs of her first day of school. Just as her father's first school day was preserved. Photos highlighting Julie's school years soon covered many pages of the album, along with Julie's dance and piano recitals. Julie in pastel tutus accented with sequins, bows, and lace. Julie with her hands poised over the piano, ready to impress her anxious parents and doting grandparents with her musical ability—ability that never succeeded beyond mediocre.

With mixed joy and sorrow, Cath had added a treasured photo of Julie in her senior-prom dress, emerald green like her eyes, soft and simple, giving her a look of timeless elegance.

All too soon, a photo of Julie in her cap and gown on graduation day joined the picture parade.

When Julie left for college the next fall, little did the Montgomerys dream she would never again live in Blakefield. But she met the man of her dreams her second year at the University of Kansas. She and Kenneth Matson, an aspiring young architect, were married the following spring.

Kenneth was a large man, tall and muscular with white-blond hair and light blue eyes. His voice, soft and shy, had the lilting cadence of his Swedish heritage.

Julie's wedding was a simple one, attended only by family and close friends. Her determination to do things in her own quiet non-flashy way encompassed what she proclaimed as "her day," and no amount of coaxing and complaining by her mother and maternal grandfather could persuade her to plan the large, ostentatious wedding they tried to thrust upon her.

The small dignified and tasteful ceremony fit the charming couple perfectly, thought Cath and Jack.

Julie and her husband moved to Minnesota immediately following their wedding, much to the dismay of her father and grandparents—and the anger of her mother. There, Julie attended art school, and Kenneth began his successful career as a commercial architect. There they built their lovely home overlooking Lake Minnetonka—the home where Cath experienced so much happiness.

Cath treasured the photos of Julie now more than ever. Julie was her greatest solace.

Chapter Thirty-eight

Such a gorgeous morning this is, thought Cath. *I don't think any time of the year is prettier than early June.*

Roses and clematis were climbing outside her window, and the color, as well as the fragrance, was breath-taking.

I feel really good this morning—a bit like a child with spring fever. I love summer, especially early summer, and things seem to have settled into a less threatening routine since my trip to Minnesota. Rennie hasn't locked me in my room once during the nearly nine weeks since then. Maybe she's grown tired of playing the game of bully. Or maybe she started to be afraid I'd tell someone. Whatever the reason, I'm grateful.

She had begun to relax more, to feel like herself. She was reading a great deal again, and she spent more time outside, more time walking through the neighborhood. It was a beautiful park-like neighborhood with tree-lined boulevards and an array of flowerbeds.

During one of her walks this week, Belinda Harris stopped her and invited her over for brunch today. Some of her old friends— friends from years past—would be there. Most were widows like herself, and they had drifted apart since their husbands died. Particularly, since Cath moved in with Matt and Rennie.

"Thanks so much for the invitation, Belinda. Of course, I'll come; I'd be delighted," Cath responded to the invitation with pleasure and excitement.

Belinda, who lived three doors down from Matt and Rennie's home, was younger than Cath, but not as young as Rennie. Through a common interest in flowers and gardening, a strong friendship had grown between her and Cath.

She had been walking by Belinda's home for some time, and always, except for the most bitter weeks of winter, she'd see her working in the yard. Belinda seemed to have an endless regimen of planting, trimming, digging, and replanting that made her gardens the pride of the neighborhood.

Recently Cath had learned that not only did she and Belinda share an appreciation for gardening, they had some friends in common. Friends who were coming to the brunch.

Cath was especially excited about seeing Peggy Reynolds. At one time, Peggy and her husband, Daryl, had been very close friends of hers and Jack's. Thinking about the times the four of them spent together brought a smile to Cath's lips and a warm feeling inside. Time and the deaths of both their husbands had gotten in the way of their friendship. Cath was delighted for the opportunity for its renewal.

She had waited for this day with great anticipation. The beautiful weather just added to her pleasure. She had even sacrificed her precious one daily cup of coffee at breakfast this morning, wanting to wait until she could join her friends. She found herself humming along with an old tune playing on the radio.

Cath selected a cobalt-blue linen dress, perfect with her coloring, and its matching jacket was full enough to hide her too-thin body. She had regained some of her weight-loss since her visit to Minnesota, so was not quite as thin as she was when Julie could feel it with a hug.

Cath was correct in her guess that Rennie had ceased her imprisonment of Cath because she was afraid she might tell someone. Rennie had feared that Cath might tell Julie when she visited Minnesota in April—scared to death that she would. She could hardly believe her good fortune when there was no aftermath of that brief visit.

And when Cath didn't bring her tale of woe to Julie, Rennie was quite sure she wouldn't tell anyone. No, if Cath wouldn't tell Julie, she would tell no one. Of that, Rennie was quite sure.

After all, Cath and Julie had been each other's confidante for as long as Rennie could remember. That realization, as always, filled her with unbridled jealousy and fury.

But Matt had been extremely solicitous of his mother lately. He had really been concerned about her the night she made the abrupt decision to take a trip to Julie's, and that event seemed to sharpen his awareness of her needs. He picked up on her every mood and quizzed Cath often about how she felt.

Rennie couldn't take the chance that Matt would figure it all out—would come to understand that she may have relented to his determination to move his mother to their home, to *her* home. But she hated it and vowed she would make Cath sorry she intruded on what had been her nearly perfect life.

Matt had relaxed his ultra-concern over his mother for about a week now, apparently convinced that she was fine, that his fears about her were unfounded.

It was close to eleven o'clock, and Cath was just putting the finishing touches on her hair. She had even applied a small amount of make-up for the occasion. Although only a neighborhood brunch, this was a very special occasion for the seventy-eight-year-old widow who had had an incredible year battling illness and abuse.

As she looked at herself in the full-length mirror attached to the back of her door, Cath smiled. She was very pleased with what she saw. Most of all, pleased because the reflection she saw appeared happy.

She picked up her purse and patted her hair one last time. *Naturally curly curls need a lot of patting, especially when they turned white,* she thought, critically.

Cath put her hand on the door knob, ready to head out the door and her much anticipated outing. She turned the knob and pulled, but it wouldn't open.

The door was locked.

Chapter Thirty-nine

Cath changed that day. She crumbled inside.

She'd had had many episodes of despair throughout the year, even occasions of a seeming dementia when she did things like stuff toast and jelly in her robe pockets and later, have no recollection of having done so. But she had always managed to snap back. Her spirit, her determination, her resolve gave her an unconquerable resilience.

Now she relinquished them all—the spirit, the determination, the resolve.

The moment she knew she wouldn't be going to the brunch after all, that she would not be having an anticipated reunion with an old friend, her shoulders slumped and her body sagged. She appeared to age by at least ten years.

She might have had a number of different reactions to her forced change of plans. Cried out and pounded on the door. Used the phone to summon help.

But Cath simply resigned herself to her plight. Months of systematic abuse had simply worn her down.

She didn't call for Rennie. What good would it do? She knew Rennie wouldn't unlock the door.

And the other options were just not acceptable to her. Rennie knew Cath was excited about her social excursion this morning. She had listened to Cath speak with great animation about it at dinner last night. Matt had been pleased to hear his mother's plans, also, and especially delighted to hear she'd be seeing Peggy Reynolds.

He remembered when his mom and dad and Peggy and Daryl Reynolds had seen a lot of each other. He even remembered when he, as a young adolescent, had a terrible crush on their daughter, Beth—four years his senior.

"Peggy Reynolds? Wonderful! How long has it been since you've seen her, Mom?"

"At least fifteen years. We—your father and I—saw them often when Daryl was alive. But after his death, Peggy spent most of her time in Maine with Beth and her family, and then your dad died, and . . ."

Cath shrugged, indicating, Matt supposed, that friends grew apart when half their number was gone.

"I'm glad you're getting out to be with friends," said Matt, obviously pleased with his mother's opportunity for socializing.

"So am I. It'll be fun catching up on all that's happened in the intervening years. And I'll be meeting some new people. Some live close by," she added with a big smile.

Cath was visibly enthusiastic. It was evident in her lively speech—in her entire demeanor. Watching his mother, Matt realized that she'd come a long way since she was sick-unto-death last year. He could scarcely recall his concern of last spring—when it had seemed to him that Cath was clinging to him, and he had feared that she was failing.

Now Cath's enthusiasm and animation were gone. Completely gone. It seemed to take all the energy she possessed just to move.

She tottered slowly to her closet and removed the ensemble she had so carefully selected for the day, the outfit that had so pleased her. She carefully hung up her jacket and dress. She folded her gala floral scarf and laid it in the drawer; she placed her earrings in her jewelry box.

Her movements were painstakingly slow and deliberate. Silent tears coursed down her face as she robotically went through the motions of undressing. Her limbs felt weak, and her hands trembled.

She wasn't sure she could speak, but she felt she must. She must speak to Belinda. A lifetime of courtesy did not immediately disappear—not even when one was engulfed in despair.

Cath mustered as much composure as she possibly could. Wrapping her robe around her, her head bowed as if in prayer, she folded her arms across her chest, hugging herself. She went to the bed and sat on the edge, quiet and immobile for a few minutes.

Then she lifted the receiver and dialed Belinda's phone number.

"Belinda? This is Catherine Montgomery. I can't believe I woke up with a dreadful sore throat this morning. I'm so sorry, but it looks as if I'm not going to make it to your brunch after all."

"I'm sorry, too, Cath. We'll miss you. You do sound a bit . . . well, you just don't sound like yourself. Do take care, and we'll make it another time."

"Thank you, Belinda. 'Bye," said Cath in a choked voice.

She hung up the phone and lay back on the bed as her tears continued to fall.

Chapter Forty

Cath didn't join Matt and Rennie for dinner that night, pleading a sore throat—the same excuse she had given Belinda.

"I'll have Rennie bring you some hot tea, Mom. That'll help your throat. And if it's not better tomorrow, you're definitely going to see Jason. What would you like with your tea?"

"Nothing, Matt. Just the tea would be fine."

Matt, not Rennie, brought the tea to her.

After he left, Cath lay in the darkness, enveloped in sadness, mourning a life all but lost. Hers.

It seemed impossible that she couldn't stop what was happening to her. This was Blakefield. She'd lived here or near here all her life. This was her son's house.

Her own son!

Yet, she felt helpless to stop the abuse.

I can't let anyone know—I just can't!

No amount of pain could equal the agony that the loss of her dignity would inflict upon her if others knew.

Never again did Cath allow herself to become excited about the promise of an interesting or fun-filled day. Becoming quiet and remote, she showed little enthusiasm about anything.

She talked little and laughed less. Neighbors who had enjoyed watching her spirited gait as she walked by their homes now noticed how slowly she ambled by—the few times when she went for a walk at all.

Although she still sometimes joined Matt and Rennie for breakfast, on the remainder of most days, she stayed in her room. Sometimes by choice, other times by forced confinement.

She ate little. She felt numb and detached—perhaps too detached to any longer care. There was no longer any fight evident in Catherine Montgomery.

And yet, she felt no hatred for Rennie. To Cath, Rennie was still the girl that Matt had chosen—still the high-spirited child she was when Harold Spaulding first brought her to Blakefield.

Spending yet another solitary day in her room, Cath thought about Rennie and how their relationship had eroded. She sat down in a chair by the window and watched a slow drizzle drip down the pane.

She pulled her album into her lap and opened it to the many photos of Matt and Rennie. *What an attractive young girl she was,* reminisced Cath. She wore her chestnut-brown hair long, usually tied back with a bright-colored bow, and long dark lashes that brushed her cheeks when she fluttered them coyly—which she did often—framed her lovely almond-shaped brown eyes.

It was two years before Matt's graduation from high school when the Spaulding's moved to Blakefield. Harold Spaulding had purchased the highly successful tool company sprawled across several acres on the edge of town, as well as the beautiful Merriman estate, also on the edge of town.

Matt was swept off his feet the first time he saw Rennie Spaulding.

"Mom, guess what, there's this gorgeous new girl who's just moved to town, and she's in my second-period American History class. Besides being pretty—really, really pretty," he emphasized with exuberance, "she's sophisticated, coming from Chicago and all, and I understood she's rich, too."

"And is that important to you, Matt?" asked Cath, amused by her son's obviously smitten state.

"No, Mom, of course it isn't." Matt grinned sheepishly, knowing how lovesick and foolish he must be sounding. But he just couldn't help himself. Renata Spaulding was the most perfectly wonderful girl he had ever met.

"Oh, Mom, I almost forgot. She's really a terrific pianist. Jason said she accompanied the choir last Thursday for their cantata practice and was really good. I guess Mr. Blythe's going to have her fill in while the usual accompanist's visiting her sick mother in Wisconsin. And you know how picky Blythe is about his spring cantata. Man, do I wish I could sing so I could go to choir practice. But since I sound like a pond frog every time I try, I guess that's out.

"Anyhow, Jason said she really knows music. The only problem is, he couldn't keep his eyes off of her and lost his place a few times. The other guys did too, I guess, because their parts didn't sound too good. Blythe got a little hot under the collar about the bad practice, so they had to have another after sixth period. Jason didn't mind though, because he got to see Rennie again."

Matt paused briefly. "Rennie. That's her name. It's really Renata, but she likes to be called Rennie."

Jack walked into the room during Matt's animated report of the new girl, and noticing Matt's flushed cheeks and fervored speech, thought, *This young pup thinks he's in love.*

"It sounds like you and your buddy might be in competition for the attention of the fair maiden," said his father.

"Yeah, sort of. And she's really nice to everyone, so it's hard to know if she likes one of us more that they other. But we'll work it out."

And work it out they did. Renata Spaulding, known to most as Rennie, chose Matt—much to Matt's delight.

Rennie chose, and Rennie got. She generally got what—and whom—she wanted.

She never made any pretense about who she was. Rennie was the first to admit that she expected to have her way, expected to be the center of attention.

No, Cath really couldn't bring herself to blame Rennie just for being who she always had been, just for being herself.

Matt finally garnered the courage to ask Rennie out just before Thanksgiving, and by Christmas that year, he was no longer dating anyone else. Photos of the young pair began to deck the pages of the album during his senior year. Matt and Rennie in their swimming suits at an end-of-summer pool party held just before school started. Matt and Rennie horseback riding. Matt and Rennie sporting Halloween costumes—Anthony and Cleopatra—as they left for a party at the high school. Matt and Rennie decorating the massive

Christmas tree at the Blakefield Country Club, where Harold Spaulding was a member.

Cath had to admit that they made a striking young couple. Very striking indeed.

"I think I hear wedding bells in the distance for those two," said Spence as he chatted with his sister one day after Rennie and Matt had just left for some social event.

"I suppose you're right, Spence. They're together all the time. And she is a lovely girl. A bit spoiled, however," said Cath, frowning.

"She is that, all right," he agreed. "I understand that when Spaulding's wife died, he was devastated. Put all his time and energy into his work and his money into Rennie. Even before that, she had the best that money could buy. She's been to boarding schools, private camps—even went to Europe a couple of years ago with Spaulding's sister. But, Cath, you can't hold that against her. After all, the poor kid's motherless. I think her dad's just been trying to fill the emptiness left by his wife's death."

Spence took a sip of tea as Cath remained quiet. "Anyhow, Sis, Matt's graduating in two months. He's a big boy now."

"I know, Spence. I only hope he's not so love-struck that his plans for the future get ruined. He's been talking law school for four years. I'd like to see him follow his dream."

"He will, Cath. You didn't raise a dummy, y'know. But I'd be willing to bet his dream now includes Miss Renata Spaulding." He took his cap off the back of the chair and placed it firmly on top of his bleached-white hair. "Well, I best be getting back."

Spence kissed his sister lightly on the cheek and headed back to the farm—the farm where he and Cath had grown up, where he had lived alone ever since his mother died.

That had been a heart-wrenching year for Cath. First her baby girl, then shortly after, her mother. Sarah Rowan died as she had lived. With dignity. Quietly, in her sleep.

Cath had worried about Spence after Sarah was gone. She hated seeing him alone all the time. But she finally accepted the reality that Spencer Rowan was a solitary soul who loved the land and really needed little else to make his life full and complete.

After he left, she pondered over what Spence had said, and she knew he was right. Cath, too, could almost hear the wedding bells ringing for Matt and Rennie.

Chapter Forty-one

As predicted, Matt Montgomery asked the vivacious Rennie Spaulding to marry him—even before he completed law school.

Cath watched her son through misted eyes—Matt and his beautiful bride beside him. Rennie's wedding dress was spectacular. It had been her mother's, imported by her mother's wealthy parents from their homeland. Rennie looked every bit the German princess in yards and yards of ivory satin encrusted with pearls. An eight-foot train trailed behind her, and a veil of pure silk netting cascaded down her back. She carried a massive bouquet of trailing pink and red roses, and baskets of roses were so numerous throughout the church, their fragrance filled the air like early morning in a rose garden.

The church was packed. On one side were the many relatives of the Rowans and Montgomerys, the countless friends Cath and Jack had acquired during their lifetime in Blakefield, plus co-workers and employees of Jack's. David Lakey, the director of the gallery in Omaha where Cath showed her paintings also came—much to Cath's pleasure.

Those seated on the bride's side represented the socialites of Blakefield, acquaintances of Harold Spaulding through his active support of the area's only Country Club, as well as presidents and chief executive officers of companies he dealt with—clients and suppliers alike.

Matching the Blakefield high society in glamour and style were Harold and Rennie's friends from Chicago. It was apparent to all observers that the Spauldings had indeed been long accustomed to the top end of the social strata. Jewels of all descriptions flashed from the fingers, wrists, and necks of the female guests, complementing suits and dresses fashioned by only top-notch designers.

Harold's younger brother, Matthias, was there, along with his stylish wife and their two children. Mathias managed the business that Harold left when he abandoned Chicago. His two sisters,

Rachel and Barbara, came from Boston with their husbands. They, too, were paragons of style.

Only one person represented Rennie's mother's family, however, Rennie's Aunt Fredricka. Harold Spaulding had not maintained contact with his wife's family after her death. It was as if he blamed them for his loss.

Fredricka was so charming that Cath warmed to her immediately. She was the youngest of her many siblings—several years younger than Rennie's mother, Magdalen. In fact, it appeared to Cath that she wasn't much older than Rennie.

Her attire was much less ostentatious than that of Spaulding's Chicago friends and new friends of the Blakefield Country Club set. The soft blue of her dress complemented her kind, blue-gray eyes and ash-blonde hair, which she wore in a blunt cut, just brushing her shoulders. Her only jewelry was a small string of pearls.

Fredricka's entire demeanor spoke of elegance.

Rennie seemed truly delighted to see her aunt, and tears not often shed by her glistened in her brown eyes as the two embraced. Fredricka was said to look very much like her deceased sister, and her appearance brought the essence of Magdalen to Rennie's wedding.

Harold Spaulding remained cool and distant towards his sister-in-law. Fredricka appeared not to notice. But she did notice, and she thought of the last time she had seen Harold and Rennie. Not too long after her sister, Magdalen, had died. Rennie had such a difficult time after her mother's death. She was just a totally lost child.

Now the child had become a woman—a bride.

The wedding-day morning had been drab and gray, with a soft mist beginning during the night and falling until almost noon, threatening to make the festive day a wet sodden one. But at noon the curtain of damp grayness rolled back, and there was the sun— almost as if keeping a promise to shine on the wedding of Renata Spaulding and Matthew Montgomery.

Soon the joyous strains of the wedding recessional filled the church, and a smiling Mr. and Mrs. Matt Montgomery marched back down the aisle. Shortly thereafter, they joined their families and friends at an elaborate country-club reception, complete with orchestra and a buffet so elegant that even their most elite guests would speak of it for weeks to come.

"I'm so happy, Mom," said Matt, whirling his mother around the dance floor as his bride danced in the arms of her new father-in-law.

Cath smiled up at her handsome son, relishing his happiness. Inside she prayed that it would be a good marriage. That life would continue to be kind to Matt, her only child.

Bulbs flashed, as countless photos were snapped of the young couple and the festivities. Many would adorn the walls of Harold Spaulding's spacious, but now almost empty, home. Many would go in Cath's album, which had continued to grow over the years.

One evening, she laid the photos of that memorable day end to end across the dining room table. There were so many that the entire surface of the table was covered. She took her time—several hours—selecting those that best captured that joyful day.

Even now, so many years after Cath had smiled through tears as Matt and Rennie repeated their wedding vows, she could relive that day vividly as she paged through the album of photographs. She could almost hear the peal of the organ and smell the heavy scent of the hundreds of roses arranged throughout the church. She could feel the happiness of her son—totally, completely, in love with his beautiful bride. The very, very lovely Mrs. Matt Montgomery.

Cath looked at a photo of Rennie, her aristocratic flawless face framed in a frothy cloud of veil, her eyes sparkling with joy and excitement. Eyes that now looked at Cath with hate.

Chapter Forty-two

Matt was out of town for long periods of time once again. His firm's law practice continued to grow, and success equated to incredible demands on his time and long periods of absence from Blakefield. His vow to refuse to be trapped by unrealistic demands from his career, made following his illness the preceding winter, was long forgotten. He worked harder than he ever had.

When he was home, he was weary and stressed. He often had to deal with Rennie's tantrums because he gave her so little attention. And justifiably, he admitted, promising to be there for her more often and to be more attentive to her when he was—a promise rarely kept.

He simply had no time left for Cath.

He saw that she appeared to be fading. She neither looked nor acted like herself. And he did question her often about how she felt—questions that fueled Rennie's consuming anger.

"Mom, are you okay?" he asked as he watched her break her toast into eight small pieces and then eat only two. Her hand trembled as she raised her coffee to her lips. "Mom, are you sure you're okay?" he asked again.

"Mom, maybe Rennie could help you with your hair," he said as he noticed how unkempt it looked—a comment that brought him a scathing look from his wife.

"Mom, are you sure you're feeling all right?" he asked when Cath said she wasn't hungry and declined dinner, going instead to her room to rest.

But in response to all his probing and inquiries the answer would be the same. "Of course I'm all right Matt. Just a little tired—or not very hungry."

Or whatever else she felt the appropriate answer might be.

So Matt decided his mother was just aging and reasoned that what he saw was perfectly normal.

He noticed that Cath pored over her album daily. It was on her bedside table—filled the table, as its size had grown dramatically since the long-ago day when Sarah Rowan had presented it to

Cath and Jack.

Matt could understand why his mother so enjoyed paging through this wonderful collection of photos. He had always enjoyed looking at the album himself. When he was a small boy, he'd sit in his mother's lap while she turned page after page and told him stories about the faces he saw there.

He loved to hear about his Grandma Sarah and the farm where his mother and Uncle Spence had grown up. He laughed with his mother when she told of her Aunt Irene and Uncle Elmer's many children and the antics that kept their home alive with activities and chaos.

Even Rennie had paged through the album with Matt from time to time in their younger years, ridiculing the clothing from earlier days and looking for family resemblances. After she and Matt were married, Rennie enjoyed admiring the photos capturing her lovely and lavish wedding day. And she liked all the pictures of Julie as a baby and small child. Rennie was in many of those photos, along with her daughter, and she thoroughly enjoyed tracing her own life stages and noticing, with delight how she retained her beauty—year after year, life-phase after life-phase.

Julie loved looking at the album more than anyone except Cath, and she and her grandmother often spent hours reflecting on memories when they were together. The twins enjoyed it too, giggling over photos of their mother as a gangly grade-schooler.

Many had enjoyed sharing the joys of the photo album over the years. It had become a central thread in the lives of the Rowans, Montgomerys, and Matsons. So Matt wasn't alarmed when his mother paged through it often. She always had. His concern arose only when she began to page through it all the time.

She was becoming lost in photos, lost in memories.

Cath talked much less these days, too. At times she seemed almost robot-like, going through familiar motions without thought or enthusiasm. Always known for possessing the intensity and emotions of her Irish forefathers, she was becoming totally passive.

Most days she did nothing but page through the album.

Chapter Forty-three

Cath laid her wrinkled hand gently on the page, tracing with her fingertip the outline of the faces of the couple she knew so well—of her and Jack. "How I miss you, darling," said Cath in a voice half whisper, half sob. "We were so young, Jack, so young and unafraid."

As she quietly uttered the word "unafraid," her eyes filled with tears. Dabbing at their wetness, she shook her head in sadness. "How did I become so fearful, Jack? How?"

Cath's voice was the only sound in the room, in the house. The only sound breaking the ethereal silence that surrounded her whispering voice was the subtle scratching of the shrubbery outside her window, as the morning breeze brushed its small branches against the side of the house.

But no one came to see to whom Cath was speaking. She was alone—alone, isolated, and sad.

She glanced up at the face looking back at her from the mirror across the room. An old face. Hers.

She rose from the chair where she had been sitting, reminiscing with her photo album, and walked over to the mirror. Although the resemblance to the young girl in the wedding photo on page one of the album was apparent, the heart-shaped smiling face was now solemn and wrinkled. Her pale skin hung loosely on her cheeks, and her eyes no longer sparkled. Her hair, curly and white, framed her sad, thin face.

Cath touched her reflection in the mirror. Gently with her fingertips, just as she had touched the photo. She leaned forward and touched her forehead to that of her likeness and sobbed—dry racking sobs that shook her shawl-draped shoulders.

When her tears were spent, and she ached with exhaustion, Cath ambled slowly to her bed, discarded her shawl and shoes, and lay down.

I'll just lie here until Matt comes home. But I can't remember if Matt is coming home this evening. Is he in town or off on another of his busi-

ness trips? Rennie would know, but I can't ask Rennie. Rennie makes me afraid.

Matt. Please come home tonight, Matt.

Cath closed her aching red-rimmed eyes, and thinking about her son, drifted off to a troubled sleep, dreaming of days when she was a young wife and mother.

The first day of school. Could it possibly be Matt's first day of school?

"Jack, we just brought him home from the hospital," moaned Cath, knowing how strange it would be to be "Mommy" half a day instead of the whole day as she had been for the past five years.

"Five years isn't 'just,' Cath. This is a big day. Don't go maudlin on me."

"Oh, I'm not. It's just that it's hard to believe Matt now belongs to Blakefield School District Ten half the time."

"Who's Blakefield Schoodisten?" asked Matt, coming in to the kitchen, ready for his big day, looking spiffy with his hair combed and his new shirt buttoned completely, although not correctly.

Young Matt had a real penchant for not getting buttons in their corresponding buttonholes. As he struggled to find a hole for the last remaining button on the bottom of the shirt, he was often heard complaining, "My shirt has too many buttons, Mommy."

Cath and Jack laughed, Cath's melancholy mood broken by their young son's question. She reached over and rebuttoned Matt's shirt, just as she had done hundreds of times over the past few years.

"That's School District Ten," she said, pronouncing each word distinctly. "That's the whole group your school is part of, honey, and now you're part of it, too."

Cath cupped her hand under Matt's chin, and he smiled broadly as he looked up at her, the excitement of the day showing in his eyes. His smile revealed spaces where just two days ago, teeth had been. Teeth he had wiggled constantly, trying to hasten their departure and his first experience as a recipient of the generosity of the "Tooth Fairy."

"Just a couple more photos before we leave, Matt. Why don't you sit right here," said Jack as he lifted him up on the kitchen counter, "so we can be at eye-level. Now give me that classic Matthew John Montgomery grin to save for all posterity."

Cath opened her eyes slowly. Her dreams of her son seemed so real, she expected so see a small grinning boy at her bedside. She smiled as she turned her head towards the side of the bed, and her heart quickened.

But then, she realized that she had been dreaming, and overwhelming sadness again enveloped her. Matt was no longer a little boy, the child she nurtured and protected.

Now, I need his protection, but I can't make myself ask for it.

Cath's eyelids felt heavy, and her head ached from her earlier crying. *Tears do exact a price,* she thought.

She stepped from the bed, and draping her tired, thin shoulders once more in her shawl, she sat down in the chair by the window and again pulled the thick photo album onto her lap.

Six decades after her mother had so lovingly wrapped it in yellow-rose covered fabric and adorned it with a yellow hair ribbon, the album had become Cath's greatest joy—perhaps her only joy.

Chapter Forty-four

Matt really was concerned that his mother had stopped reading again. He feared it was her eyes. His grandmother had had failing eyesight, and so had his Uncle Spence. Losing her vision certainly would explain a lot—even her changed personality.

"Mom, I'm going to make an appointment for you to see Dr. Haven—you know, the ophthalmologist. I don't think you're seeing so well these days," said Matt one evening when he had interrupted her "album reminiscing."

For a moment, Cath just looked at him—she had no idea what he was talking about. "I see just fine, Matt. Whatever gave you the idea I don't?"

"But Mom, you don't read anymore," blurted Matt. "You've always loved to read, and I thought . . ."

"And I will again. It's just that I'm not in a reading mood lately. I'm sure I will be again soon." Cath patted her son's hand, trying to reassure him there was nothing wrong. She smiled the saddest smile.

Matt saw only the smile. He didn't notice the sadness.

"Okay, if you're sure. Maybe I'll check out Barnes & Noble and see if I can find a couple of really good books you might enjoy."

"That would be nice, Matt," Cath said listlessly.

After Matt left, Cath thought about what he had said—about her no longer reading. And he was right. She had always loved reading. Right from the beginning.

Before high school, before she met Jack Montgomery, Cath attended a small country school not far from her family farm. Even as a very little girl, Cath walked the two miles to the small, square, white school building. At least it was white once. By the time she attended, it had become a sort of a weathered gray.

Cath loved school. From day one, she loved it. Going to school for the first time was a memorable experience for the eager little girl. Everything about it was exciting—even the trek along the well-worn path to get there.

She gripped her little lunch pail with a small hand still browned from the summer sun. She thought it wonderful that she had her own pail, her very own lunch. Her mother had packed a thick slice of the delicious bread she baked every Saturday.

Cath loved to be in the kitchen when Mama baked bread. The fragrance was wonderful. Mama had dribbled some honey on her bread, and Cath's mouth watered just thinking about it. And she had a big slab of cheese and a shiny red apple. Her pail was so full, Mama could hardly get the lid on.

On the first day of school, Mama walked with her. Just the first day. Cath insisted on carrying her own lunch pail, but she did let Sarah hold her hand.

If Cath had looked up at her mother's face, she would have seen tears that were dangerously close to sliding down Sarah's cheeks. It was very difficult for Sarah to part with this little one of hers.

But Cath didn't notice Sarah's sadness. She was too excited, too energized, and too full of questions.

"I'm going to read a book when I get home tonight, Mama. Just like you."

"Well, honey, you might not be able to after just the first day—it usually takes longer than one day to learn. But if you listen carefully to your teacher and really work hard, you'll be able to read before you know it."

Sarah smiled at her young daughter, her spirits lifted by Cath's eagerness and excitement.

"I will, Mama. I'll work really hard."

And she did.

From the first day of school, Cath loved reading. A love that never left her. Only now, it seemed like she simply didn't have the energy.

Chapter Forty-five

Summer had burst upon Blakefield, as sunny day followed sunny day. An ideal time for Cath to feel better about life—to walk, to sit out on the patio and read, to call friends on the phone.

But she didn't do any of these.

Occasionally, friends would call her—or stop by. When she talked with them on the phone, she was pleasant, but distant. Her friends thought she was simply not feeling well. She was, after all, not a young woman, and she had been extremely ill this past year—a couple of times.

If someone stopped by the house, Rennie would tell them Cath was resting. Most of the time she sat in her room. Much of the time she was locked in her room.

She no longer struggled to get up and out of her room before Matt left. No longer did she walk out with him as he left for work, ready to take one of her much-loved strolls through the neighborhood.

Matt gave no thought to the fact that his mother wasn't going out early in the morning as she had done in the colder days of winter and early spring. He simply presumed she went later.

He didn't ask.

Cath hadn't seen Brenda Harris since her canceled appearance at Brenda's brunch. She had only walked a couple of times since then—both times going in the opposite direction from the Harris home. Her heart was really not into talking with anyone.

She did speak to Julie on the phone, however—whenever she had an opportunity to do so. Of course, she told Julie nothing about her plight.

She would practice her conversations with Julie standing in front of a mirror. She'd force a smile, hoping the smile would somehow show in her voice—that it would make her sound cheerful.

Julie mustn't know.

And then, a great and wonderful surprise! Julie called to say that she and the twins would be coming for a visit some time in late summer. Cath was both excited and frightened. Surely, Julie will be able to tell something was wrong with her grandmother.

Terribly wrong.

But how wonderful it will be to see her, thought Cath. *And the boys.* Just thinking about it brought tears, tears of joy, as well as tears of sadness.

I'll try harder. I'll eat more. I'll join Rennie and Matt for breakfast more—and take food back to my room with me.

Just in case.

Cath began to make detailed plans for their coming—plans to get herself back in shape so Julie wouldn't suspect things were amiss. She even wrote down her plans.

For a while, she was more alive, some days even animated. The planning gave her purpose and put some breath back into her life.

But then, there was a phone call from Julie. They weren't coming; they wouldn't be coming at all this summer. Jack had come down with the chicken pox. By the time Hal had joined him with "more bumps than they could count," a good chunk of their free summer days was gone.

Both the Montgomery and the Matson households were disappointed. Cath was devastated.

She slipped even further into her lonely despair.

Chapter Forty-six

Jason Miller watched Cath as she moved slowly across the room. He and his wife Paula had dropped by to show Matt and Rennie photos of their newest grandchild, David Jason. After two girls, their daughter Linda had presented them with a grandson. They were a pair of really proud grandparents.

"Not that we don't dearly love our granddaughters," said Paula. "We adore them. It's just that now there's a little boy to round out our dreams."

Cath looked at the photos along with Matt and Rennie, appropriately smiled and commented on the "sweet little boy." Other than that comment, she said nothing, however, and as soon as she had seen the snapshots, she stole away to her room.

She didn't even say good-night.

How unlike Cath, mused Jason. And he didn't like the vacuous look in her eyes. Something really wasn't right with her.

Of course, he had thought that when she contracted pneumonia, too. And look how she bounded back. It seemed then as if nothing could keep Cath down.

But something was definitely keeping her down now.

How long ago was it that he checked her over? He didn't think it was very long ago, but she certainly had changed since then. He didn't have her chart in front of him, but he knew he'd recall if he had found anything seriously wrong.

After all, this was Cath Montgomery, his "second mother."

"Matt," asked Jason while their wives were in the kitchen getting coffee and dessert, "how is Cath feeling? She seemed a bit quiet tonight."

"She did, didn't she? I don't know, Jason, I think she's feeling okay. She never complains. You know Mom. And of course, I've been out of town so much lately, I really haven't been paying too close attention to her. But Rennie tells me she's doing just fine. She sees her so much more than I do."

Great! thought Jason. It had been obvious to him for a long time that Rennie Montgomery wasted no love on her mother-in-law. *If Cath is having to depend on Rennie for her needs, she's in trouble for sure.*

"Why don't you bring her by the office tomorrow? I'd really like to check her over. For one thing, she's too thin, and another . . . . Just bring her in, okay?"

"Of course, Jason. Now you have me worried."

"I'm sure it's nothing. But if I can check her out thoroughly, I can be positively sure."

That night, as Matt and Rennie were getting ready for bed, Matt told her of his conversation with Jason and his promise to take Cath to see him the following day.

"I agree with Jason, Rennie. Mom doesn't seem to be doing too well of late. Maybe it's nothing more that her age, but she really needs to be checked over, and he would like to do it tomorrow. The problem is, I have to be in court tomorrow morning and have back-to-back appointments all afternoon. Will you take her for me, hon?"

"It's sure easy for you to make commitments that I have to keep for you, Matt."

"I know, sorry. But Rennie, you know how swamped we are these days. Please. Jason's expecting her, so I bet you won't have to wait but a few minutes to get in."

"Okay, okay. I'll take Cath to see Jason. I think it's a waste of time, though. She's just old, that's all."

With that settled, Cath was not discussed further.

In the morning, as Matt rushed out the door, he again reminded Rennie that Cath needed to see the doctor today.

Rennie assured him that she'd take care of it.

Chapter Forty-seven

Cath was anxious this morning. She was alone in the house with Rennie and this was one of the rare days when she really didn't want to spend the entire day in her room. It was a clear sunny morning. Maybe she'd even go for a walk. When was the last time she had walked?

She couldn't remember.

"I can't remember anything anymore," she said aloud in disgust.

Cath had slept late this morning—didn't even hear Matt or Rennie. Of course, she rarely heard anyone, her room set back the way it was. Most of the time, she just sensed they were up, that there was activity in the house.

But after briefly socializing with Jason and Paula Miller last night, she slept soundly, and later than usual. Having Jason and Paula in the house comforted her somehow, helped quell the fears that engulfed her much of the time. With guests, Matt and Rennie weren't quarreling for a change. It really had been a nice evening for her, in spite of her silence.

But she had gotten tired so quickly. She couldn't even remember saying goodnight to Jason and his dear wife. *But surely, I did, didn't I?* she wondered with concern.

She questioned herself, but couldn't remember.

Feeling quite well rested this morning, Cath wrapped herself hurriedly in her robe and darted out of her room as soon as she awakened. When she looked at her clock and saw the time, she feared she might be too late. She was breathless with anxiety when she grabbed the doorknob and pulled, relieved when it opened.

Relieved that Rennie hadn't already locked her in.

Cath saw Matt's car pull out of the driveway as she walked out into the kitchen, still tying the sash to her robe.

"Well aren't we a sleepyhead this morning," said Rennie sarcastically as Cath appeared at the breakfast table.

"Good morning, Rennie," said Cath, pouring herself a cup of

coffee, her hand trembling. As she carried it to the table, coffee splashed into the saucer, decorated beautifully with blue cornflowers.

Rennie didn't notice. Cath was so grateful. If Rennie had noticed, surely she would have snapped at her—ridiculed and criticized her.

Cath sat in silence, sipping her coffee. She didn't read the paper. She didn't try to converse. Sometimes, when Matt was still at breakfast, she would talk some. But she had nothing to say to Rennie, nor Rennie to her.

Cath didn't want to anger Rennie by saying something that displeased her; she felt it much safer to say nothing at all.

She simply stared straight ahead, looking out the window, just as she had done countless other mornings. An elderly woman, fresh from sleep, silently watching scenes of her neighborhood, sun reflecting off housetops, a blue cloudless sky serving as a backdrop for a rainbow of flowers, birds flitting from branch to branch.

The scene comforted her.

Cath had changed appreciably in the past few months. Since there were times when she couldn't get out of her room for adequate nourishment, she was often disoriented. She frequently appeared disheveled, and she became increasingly forgetful.

Her lovely head of white curls, previously so attractive, was now uncombed and matted much of the time. Extinguished was the spark in her eyes. They had acquired the dull glaze of the undernourished elderly, their only brightness the often appearing tears—appearing without summons or apparent cause.

Matt didn't recognize the signs of malnourishment, nor of her depression. Even though he was alarmed at times, he was only mildly so. He knew his mother really hadn't been the same since her cancer surgery and used that to explain the changes he saw. He was doing all he could, keeping her well cared for and fed—and safe from harm. At least he thought he was doing so.

Matt saw only small changes and minimized his concern when a bright experience intervened. He had been concerned last Friday evening. Cath had been in her room resting when he got home. She was pale and shaky when she came to dinner, and her conversation was fragmented and unfocused.

Yet, last night, she really seemed to enjoy Jason and Paula's visit. Unduly quiet, yes, but she had looked at the baby's photographs along with the rest of them; she had commented on them—and smiled. Matt had pushed his Friday-evening concerns from his mind last night. Until Jason said she didn't look good. Until he asked that he bring her in for a check-up today.

Today was Wednesday—the day Cath "slept in."

The day Rennie had promised to take Cath to see Dr. Jason Miller.

But Cath knew nothing of either Dr. Miller's advice or Matt's request of Rennie.

Rennie finished her breakfast and went to get ready for the day, while Cath lingered over her toast and coffee. Now alone, she rather enjoyed the quiet of her breakfast and found she relaxed tremendously during the near-hour she spent looking out the window, watching the trees and the birds. A songbird serenaded her.

As the warbling bird took flight, Cath shook her head slightly, as if trying to snap herself back to reality.

"It's about time I get dressed," she said half-aloud.

She rinsed her cup, saucer, and plate and placed them in the dishwasher. She started down the hall towards her room, feeling really quite well after all. Her earlier tension began to disappear.

I'm being silly. Rennie isn't giving me a second thought this morning.

As Cath walked down the long hall towards her own room, thinking of the day ahead and planning what she might do to make it a good day, to perhaps help lift her from the depths of sadness that seemed to overpower her most of the time these days, Rennie came up behind her. She grabbed her tightly by the arm, opened a storage closet door, shoved her in, and slammed and locked the door.

"There you old biddy," she screeched. "Now you're out of my way!"

"Rennie," called Cath pleadingly, terror in her voice. "Open the door," she begged, slapping on the it with the palms of her hands so hard that sharp pains shot up her arm. "You know I'm frightened of small spaces. Please, Rennie!"

But immediately, there was no one to hear her cries. Rennie had stalked off upstairs to her own room as soon as she locked the closet door, and any sounds from downstairs were soon drowned out by the shower in her bathroom.

An hour and forty-five minutes later, Rennie emerged attractively dressed in a fern-green suit with shoes to match, a white silk scarf scattered with green polka dots tied carefully around her neck. Jade earrings, an anniversary gift from Matt, completed her ensemble.

She walked across the entryway, her footsteps softly clicking on the tile floor. She walked through the kitchen and into the garage without slowing her steps, without even glancing towards the door further down the hall, the door she had locked.

The door holding Cath prisoner in a small dark closet.

Soon she backed her car out of the garage, down the driveway, and disappeared down the street.

Cath's cries for help and pounding on the door had ceased during Rennie's lengthy grooming session. If Rennie had bothered to stop by the closet door to listen before she left for the day, she would have heard a soft whimpering—a sound very much like a crying kitten.

Cath had never liked small dark spaces. Her claustrophobia, along with the shock of being abruptly pushed into the closet, had her heart racing. It pounded so loud and fast that she could almost hear its rhythm in the confined space of the closet. Her arm, which Rennie had so strongly squeezed, throbbed with pain.

The closet was used for general storage. A vacuum cleaner stood in one corner, and a large electric roaster, used only rarely, was on a shelf, along with some cleaning supplies and a stack of old worn but clean towels kept for cleaning and polishing purposes.

It was a small closet, but it did have a good high wattage light bulb to assist searching for just the right thing. Unfortunately for Cath, the light switch was outside the door.

Cath was enveloped in total black darkness.

She huddled against the door, as if her closeness to the opening would expedite her release. But even in her terror and disorientation, she knew she would not soon be free. Her multiple experiences locked in her own room had proved that.

And this would be worse. No light. Only stale air.

She was hot. She had no access to a bathroom and already she had the need of one. Oh, how she wished she had been locked in her own room. There it was light, and there was somewhere to sit or lie down. There she could move around.

And there she had her album to keep her company.

Cath remembered when Matt installed the lock on this closet. She and Jack had just stopped in and were visiting with Matt and Rennie when three-year-old Julie walked by, her arms laden with cleaning supplies.

"Made a mess," she announced in her young-child, determined manner as she marched by her parents and grandparents.

"Just what do you have there, Missy?" asked her mother, catching up to her and placing a restraining hand on her shoulder.

"Told you. I made a mess," responded Julie indignantly.

"So I gather," said Rennie, eyeing the many supplies Julie had clutched in her small arms.

Matt took the cleaning materials from her and said, "Why don't you show me, honey, and we'll clean it up together." He placed all the supplies but one on the counter, took his daughter's hand, and went to inspect the "mess."

About ten minutes later, he came out and announced that it wasn't serious. "The two of us had it cleaned up, pronto." Then he walked over to the counter and examined the materials his young child had been hauling off to her room. "My God!" he exclaimed. "We can't have this sort of stuff around where she can get into it!"

That very afternoon a lock went on the storage closet door. A lock placed too high for little fingers to reach.

A lock that now held seventy-eight-year-old Catherine Montgomery prisoner.

Cath had not used the bathroom when she first arose. She had been too eager to leave her bedroom, too frightened that she'd be unable to open the door, worried that she might already be locked in her room. Now, she wished with all her being that she had been—that she had access to her bathroom.

Her bladder ached, and she had no choice but to release the pressure within her. It began only as a dampness on her clothing, but soon was a steady stream.

Catherine Rowan Montgomery, a proud and dignified lady, was reduced to a huddling whimpering old woman awash in her own urine.

Even in her isolation, Cath felt embarrassment. The strong odor in the closed quarters made her feel ill, and she struggled to hold down the breakfast she had so recently enjoyed. Sobs racked her body—soft but deep sobs, which shook her entire frame.

After a while her sobs ceased, but silent tears continued to fall unchecked. She remained huddled close to the door with her head, aching and throbbing, resting on the hard surface of the wood. The air was so stale and close she could scarcely breath, and it was intolerably hot. Whether because of the heat, stale air, or her exhaustion from the trauma and tears, Cath fell asleep.

Mercifully, she slept.

Chapter Forty-eight

Rennie pulled into the garage at just past three o'clock in the afternoon. She had had a delightful day—the kind of social day that so easily lifted her spirits. She was humming when she came into the house, Cath long forgotten.

As she walked down the hall in her fashionable impeccably clean home, she became aware of an odor. An unpleasant odor, coming from the closet. Only then did Rennie remember.

She unlocked the door and abruptly pulled it open. As she did so, a sleeping Cath fell out onto the floor.

"How dare you, you dirty old woman!" screamed Rennie, pulling Cath to her feet, clutching again the arm she bruised when she pushed her into the closet that morning.

The pain aroused Cath, but only to half-awake and seriously disoriented. She cried out.

"Get out of my sight!" cried Rennie as she pushed Cath down the hall towards her room. "Thanks to you, I now have to scrub the floor."

Cath dragged herself down the hall in a daze, running her hand along the wall for support as she went. She was so weak and disoriented, she could barely stand, let alone ambulate.

Twice her knees buckled, bringing her down hard on the floor. Each time she uttered a feeble cry of pain.

But no one heard her cries.

Rennie was flinging her clothes everywhere in her own room, muttering in anger. "I can't believe this. My perfectly wonderful day ruined. All because of that disgusting old lady. Dammit, dammit!" she screamed.

She quickly donned clothes more suitable for scrubbing—not something she frequently did herself. Even in jeans and t-shirt, she looked elegant. Of course, both jeans and shirt bore the name of a fashion designer.

"Damned old woman. I won't have it. I just won't have it! This is my house, and some old woman isn't going to ruin it for me."

She stormed out of her bedroom, banging the door behind her. She gathered the cleaning supplies and set to remedy what she regarded as an intentional affront to her by Cath. She had absolutely no understanding of what had happened—and why.

Her clean up was not a monumental task. In minutes, she had the small patch of floor scrubbed and deodorized, the offensive odor only a memory.

When she reached her own room, Cath closed and locked the door. For a while she leaned against it, hanging on to the doorknob for support. Her body sagged, and her breathing was labored.

She inched over to a chair and sat down. For a brief moment, she just sat, not moving. Then, she removed her wet nightgown and robe and rose to drop them to the floor.

Shakily, she stumbled into the bathroom, and filling a glass with water, she drank it, quenching somewhat her day-long thirst. Next, she filled the bathtub.

Cath was so weak, she needed both hands to turn the faucet handle. When the tub was nearly filled, she stepped in, trying to hold tightly to the safety rail for support. But she was unable to keep her hold, and she slipped sidewise, slamming her bruised arm against the faucet. She cried out in pain and again grabbed the rail to prevent a complete fall into the water.

Cath then eased herself down, stretched out the length of the tub, and let the warm water lap gently over her. She closed her eyes, tears streaming down her cheeks, falling like raindrops into the water.

Picking up the soap, her favorite lavender soap, she inhaled deeply the familiar fragrance. The steam from the bath, mixed with the lavender scent, rose to clear the smell that had enveloped her during her day of confinement. The steam helped ease her muscles, cramped from lying on the floor, and as some relaxation swept over her, her day-long fear began to fade.

It was displaced by despair—total, complete, and anguished despair.

Life has become too hard. I can't deal with this—this anger, this hate, this rejection. I can't do it. I just can't.

Cath sat in the water until it began to feel cool. Then, she stepped gingerly from her bath, again grabbing the rail for support, more successfully this time. She donned a clean gown and brushed her hair. She looked in the mirror, and an elderly woman's face looked back at her. The eyes were filled with indescribable pain and sadness.

Cath opened the door to the medicine cabinet and removed a bottle of pain pills. She again filled a glass with water and carried the bottle and the water to a chair next to the table by her bedside—the one where her photo album lay.

There she sat.

She opened the bottle of pills, struggling somewhat as her shaking hand had difficulty gripping it. She poured the pills into her hand and placed them one by one in her mouth, taking a swallow of water after each.

Then, she opened the photo album and began reliving her life, once filled with such joy, and now, filled with so much pain and sorrow.

Cath's hands were shaking badly, but with sheer determination she turned yet another page of the album. Her precious photo album—the quilted fabric worn through in spots, the once colorful yellow rosebuds faded, the embroidered names no longer recognizable.

Photos of Matt graced this page—Matt on his first day of school. His little-boy smile with two missing front teeth grinned up at her.

Next, she found Jack's photograph. Jack breaking ground for a new store—the one at the shopping mall. How she had always loved that picture of Jack.

Her tears were flowing freely now, dropping on the pages, leaving dark splotches staining her memories.

The album, smooth from age and scuffed at the corners, began to slide from her lap. Struggling to hold it, she turned to another page—a montage of smiles and laughter. Matt's wedding day. Matt and Rennie's. Such a happy day. The wedding of her only child—

Matthew John Montgomery.

Cath's fingers scratched at the edges of the thick pages, trying to turn one more. But she was unable to summon the strength. Her vision had become blurry, and her hands were growing numb.

The album slipped to the floor, landing with a thud, some of the photos, old and yellowed, breaking loose from their pages.

Half-buried in the scattered remnants of her memories lay a bottle—a pill bottle. Empty. The label bore the name, "Catherine Montgomery," and the instructions, "Take Two Daily for Pain."

Her head, white with wisps of unkempt curly hair, fell to her chest, and her arms, one discolored with fresh bruises, dropped to her sides. A small sob escaped her lips as she whispered, "I'm coming, Jack. I'm coming."

Chapter Forty-nine

The melodic chiming of the doorbell interrupted Rennie's banging of pots and pans in the kitchen.

"Now what!" she exclaimed, still inwardly raging at Cath. Wiping her hands on a towel, she stomped to the front door and whisked it open, prepared to verbally attack whomever she faced.

There stood Julie.

"Hi, Mom," she said brightly, as if it were not at all unusual for her to jaunt from Minneapolis to Blakefield for dinner.

"Julie! What are you doing here?"

"What kind of welcome is that?" asked Julie, laughing and hugging her mother. "If you'll let me in, I'll tell you all about it."

"Of course, c'mon in," said Rennie, returning her daughter's hug and stepping aside. "It's just that you really took me by surprise. You don't generally 'just drop by.'"

"I suppose I should have called to let you know I was coming, but it was very last minute, and I thought a surprise would be great fun."

"I'm surprised, all right," said Rennie, a smile finally breaking through the frown that she had been wearing ever since arriving home and discovering Cath's "accident."

"Well, Steve and Amy Borg were driving to Kearney, and since they were practically going right by here, they offered to haul me along. Isn't it great? You remember Steve and Amy, Mom. They own that great property just to the west of us. You met them when the twins were born."

Rennie nodded.

"Anyhow, Kenneth's up to his ears working on the plans for a new mall in St. Cloud, and Gen offered to take the munchkins for a couple of days. And of course, they were delighted to have a short vacation with Grandma and Grandpa on the farm. So here I am."

"I'm glad to see you, Julie. And won't your father be surprised."

"I'm sure he will be—and Grandma Cath. Where is she, by the

way? In her room?"

With the mention of Cath, Rennie's face clouded, and again she frowned. "I suppose so. Where else would she be?"

Julie looked up sharply, noting the change in her mother's voice when she mentioned her grandmother. She groaned inwardly and thought, *Please, Mom, not this time. No, I refuse to let her ruin this visit for me.*

Still wearing her smile, she said brightly, "Well, I'm going back to see her. Be back in a minute, Mom."

Julie walked briskly towards Cath's room. She could almost feel Rennie glaring after her.

Rennie was indeed glaring at her, but only for a moment. She had started for the kitchen, ready to resume her dinner preparations when Julie's scream broke her stride.

"Julie, what is it?" she called as she ran towards Cath's room. "What happened?"

"Mom, call 9-1-1!"

For a moment, Rennie just stood there staring at the scene. Cath was lying on the floor, Julie bent over her grandmother, pushing on her frail chest and breathing into her mouth—her eyes filled with terror.

Rennie could feel the blood drain from her face. She scarcely recognized her own voice as she asked in a tone just barely above a whisper, "Is she dead?"

"Dammit, Mother!" Julie screamed. "Call 9-1-1. Now!"

Julie's brisk order snapped Rennie out of her stunned state, and she quickly reached for the phone and dialed. After hurriedly giving the necessary information to the dispatcher, she knelt beside Julie and again asked, her voice quavering, "Is she dead?"

"I do feel a slight pulse. At least I think so," said Julie, still vigorously administering CPR. She whispered softly, "Grandma Cath, Grandma Cath—wake up. Please wake up."

They could hear the sirens coming closer. Rennie rose to her feet and woodenly walked to the door. "I'll let them in," she said in a frightened voice.

In moments, Cath, tubes in her arms and an oxygen mask on her face, was whisked away, sirens wailing. Julie sat in the ambulance by her side, gently caressing her forehead. Tears coursed down her face, and she continued her entreaty. "Please, Grandma Cath. Please wake up."

"Get in touch with Dad," Julie had ordered her mother as she followed the gurney out of the house and into the ambulance. Rennie, her face blanched white, had only nodded.

She watched the ambulance speed away and went into the house to call Matt. She was able to reach him immediately. Then, she slumped into a chair, put her hands over her face, and cried. Copious tears.

Tears of terror.

When the medical attendants were preparing Cath for the injections and tubes, they had bared her arms. There, plainly visible on her right upper arm, was an ugly bruise—deep purple and clearly showing the imprint of someone's fingers. Although Julie said nothing, Rennie knew she saw the mark.

Chapter Fifty

Matt had been on his way home when Rennie called. He was barely able to hear what she said and wasn't sure he comprehended what he did hear. But there was no mistaking the urgency in his wife's voice. And he did understand "Cath" and "hospital."

In minutes, Matt's car skidded to a quick stop in front of the emergency entrance to Blakefield Memorial. He all but ran to the first nurse's station he could find and breathlessly, asked where they had taken his mother.

He was gently guided to a waiting room, where he found Julie, her face pale and tear-stained.

"Oh, Daddy," she cried as soon as she saw him. She wrapped her arms around his neck, fresh tears flowing. "It's Grandma Cath," she whispered, choked with sobs.

"I know, honey," soothed her father, his voice filled with worry. "Your mother told me when she called. Is it her heart?"

Julie shook her head. "No," she whispered sadly. Between her sobs, she tried to explain the empty pill bottle and the dark purple bruise on her grandmother's frail thin arm.

"Oh, my God," he moaned, burying his head in his hands. "Oh, my God."

At the moment, Matt Montgomery was the picture of defeat. Seated in a hospital waiting room, slumped over, his elbows resting on his knees, his graying head bowed low and covered by his hands, he realized that his mother had tried to take her own life. Had tried to kill herself—had, perhaps, succeeded.

Julie rested her hand on his back. They sat like that for a long time, father and daughter, each overwhelmed with sadness, each fearing for the life of someone they loved.

Mom. Oh, Mom. What was so bad that you couldn't face it?

But even as he asked himself the question, he knew the answer. Rennie. It was because of Rennie she did this. And he had let it happen.

Self-loathing filled him. He had felt for some time that Rennie was neglecting Cath—maybe even mistreating her. But he had no proof, and neither one would tell him anything. But something heinous must have happened to have pushed her to attempt to take her own life.

Mom, why didn't you tell me? I let you down. I was the protector, and I didn't protect. I didn't take care of her for you, Dad. I'm so, so sorry.

Matt's self-incriminating reverie was broken by Julie's voice. "Dad."

Just as she began to speak, Dr. Jason Miller walked through the door, an angry scowl nearly hiding the concern in his eyes. "Sit down, Matt," he ordered as Matt started to rise. "We need to talk."

"Is she . . . ?" Matt couldn't bring himself to say the word.

"No, friend, she's not dead, but it was mighty damned close. Matt, what in the hell has been going on here? Your mother tried to kill herself. At home—in your home! Good God, Matt, can't you even protect your own mother in your own home?"

Jason unleashed his anger on his friend—his oldest and dearest friend. Matt said absolutely nothing in his own defense.

For a moment no one spoke. The only sound in the hollow quiet of the room was Julie's soft sobbing.

Jason looked at his friend, placed his arm across his shoulders and sighed. "We were able to save her, Matt. It's going to be a long haul to recovery, but she's alive."

With the news that his mother was alive, Matt again buried his head in his hands—and cried.

Jason sighed again and continued, "She's had a stroke, Matt. It didn't kill her, which is amazing considering all the drugs she ingested, and I can't promise she won't have another one that will. We're watching her closely—very, very closely."

Matt kept his head bowed.

"The hospital will initiate an investigation of abuse, Matt."

Jason's words were expected. Matt could only nod.

"It was Rennie, wasn't it." Not a question. Just a statement of fact. A fact that any of the three in that room might have stopped—but didn't.

Again Matt nodded.

Julie's mind had been racing back to her earlier concerns. She had felt something was wrong at Christmas—and again when her grandmother made her surprise visit in April. She, too, was enveloped in self-incrimination.

Dr. Jason Miller knew he had not delved deeply enough into his questions concerning Cath's seemingly failing health. Why? Why? All he could do now was to ask himself why. He felt he was not blameless in permitting this dreadful thing to happen to this dear lady he held in such high regard.

With yet another sigh he said, "You two can go in to see her now. Just don't make it too long. Cath has had a very tiring day."

He looked Matt in the eyes as he said the last and saw incredible pain. Grabbing his friend in a long hard embrace, he said, "I'm so sorry, Matt. So sorry."

Then he gave Julie a quick hug and left.

Matt and Julie, hand and hand, lending support to one another, walked slowly into Cath's room. Cath's white curls were splayed across the pillow, framing her pallid face. Her eyes were closed, and her breathing was so soft, if Matt hadn't just been told she was alive, he would have doubted it.

The loose sleeve of her hospital gown had pushed up as she slept, revealing the large bruise with its finger-shaped outline—made by someone's hand, Rennie's hand.

Nausea overcame Matt, and he quickly swallowed the bile rising in his throat. "Damn Rennie," he whispered as forcefully as he could. "How could she?"

They walked slowly and quietly to Cath's bedside, both thinking how many times in recent months they had done so. Julie's eyes stung with tears she was holding back with great effort.

Matt reached for his mother's hand and tenderly held it in his. She opened her eyes, looked first at Matt, then at Julie. And then, she smiled—a crooked smile.

The stroke had paralyzed the left side of Cath's face.

Chapter Fifty-one

Julie and Matt sat in an otherwise empty waiting room, a wall clock quietly ticking away the seconds of the late evening hour.

"Daddy, my mother did this. My mother," she repeated, gulping her swallowed sobs. "How could she be so cruel? How can I possibly still love her?"

Matt took her hand in his and squeezed so hard Julie winced. "I don't know any of it, Julie—how she could be so cruel, how you—or I—can go on loving her. Or why I didn't see it happening? How could I be so blind—how could I?"

He broke down again, his deep sobs shaking his frame. Julie put her arms around her father and held him to her chest like a child, until his sobs subsided.

It was nearly dawn before the two had their emotions in check enough to discuss what had taken place.

"One of the reasons I wanted Mom to live with us, Julie, was so I could monitor her health. But I really got lax about it—I got too busy at work, and it bothered your mother if I asked about it at dinner. Just feeble excuses. All I have is feeble excuses."

"Do you think Mom hurt her before this? Wouldn't you have known?"

"I don't know, Julie. I honest to God don't know. It's possible, but I never saw any marks on her. I suppose she might have hurt her where it wouldn't show."

Matt pounded his fist on the coffee table in front of them. The loud bang resonated throughout the room, bouncing off its emptiness. "Damn! I don't even know if my wife was hurting my mother. Jason's right—what kind of home do I have anyway?"

"Dad, this isn't your fault—no more than mine. I knew something had to be wrong, even at Christmas. She seemed afraid of Mom. Mom sort of seemed afraid of her, too. It just didn't make any sense, so I dropped it. I didn't even ask her about it, Dad," she wailed with self-accusation.

"I didn't notice, not at Christmas. But since then, for some time now, Julie, she's seemed overly quiet, remote—rather sad, not like Mom at all. Even though I'd ask her if she felt all right, I never really investigated why—why the changes." Matt sighed. "What kind of son am I, anyhow?"

"Did Dr. Miller ever find out why she'd gotten so thin?" asked Julie.

"No, it disturbed him, but he couldn't find anything wrong, any medical reason for it. Jason saw her a lot this year, and every time he did, he gave her a clean bill of health—more or less. I think I just convinced him she was getting old—or he convinced me. I don't know—maybe we convinced each other."

He ran his fingers through his hair. "Jason wanted to see her today—or yesterday," he said, glancing at the clock, realizing it was close to morning of a new day. "Your mother promised to bring her to his office, but instead—this." Matt's voice broke, and for a brief time, neither he nor Julie spoke.

"Grandma Cath's thinness bothered me when she came to visit in April—at first. But she seemed so happy and cheerful, I didn't worry about it for long."

"That April trip. I was amazed at how suddenly she decided to make that trip—and how she seemed to cling to me. I was leaving town for a few days, and she apparently didn't want to be alone with Rennie. Easy to see now, but I sure as hell was blind to it then. I even tried to persuade myself that she was losing her eyesight, trying to think of reasons—of excuses—for the changes in her." He shook his head from side to side. "Excuses. Why didn't I try to find the reasons?"

Just then, Kenneth walked into the room, and Julie ran to him. "As soon as I settled the boys in at Mom and Dad's, I got a late-night flight out," he said, enfolding his wife in his arms, then, reaching over to his father-in-law and tightly squeezing his shoulder. Can you fill me in on what's happening? But first, how is she?" he asked, his question tentative, fearing the worst.

Matt told Kenneth all that had happened to this point—Cath's suicide attempt, the bruises on her arm, the stroke. The story took some time; Matt's voice broke often in the telling.

Julie didn't speak at all, just listened to her father tell the tragic story. She remained close to her husband, her head against her chest, a picture of exhaustion and sadness.

Chapter Fifty-two

As Jason had predicted, Cath slowly recovered. But there were permanent changes in Catherine Montgomery. Her winning smile was now confined to one-half her face. The other, the left side, was frozen forever in expressionless sameness.

When his mother was well enough to leave the hospital, Matt moved her into a small house of her own. A full-time nurse and companion was with her night and day.

And he was with her as much as he could possibly be. He, too, made the small house his home.

Matt knew the moment he realized what Rennie had done that he would leave her. He went home only long enough to pack his bags.

Rennie stood by the door, her always perfectly coifed hair disheveled, her always perfectly made-up face, pale and tear-stained.

"Please, Matt," she entreated, "let me explain."

Matt held up his hand, palm toward her as if he were stopping traffic. "No, Rennie, it's too late." His voice nearly broke as he spoke those words, so final in their declaration.

Picking up his bag, Matt walked out the door. Just as Rennie had always feared he would do if he found out.

He left without ever looking back.

Epilogue

The spark of living in Blakefield left Matt. It was the only home he had ever known, but now, to him, it seemed tainted. Within six months of his leaving Rennie, he resigned from his law practice, and he and Cath moved to Albertville, a small suburb of Minneapolis, not far from Julie's home.

He was home more often now, working as a legal consultant with a small law firm. His mother needed nursing care less frequently, but he made certain that when he wasn't there, she was attended to—kindly and generously, with loving care. They visited quietly in the evenings, sometimes with Julie and her family, but often alone.

Both Matt and Cath took great delight in the twins, now nearly pre-teens, getting taller each day and beginning to show signs of the young men they would become. Cath seemed to enjoy her peaceful life in suburban Minnesota, as did Matt. But she was never able to shed her sadness over the dissolution of her only child's marriage, no matter how many times others attempted to alleviate her feelings of guilt.

And Matt missed Rennie—he had loved her so. However, he saw her rarely after leaving Blakefield.

As Dr. Miller had promised, the hospital initiated charges of elder abuse against Rennie. Three days after her brutal treatment of Cath, she was arrested.

She was at the piano, her fingers wandering over the keys, playing portions of familiar tunes. Her mind wandered along with her fingers, her thoughts mostly on Matt, on their relationship.

Our life was so good, we were happy doing the things we wanted to do, when we wanted to do them, enjoying the haven of our own home. Why did she have to move in and ruin it?

Tears brightened her eyes, and she brushed at them with fists. Just as she was miring in self-pity, the doorbell rang, the pleasant melody intruding on her thoughts and filling her with the hope that it might be Matt.

She all but ran to the door, jerking it open hurriedly. Her lovely face fell as she saw two policemen. They informed her of the charges against her, advised her of her rights, and handcuffed her well-manicured hands behind her back—in spite of her shrill, piercing objections.

At first, Rennie was angry and humiliated, screaming insults at the arresting officers. But as she walked into the jail, handcuffed, true terror overtook her, and she began to sob.

As soon as she was allowed to do so, she phoned Matt. "Matt, this is terrible. I've been dragged off to jail like a common criminal. Locked up! You have to get me out of here—you just have to. I can't bear the thought of being locked up."

She sobbed softly into the receiver. "Please help me, Matt. I'm your wife, for God's sake," she begged when he didn't reply.

Matt sighed. "I'll call Loren Baxter. He's a good attorney and will give you whatever help you need."

"And please, Matt, tell him to hurry. Please."

Matt hung up before her second please. He felt like his heart would break.

The charges against Rennie were eventually dropped. Neither Cath nor Matt would agree to testifying against her in court.

Nearly four years after her suicide attempt, at age eighty-two, Catherine Rowan Montgomery died quietly in her sleep, just as her mother had before her.

With dignity.

Author's Notes

Elder abuse is one of the fastest-growing forms of domestic violence in the U.S., a hidden phenomenon that affects hundreds of thousands of older Americans. The exact number of incidences of abuse is unknown; far too many occurrences go unreported to determine an accurate statistic. One estimate, however, places the number of seniors mistreated or abused at 1.5 million per year. And with a rapidly growing elderly population, the numbers will most certainly rise.

Elder abuse takes many forms. It may be—and all too often is—physical mistreatment and battering; it may be psychological; it may be financial. Some unfortunate seniors are victims of all three.

There are many different profiles of the abuser, but the abuse is most often inflicted by younger family members responsible for the elder's care. The profiles of those abused are also greatly varied, but the typical abuse victim is over age seventy-five, usually female, with one or more disabilities, such as confusion, incontinence, and wandering—the most vulnerable.

Most civilized people find the thought of elder abuse repugnant and would never participate in such an ugly practice. Few do. But in such a highly populated world, those few who do take part in these unspeakable cruelties number in the thousands. Consequently, far too many elders are neglected, cheated, hurt—and even killed.

Far too often, symptoms of abuse are ignored—or merely written off as signs the abused is "growing old." But mistreatment may result in depression—or other major behavior or psychological problems. Elders deprived of proper nutrition will frequently experience memory loss, and in extreme cases, exhibit signs of dementia.

Many don't have the means or the ability to speak out in their own behalf. Others have both means and ability. But the fear of losing their dignity, of being pitied, is so strong, they would, like Cath, prefer to die.

Some experts estimate that only one out of fourteen elder abuse incidents is reported to the authorities. And many of those that are reported don't result in conviction for the abuser. Like other domestic-violence cases, the abuse is often difficult to substantiate, the abused often too frightened to accuse their abusers in court.

But elder abuse is a crime—an ugly crime. If convicted, the abuser may be sentenced to jail. The length of time of incarceration will depend upon whether the crime charged was a felony or a misdemeanor.

For those abusers who, unlike Rennie, abuse not out of selfishness or cruelty, but out of desperation, there is help available. The woman, for instance, who works eight plus hours a day, comes home to three children and her aging mother, and just can't cope with her mother's incontinence—so she strikes her. Respite programs or eldercare facilities offer relief, and counseling is available through social service agencies or churches in nearly every community.

There are alternatives to abuse.

Suicide is high among the elderly. Although only thirteen per cent of the population is, at this time, considered elderly, twenty-five per cent of suicides are committed by older individuals. The reasons are myriad: loss of spouse and other contemporaries; diminished economic resources; poor health and its oft-accompanying pain. And unfortunately, abuse.

More than thirty-five percent of elder abuse victims suffer psychological abuse. Their sense of self-esteem can become so eroded, they lose their will to live.

Cath's story is fiction, but in reality, it is a composite of the stories of many—the many older citizens who need everyone's compassion and understanding as they come to the end of their years.

They have raised their families, concluded their careers, championed their causes, and supported their communities.

Now they ask for understanding for shortcomings intensified by age, care for bodies that now frequently fail them, and protection from danger. They deserve that.

So did Cath.

S. W.